To Jojuan

Return of Bliss

Hugh Harris

Return of Bliss

The Dinkel Island Series
Book 2

TATE PUBLISHING
AND ENTERPRISES, LLC

Published by Tate Publishing & Enterprises, LLC
127 E. Trade Center Terrace | Mustang, Oklahoma 73064 USA
1.888.361.9473 | www.tatepublishing.com

Tate Publishing is committed to excellence in the publishing industry. The company reflects the philosophy established by the founders, based on Psalm 68:11,
"The Lord gave the word and great was the company of those who published it."

Published in the United States of America

ISBN: 978-1-62994-291-9
1. Fiction / General
2. Fiction / Thrillers / General
13.12.12

Dedication

To Nancy Morath, a former music director
who taught me to love gospel music.

Acknowledgement

I am indebted to the members of the Aspiring Writer's Critique group at the Lifelong Learning Institute in Midlothian, Virginia, for their insights and encouragement as I shared the development of the story contained in these pages. I am also indebted to the various gospel music groups whose concerts inspired me during my pastorate at Willis United Methodist Church in Henrico County, Virginia between 2005 and 2010, and to The Cabin Friends Quartet in Halifax County, Virginia. As always, I thank my wife, Sharon, for her patience with me while I've lived with my feet planted in two different worlds during the writing of this book.

Introduction

"Weeping may linger for the night, but joy comes with the morning."

Psalm 30:5b NRSV

1

Grief Runs Deep

It was deep into the early morning hours when Dinkel Island artist Stan Grayson sensed Lillie's presence beside him. As he reached to enfold her in his arms, she took his hand and very gently slid out from the covers, pulling him to her. She was magnificent, as always, her auburn hair flowing in a breeze he hardly felt. Her skin was free of wrinkles and age spots, almost glowing as if she was the very essence of life. She didn't speak, but touched her finger to her lips and beckoned him to flow out of the room with her. He was so caught up in her presence that suddenly everything was bright, with a welcoming warmth, and they drifted in the air just above the crepe myrtles with their violet and white blossoms.

Lillie spoke in a whisper that almost sounded like the wind. "Let go, honey, come with me. Embrace the beauty." Stan realized they were flying—but they couldn't fly! He began to get a sinking feeling, but Lillie spoke again, "You can do it!" How many times had she said that over their years of marriage, with Stan wanting to step back in the face of impossible situations, and Lillie calming him, lifting his spirits as she gently yet firmly showed him how to stretch just a little farther. "Keep your eye looking ahead, honey, don't look down."

For a moment Stan closed his eyes and then opened them to see that they were above the pines now, soaring, her luminescence drawing him forward. She was drawing him into herself, not sensuously, but in some deeper way that fueled a positive energy. It felt like an electrical surge. Stan looked down and saw the docks outside Pappy's Place, and there was his boat, the Lillie Plume, and wait! What was going on? Someone was scraping the name off Stan's boat. Stan felt himself tumble and roll in the air. He was falling away from her.

"Come back!" Lillie said. The aura of her presence filled his spirit again, and he looked up to see her smiling, reaching for him. He was falling but her arm seemed to extend enough for him to reach it, and he grasped her hand. Then there they were, soaring again.

"Don't look back, honey, keep looking forward," Lillie said.

"But what's happening to my boat?"

"That's just your fear playing games with you," Lillie said. "Don't play to your fears. Believe in yourself."

Somehow when Lillie whispered her encouragement, Stan felt strengthened and confident. They continued to soar, doing rolls in the air, and somersaults, and dives. They laughed and soared with the gulls and her radiance was as if it were that of the sun itself. The lightness of the moment fueled his spirit.

"Let's go higher," she whispered, pointing to a bank of clouds. Suddenly they ascended and entered a thick world of liquid cotton. Then Lillie let go of his hand, and seemed to mysteriously fade into the billowing whiteness. Stan found himself engulfed by a brilliant glow as Lillie's whisper lingered, "I love you! Hold onto our love. Let it lift you." Then the aura faded as she dissolved into the cloud, and Stan felt deep grief tugging at his soul. He reached out in vain to pull her back. He felt cold and alone, tumbling again, still reaching for Lillie's presence, but she was gone. A deep emptiness pried at the hinges of his soul as tears dampened his awakening eyes. Another night of grief faded with the light of dawn.

Rubbing his eyes and squinting, Stan realized that he had left the bedroom shades open so that the morning sun shining through leaves outside his window sent shadows dancing across his face. He looked at the digital clock on the night stand—it was 6:30 a.m. The sensation of Lillie's presence lingered. He reached over to feel the empty space where she had once slept. His mind began to dwell on the years they had spent sharing each morning's fresh light and promise. It had been nearly three years since a highway accident had snatched her away from him. He felt like he should have been past the grief by now—but it seemed to hang on.

Stan got up, exercised and shaved, then headed out for his daily two-mile fitness trek around the neighborhood. The sun cast refreshing shadows along his path as he went down toward the docks and jogged along the pier behind Pappy's Place. There was not a cloud in sight. *It's gonna be a beautiful day*—he said to himself—*but a hot one.* As soon as he got back home he showered, ate breakfast, and then drove over to the Grayson-Plume Gallery.

∾

Rev. Edward Heygood, who had served as pastor of the Dinkel Island Wesleyan Brethren Church in the mid-nineteen-eighties, pulled into the parking lot behind the gallery. *It feels good to be back* he thought as he stepped out of his car, breathed in the salt air, and took in his surroundings. He and Stan had formed a deep bond of friendship over the years—a bond that had been reinforced when each had lost his wife and experienced emotional support from the other. Ed's wife, Sally, had died of cancer a year after Stan's wife had died. Having just retired from the ministry, Ed was returning to Dinkel Island at Stan's invitation.

The moving truck had pulled in right behind Ed and the driver walked toward him. "Where do you want us to unload?"

"Through that door and then upstairs," Ed said, pointing toward the gallery's rear entrance. "I'll see if it's open." As he spoke Stan Grayson pulled into the parking lot.

"Man, you made good time," Stan said as he got out of his car. "I thought you wouldn't be here until after lunch."

"You know the old saying, 'the early bird gets the worm,'" Ed said, laughing and embracing his friend. "Not that I'm expecting to find worms in the apartment."

"And you won't, I promise."

Once Ed and the movers got into their work Stan excused himself. "I've got a ton of work in the gallery," he said. "When you get finished come on down and we'll go to lunch."

"You got it," Ed said, and they went their separate directions.

As the movers did the heavy work, Ed got in touch with his feelings about this return to Dinkel Island. The place had a charming uniqueness among Chesapeake Bay communities. For one thing, it was not a true "island," but a peninsula connected to the mainland by a narrow, marshy land bridge. At high tide the marsh grass was almost swallowed up by sea water, hence the feeling of an "island." The community was part of Nor'easter County whose seat, Potomac City, was seventeen miles away. Once a center of thriving truck farming, and later a hub for watermen working the bay, Dinkel Island was now becoming a cultural hub for an expanding industrial and commercial community that embraced the acreage just across the Crabber's Creek Bridge.

It'll be a lot different, Ed thought. *Dinkel Island has changed and so have I.* He thought back over some of the adventures his pastorate had involved. *I wonder what lies ahead?*

When the movers had finished, Ed saw them out and then went into the gallery where he found Stan and Molly going through paperwork. Molly Pringle was Stan's right hand person but Ed had never met her, although Stan had told him enough about her that he felt as though he knew her. He took in her presence. She had medium blue eyes, honey-colored hair, a trim figure and a flirtatious manner. Had Stan not told him that she was a fifty-six-year-old widow, Ed would never have guessed it from her appearance.

"The total number of artists registered is still three short of the available spaces," Molly was saying as Ed walked up, "and I've sent emails to the waiting list. Haven't heard back yet, so I need to send a reminder today."

Stan looked up as Ed entered. "Let me introduce you to an old friend of mine, Ed Heygood," he said to Molly. "He's the one I mentioned who is renting the apartment upstairs. He just moved in."

Turning to Ed he said, "We're working on last minute details for the Art Extravaganza. It's gotten a lot bigger than it was when you were here before."

"Oh, I remember Dinkel Days and the Art Extravaganza," Ed said. "I guess that's coming up in a few weeks, isn't it?"

"Yeah," Stan said. "Lillie started this thing and managing it came naturally to her. Not so with me. If it weren't for Molly I'd have stepped back from it long ago."

"I've heard a lot about you," Molly said as she and Ed shook hands. "If only half of it's true then you're quite a guy!"

"Consider the source," Ed said. "Don't believe everything you hear."

Stan changed the subject. "Let's take a break, Molly. It's time for lunch. I want you and Ed to be my guests."

"See there," Molly said, shaking her head mockingly. "That's why he can't manage the art show—he's always jumping off on something else."

"I'm the boss around here," Stan said. "I say it's time to take a break."

"Well, boss, I respectfully decline. Somebody's got to get the work done. Besides, I brought lunch with me today—its back in the fridge. I'll just stay here—y'all have a good time."

"Well, okay," Stan said. "It's your loss! Really, I do appreciate all your time and effort. Oh, we need some more volunteers for the show days, so let's be thinking about who to call on for that."

"Look, Stan, I can see this is a bad time for you to leave," Ed said. "I can get myself some lunch—you don't need to interrupt things for me."

"Hey, who said anything was for you? I'm hungry and I'm just goin' out to take care of myself. You can tag along if you want to."

"Tag along, eh?" Ed interrupted. "I was just offering to look after you, old man—after all, somebody's gotta do it!"

Stan laughingly straight-armed Ed. "That'll be the day! You lookin' after me. Why do you think I had you come to live here—you're the one somebody's gotta look after."

"You two guys get out of here!" Molly said.

"Okay—we're outa here," Stan said. "Be back in an hour or so."

⌇

Stan and Ed walked over to the beach front and ordered hot dogs from a vendor, then went to one of the tables with an umbrella that the town had provided for the summer season. After brushing some sand off the table they sat down and took in the atmosphere. Two kids who were wet from the surf rushed past them, followed by a wet dog that paused to shake itself near the table, showering Ed and Stan.

"Just what I wanted to season my food," Ed joked.

"Can't beat Pleasant Beach for personal service," Stan said. They laughed and Ed took in the beach sounds as sea gulls cried out, darting through the air looking for food morsels. Time seemed to stand still for a few moments as each man soaked in the atmosphere.

Ed broke the silence. "I can tell you really miss Lillie," he said. "I know how that is, myself. When you have a really good partnership and then lose your partner, it takes a long time to recover. And sometimes I wonder if you ever really do recover."

Stan had a distant look in his eyes for a moment and then said, "You know, I thought I'd get past the grief by now, but it doesn't ever go away. I wake up in the morning and feel like Lillie's been right there with me in the bed all night, and it takes a few moments to get myself in gear. I never used to be that way. Do you ever go through that with Sally?"

"Well, sometimes I do. I think you and Lillie were so much of each other's completeness, though, that it's been a different dimension of loss for you. And it was so sudden. With Sally we went through death's process for months as she tried to beat the cancer. I mean, it was still very harsh when death actually came, but I'm not sure the grief is the same as what you're feeling."

"Lillie was the key to so much that has been good in my life," Stan said. "She was the brains around our house and in the business. When she did something it was top notch, and it always went well—and was always profitable. That woman had a knack with organization and finances."

"I remember," Ed replied. "We used to say anything she touched turned to gold."

"You don't know the half of it, Ed. I tell myself I need to get to know some other woman, but I can't get away from Lillie in my spirit. I hear her voice floating around when I least expect it. I've cut way back on what I do around the gallery and studio, thinking I need to get away from the memories, but it all stays with me. I even bought a boat and go out fishing quite a bit, and when I'm coming in I often think I see her standing on the pier, waving to me. Sometimes it's more than I can take."

Ed reached over and put a hand on Stan's shoulder. "I know exactly what you mean, my friend. Grief runs deep and it's very persistent with me, too. The only way I can deal with it is to embrace it—I mean, accept it and try to connect with all the best of Sally that is with me, and give thanks for it. Over time I've learned to enjoy those bits of memory that pop up, and my hope for you is that you'll find that kind of peace, too."

"I don't know," Stan said, "I just don't see how you do that. Maybe I'll learn someday."

The next day Ed was in the Food Lion check-out line when a voice behind him said, "Aren't you Pastor Heygood?"

He turned to see a mature woman who looked to be in her late sixties. She was stylishly dressed and had attractively fashioned silver hair. A spark of recognition charged between them.

"Why, Fanny! Fanny Morris!"

"I'm surprised you recognize me," she said. "I've gotten a lot older since I saw you last, but you haven't changed a bit. I'd know you anywhere."

"Oh, I don't know about that," Ed said, laughing. "I've lost a lot of hair and what I have doesn't look anything like it used to—not to mention a few extra pounds I'm carrying around the middle. But I'm glad you said something. It's good to see you again."

Ed's mind raced through images of Fanny and her experiences when he'd been her pastor. She had been housekeeper for Harper Jauswell, a very cranky man whose change of heart had turned around his life and the lives of others who knew him. One of those had been CJ Crumbold, a criminal who had tried to defraud Harper by claiming to be his nephew. Fanny had fallen in love with CJ, and then been deeply hurt when his criminal intentions surfaced. CJ had been one of those affected by Harper's change of heart, and had experienced his own change, and with it a call into the ministry. Fanny had finally been able to forgive him but they had never resumed their relationship.

"Don't you want to go ahead of me?" Ed said. "You have so few things and I have a full cart."

"Oh, no," Fanny said. "I don't mind waitin'. Besides, it gives us a chance to talk."

"Okay," Ed said. I guess you know that Sally died last year."

"Yes, I was sorry to hear about Sally. She was such a fine person and we all thought so much of her back when y'all was here. How are the kids?"

"They're grown now, of course, and have moved away with families of their own. We get together on holidays, and we skype to keep in touch. I know Harper died a few years ago—are you still living in the Jauswell house?"

"Yes, Mr. J was very generous to the church and to me. He left me his house and all his money and property, after a donation to the church. It was kinda overwhelmin', but I've learned how to handle all of that."

"I can imagine."

"A few years ago I met a man named Leonard Grant, and after a while we got married. He was a good man, and treated me nice. We moved to Richmond, but I kept the house here, and last year he had a sudden heart attack and died. So I'm back in Mr. J's old house."

"I'm sorry about your loss, Fanny."

Fanny's eyes swelled for a moment, then she said, "Sometimes it seems like I'm always on the losing end with men."

"I'm sure it must feel that way," he said, softly. "I'm so sorry you've had to go through all of that."

Fanny sniffled then half-chuckled, "Listen to me going on about myself when you've had your losses, too."

"That's okay," Ed said as the cashier asked for his MVP card and he began unloading his cart. After checking out he waited for Fanny and they walked to the parking lot together, chatted a few more minutes and then drove off.

19

When Stan heard Ed come in he went up and knocked on his door. When Ed answered he said, "I hear you been talkin' to Fanny Grant."

Ed looked puzzled. "How'd you hear that?" he said.

"Dinkel Island might be growin' and changin'," Stan said, "but it's still a small town with a very active grapevine. Molly told me—she answered the phone and when she hung up she said it was Sarah Jones calling about, as she said it, 'some old preacher from the past who was talkin' to that Fanny lady, the one who lives in the Harper Jauswell's old house.' So I knew that had to be you talkin' to Fanny."

"You're a pretty good detective!" Ed said. "Who'd you say called…Sarah Jones?"

"Yeah, you remember her. Sometimes people call her 'Mrs. Grapevine,'"

"So she's still doin' that! She must be up in years by now. She had to be in her fifties at least when I was here."

"I think she's in her eighties now, and yes, she's still the same Sarah. I guess Fanny is the first of your old flock that you've talked to so far, isn't she—I mean other than me, of course?"

Ed told him about their conversation in the parking lot. "She asked me about CJ Crumbold. I told her he was up in Potomac City now."

"Hmmm," Stan mused, "Wouldn't it be great if those two could mend their fences and get back together. I heard that she said she wasn't cut out to be a preacher's wife."

"I know," Ed said. "CJ told me about that—it was tough for him, but he kept his commitment to the ministry and went on without her."

Stan remembered everybody's surprise when CJ announced his calling. "Speaking of not being cut out for something, CJ was the last person I would've expected to become a pastor," Stan said. "God does work in mysterious ways."

"I guess you could say that about everybody who's called into the ministry," Ed said and then excused himself to get back to putting away his groceries.

Stan went back downstairs to his studio. The day stretched into evening without another opportunity for the two of them to talk. When he got home Stan grilled himself a T-bone steak, then settled down to watch a baseball game. The house felt empty, just as the apartment had before he moved, so he finally went to bed.

Having Ed back in town had certainly stirred up a lot of memories, including those of his years with Lillie. *It was Ed who married us that day at the Wedding Pier,* he recalled. *He and Lillie were the two people who made the biggest difference in my life.*

Stan lay in bed picturing Lillie, imagining her in the next room as though she would appear at any moment. Deep sadness wrenched his soul. *Oh, Lil—I miss you so much* he whispered as he sought the solace of sleep.

2

A Mysterious Catch

"There's nothing like the feeling of a Saturday morning," Ed said as he and Stan walked down the pier from Pappy's Place toward Stan's boat. Seagulls with wind-ruffled feathers perched atop pilings scouring the landscape for food morsels. Nearby two watermen talked with an old-English twang as one of them painted the trim on his boat. The tranquility of the moment was interrupted by the roar of an outboard motor that soon faded into the distance. It was a rich moment that Ed wanted to flag in his memory bank.

"Guess I never thought much about it," Stan said. "I've always thought of Saturday as the time to run errands or do chores and such. Never thought about how it feels."

Ed reached back through the years in his mind. He remembered the frantic Saturday activities when the kids were growing up, and the ever-present last-minute tasks getting ready for

Sundays in the pastorate. "Maybe it's just me"—he said—"but I always think of Saturday as a change-of-pace time when I break out of normal routines."

"I guess fishin' qualifies for that. I probably shouldn't tell you this but I haven't had much success catching fish lately. Maybe havin' you along will change that and put a little excitement into the day—as well as some fish in the fryin' pan."

Ed laughed. "Don't sweat it, whether we catch anything or not the day will be a welcome change of pace for me."

"Here we are," Stan said as they walked up to his 1990 Grady White Gulfstream 230. "She's an old-timer. I bought her used but in excellent condition and she's held up really well. A little bigger than what I wanted, but I wouldn't change now."

"I must say, I'm impressed. This looks more like a yacht than a fishing boat."

"Oh, it's a fishin' boat all right—at least for me. It's just the right size to be stable in the water, yet to get in and out of some of the creeks. It's twenty-three feet long."

They climbed aboard, unsnapped the vinyl curtains into the cockpit area and Stan showed Ed some of the features of the boat. "I bought this depth finder last year. That should help us find some fish today."

Stan turned on the bilge pump and told Ed to take the bait and food down into the cuddy cabin. Ed was impressed again with the vinyl cushions, storage bins, portable commode, fold-down spare bunk and even a small sink.

He went back topside as Stan started the motor and then had him release the mooring lines. They were quickly out into the no-wake zone which gave Ed a chance to take in the beauty of the shoreline, as well as the cliffs he could see across Tranquility Bay at Lighthouse Point.

"I remember when you wrote me about buying this boat. I was surprised at the time. You handle this thing like you've become an old sea dog," Ed said.

"I guess I surprised myself," Stan said. "I've been doing paintings of boats and hanging around watermen for years, so the summer after Lillie died I decided I needed something to take my mind off of her. Now I'm sort of living what I've been painting."

As they moved into the channel Stan opened up the throttle and the boat planed out. "I thought we'd run to Windmill Point and see what we can find off the shelf."

"Sounds great to me," Ed said.

"This baby'll do 30 knots easy," Stan shouted over the noise of the motor. A southeasterly wind created a one-foot swell and the boat handled the sea with a rhythmic rolling motion. Once they reached their destination Stan cut the engine and they drifted just off the shelf at Fleet's Island with their lines out. The sun bore down on them relentlessly, their only relief being a gentle breeze.

"So what are your plans now that you're retired, Ed?

I wish I knew the answer to that, Ed thought. "I don't know, really," he said. "I have thought about maybe doing some writing."

"Oh! I'm surprised. I mean, that sounds like a lot of work. I thought maybe you were gonna take it easy."

"I'm just like you, old man. I'll never sit back and 'take it easy.' Yeah, writing is probably hard work, but it's different. It's just a thought right now."

"What would you write?"

"It wouldn't be theological stuff—I guess I really think about trying to write short stories, either from my experiences or perhaps fiction."

"I'll be interested to see what you come up with." Stan paused and consulted the depth finder. "There's nothing much down there and we've been drifting back and forth for over an hour. Let's break this off and run up into the Rappahannock River. Maybe we'll find better luck up there."

"Sounds like a plan," Ed said as he reeled in his line and stowed his gear.

Stan started the motor and they moved on. "I'll check a couple of bands on the radio while we're runnin' and see if there's any chatter about fish bitin."

They passed a regatta of small sailboats and then saw a number of power boats with people fishing from them. They joined that group but caught nothing, and it appeared the others weren't doing much either. There wasn't much encouragement over the radio and after a while Stan said, I guess we'd better call it a day."

As they headed back out the Rappahannock Stan said, "I had sort of hoped to put a little excitement into your life with a good catch, but I guess we'll have to stay dull and dismal until another fishing day comes up."

Just north of Windmill Point Stan cut back the engine and pointed out to into the bay where a whole flock of gulls were screaming and diving in the channel.

"Look at that! Something's going on out there. Let's check it out—maybe we'll have fish for supper after all."

Just as they got there, however, the gulls suddenly scattered and flew off.

"Must have been some blues feeding near the surface. About all that's left now are the pieces," Stan said, and they turned back toward Tranquility Bay and Dinkel Island. As they approached Lighthouse Point, Stan noticed some activity on the depth finder. Again he cut the engine back and they went slowly in toward shore.

"Seems to be some fish down there," Stan said. "Do ya wanna throw in the lines again?"

"Sure," Ed said, so they stopped off the shelf and cast their lines. It wasn't long until Stan got a strike and pulled in a croaker."

"Better'n nothin'," he said. Then Ed got a strike and pulled in an under-sized spotfish. They threw it back and soon Ed caught a couple of croakers, and then Stan caught a spot that was legal, so they kept at it.

"You probably remember we get lots of citation spot up in here a little later in the season. They're good eatin'."

They fished a little longer and had a fair bunch of fish when things seemed to give out. Stan was about to suggest they call it a day when Ed had a hard pull on his line. Stan stowed his gear and went over to Ed.

"What you got there?"

"I don't know," Ed said, "but it struck hard and it seems to be fighting me. It gives and then pulls on the line again."

"That must be a large bluefish—must really be a big one. Or it could be a skate," Stan said. Ed worked the line and gradually pulled his catch in closer to the boat, then suddenly it seemed to give completely.

"What, did you lose him?" Stan said.

"No, there's still pressure on the line—there! I think he's coming up now. That baby is heavy—almost like a dead weight."

"Whoa," Stan said, laughing, "I don't think you got a fish at all. I'll bet that's an old tire somebody tossed in there."

Within minutes they found out Stan was partially right. It wasn't a tire, but a muddy, seaweed-laden bag of some sort. Stan got the grappling hook and they pulled it up into the boat. It was an old backpack, and it was a mess.

"Get some rags out of that storage bin," Stan said, pointing to a small door in the gunwale. Ed brought the rags and they began getting the mud and seaweed off. The fabric tore easily when they pulled at it and they found a glob of sodden papers, rotted remnants of clothing, and a small vinyl pouch that had a bulge in it and a zippered end that was corroded.

"What's this?" Stan said. "Let's open this thing and see what's inside."

They cut away the zipper and shook the pouch over their bait cutting board. A plastic box, something like a sandwich storage box you might put in a refrigerator dropped out, and when they pried the air tight top off they were shocked: it was stuffed with money—a lot of limp, wadded up bills, some of them stuck together—bills of all denominations.

"Hello!" Stan said. "Can you believe this?"

They proceeded to pull the bills apart and make a rough count "You know, there must be close to $5000 here," Ed said. "It's obviously been there a long time. You'd think somebody would have missed that."

"I'm sure they did, old buddy, but once things get in the water the tide can move them around. No telling where this came from."

Stan got out his cell phone, called over to the police station and reported their find. Chief Archie Draper came right over to Pappy's Place and was waiting for them as they docked the boat and tied it up. They showed him the money which he counted, then put it in a plastic bag. "I'll have to impound this until we can see if somebody claims it," the chief said.

"Do you think this is stolen money?" Ed said.

"I have no idea, but we'll start with what we have," Archie said. "I appreciate you calling me. A lot of people wouldn't have." He looked again at the deteriorated backpack and added, "That money had to have been dropped into the water quite a while back, maybe even a few years ago. We'll check to see if there were any unresolved reports of missing cash back over the years."

With that the chief took the money and backpack and left. Stan and Ed's fishing trip had turned into an adventure after all. After the excitement died down they cleaned their fish and went back to Ed's apartment where they fried up a great supper.

3

Joy From Confusion

At the age of thirty-four Pastor Kate Sheppard was content with her life, happy in her church and fulfilled by the inner nourishment of her calling. She was beginning her second year as pastor of the Dinkel Island Wesleyan Brethren Church, and she had mixed emotions when she heard that a retired former pastor had just moved back into town. She expected he would show up at church sooner or later and wondered how that would challenge her leadership.

She pulled into the pastor's reserved parking spot, stepped out of her car and breathed in the fresh salt air. Birds warbled in nearby trees while the Sunday morning sun promised a good day ahead. A warm smile that had painted itself on her face as she entered the church quickly faded when Herb Melloman, the church lay leader, greeted her. *Uh-oh* she thought, sensing that things weren't as peaceful inside the church as outside.

"I'm glad you're here," Herb said, "we've got an awful problem."

"What's going on?"

"Apparently a water pipe broke overnight in one of the downstairs ceilings and it has soaked one of the rooms and flooded the hallways. It must have gone on all night. There could be water damage we haven't discovered yet."

Kate went with Herb to check out the situation. As soon as they went down the stairs she smelled mildew and knew the damage was extensive. "It's clear we can't use any of these classrooms today," she said.

"I've been talking with a couple of teachers and they suggested we could do a quick shuffle and make Sunday school an all-ages-in-one-room kind of thing in the social hall. They've already started working on that."

"Good idea," Kate said. "I'll stop in there and see how things are going. As soon as you can round up some trustees let's schedule an emergency meeting right after worship so we can get this problem fixed."

"Good idea," Herb said as he went toward the social hall and Kate went to her office. Sitting down at her desk she leaned forward with her hands to her temples and prayed. "Lord, it's such a beautiful day, yet we're stuck with this problem. Help us to keep our focus on your presence so we can rejoice in your name and take things in stride. Thank you for the sunshine on the outside. Help us to trust you so that your Son can shine freshly within us and our fellowship. Amen."

Just as she finished there was a knock at the door. It was Jenny Tyrone, the keyboardist. Jenny, who had been organist since before Ed Heygood's ministry, had made a miraculous adjustment away from the organ to the keyboard and a praise band.

"Come in," Kate called out, and Jenny stepped inside. "I know you've got trouble with the plumbing this morning," she said, "and I hate to burden you with more problems, but we've lost the power to the keyboard and sound system in the sanctuary. There seems to be a short circuit somewhere that keeps tripping the breaker. What do you think we should do?"

Kate closed her eyes for a moment and rolled them toward heaven with a thought-prayer: *Lord, you never tempt us beyond what we can bear with your help, and you are greater than any need we have. What do we do now?*

She opened her eyes, smiled and said to Jenny, "What would you suggest?"

Jenny was ready with an answer. "Since Herb is setting up for a special Sunday school class in the social hall, maybe we could get out more chairs and do a very informal kind of praise service in there. What do you think?"

"Sounds great! Let's go talk it over with some other folks," Kate said, and they left the office together.

⁓

Stan and Ed arrived at church just as the morning bell began to toll. Ed wasn't prepared for what he found when he stepped inside the sanctuary. There was an expansive sense of openness and informality.

"Wow!" he said. "It looks like y'all have really gotten into contemporary worship. How's that working out for you?"

"Some of our older folks don't like it," Stan said. "Our pastor helped us explore what worship is about and our own feelings about it. When the organ needed to be replaced we decided to get the keyboard instead, and that opened the way for some other instruments. One thing led to another and we ended up reinventing how we do worship."

"That's amazing. How do you deal with opposition from those who don't like it?"

"Mostly that has just taken care of itself. You can get an electronic organ sound with the keyboard and sometimes we use traditional hymns with the organ accompaniment. Most of our folks have learned to enjoy singing the praise songs, and using live instruments also helps make it lively and inviting."

"I see you have a projector and a pull-down screen. How do you handle the visuals?"

"Oh, Kate usually has some graphics or videos that fit her sermon topic, and we put the words to the praise songs on the screen to make singing feel more spontaneous."

Ed looked around the sanctuary. "I see the prodigal son stained glass window is as prominent as ever."

"We wouldn't change that. I know what an inspiration that window has been for me and for other people over the years. I think of it as a meditation window."

"That's cool," Ed said. "I like the touch with the banners on the wall in front, too. Very contemporary, yet worshipful. I'm looking forward to the service today."

As they spoke a group of teenagers and two adults came in. "Excuse us," they said. "The service is going to be in the social hall today and we need some extra chairs."

Stan and Ed looked at each other. "I wonder what's up?" Stan remarked and then turned to one of the adults. "Can we help? What's this all about?"

"Some broken waterpipes have created a mess in the basement classrooms," they said. "Herb thinks that caused a short circuit in some of the wiring so we don't have power in here. Everything seems to be fine in the other building."

"So much for you having any impact coming back to the church, old buddy," Stan said to Ed, who shrugged and answered, "That's good. Here, grab a chair."

They followed the youth out the door and over to the social hall. That was another surprise for Ed. It was a recent addition to the church that included a state-of-the-art gymnasium/social hall/community center with a modern, commercial-sized kitchen and enough storage to allow the facility to be used in a variety of ways.

"How do you like it?" Stan asked.

"I'm impressed! I'll bet this draws a lot of people in for different community events as well as church activities."

"Oh yeah!" Stan replied. "Dinkel Island proper hasn't grown a whole lot, but we have several new subdivisions outside town with young families and lots of kids. Mammoth Baptist has a satellite church out there now, but they don't have this kind of facility. We're meeting some of the needs among the families both in and out of town."

"That's fantastic," Ed said. "It feels good to see all of this going on. I look forward to being here again."

People had been flooding into the room as Stan and Ed talked. Jenny began to play the keyboard and spontaneously people began singing praise songs. After fifteen minutes of spirited singing Pastor Sheppard, wearing a white clerical robe with a multi-colored stole, stood to address the congregation.

"Good morning!" Her voice boomed through a wireless lip microphone. "God is good—" she said, raising her arms, and everyone responded—"all the time." The people broke out in applause. Kate explained the crisis with the water and electricity and then said, "I can assure you that this is a temporary problem and all should be back to normal by next Sunday. We will need some volunteers to help with clean-up, so please see Herb Melloman if you can help. Ed was thrilled with the positive atmosphere in the room.

Following an exciting service of praise, prayer and message, Kate made an announcement prior to her benediction. "Friends, we have someone with us whom I haven't met, but some of you may remember him from years past. Rev. Edward Heygood, who just retired, has moved here to Dinkel Island, and Herb tells me he's here with us today. Rev. Heygood, would you stand and let everybody see you? I'm sure lots of folks will remember you and want to say a few words. We're glad you're with us."

After the benediction people came up to speak with Ed. The first one was Fanny Grant who beamed with joy and said, "I told everybody I could that you was back in town, and I told 'em I thought you'd be here today. I want to be the first to say 'welcome back.'"

Ed thanked her and shook hands with a surge of smiling people, and then Jenny Tyrone came up.

"It's good to see you again," she said. "Can I still call you Ed?"

Ed laughed. "Of course you can. It's good to see you, too. Boy, you've really had a lot of changes to take in stride musically. This was a wonderful service."

Greetings and reminiscences went on for a few minutes, and many people expressed sympathy on Ed's loss of Sally, whom they remembered fondly. Then a woman with a walker came up.

"I'll bet you don't remember me," she said.

Ed wouldn't have recognized Sarah Jones, but her voice was a dead giveaway. "Sure, I know who you are Sarah," he said, and hugged her. "It's wonderful seeing you again. She told him about things that had happened in her life over the years. "I can't do my Saturday cleanin' anymore like I usta," she said, "but Willy does it for me—can you imagine that!" She laughed, and then said, "and I still know what's goin' on in town."

As the crowd emptied out Kate came over to Ed. "Rev. Heygood, I'm Kate Sheppard, as I'm sure you've figured out by now. It's good to meet you and have you here."

Ed shook her hand and said, "Just call me 'Ed,' please. You had a wonderful service here today, and it looks like you did it in spite of a couple of hurdles that got thrown in your way."

"Just trusting in the Lord, and letting a lot of really good people step in and keep things going," she answered. "You know how it is in the pastorate. About the time you think things are peaceful and settled something happens. You know, when I got here this morning I was enjoying the morning sunlight and then I stepped into an unexpected mess, but God brought his Light into the midst of the mess and it all turned out fine. It always does."

4

Stirrings

The sharp ring of the telephone startled Ed as he sat drinking his coffee on Monday morning. *Now who could that be?* He glanced at his watch as he answered.

It was Fanny Grant who said, "Good mornin', Ed. I hope I'm not disturbin' you—I know it's kinda early."

"Oh, you're not disturbing me," he said. "It's not early for me."

Fanny sounded relieved. "I'm glad I ain't botherin' you, and you might think this is kinda forward of me, you not bein' back in town long and all"—she paused a minute, then continued, "I was wonderin' if you'd like to come over and have lunch sometime this week—here at the house, I mean."

The invitation caught Ed off balance. He had been thinking about the mysterious money he and Stan had found in the bay on Saturday. Having lunch with Fanny, or any one else for that matter, was the farthest thing from his mind. He started to decline but then changed his mind. *Maybe I need to lighten up. It would be fun to get re-aquainted with Fanny. I can see she's changed a lot over the years.*

"I guess I could fit that into my schedule," he said with a slight chuckle. "I really don't have too much going on here yet, so sure, I'd love to. What day did you have in mind?"

"Actually, I sort of wondered if you could come today," Fanny replied.

Again Ed was surprised, but he said, "Sure, what time?"

"Is 12:30 okay?"

"That's just fine," Ed replied.

"Good! Oh, it won't be anything fancy. I thought I'd make some sandwiches. Do you like smoked turkey breast on whole grain bread?"

"Sure, anything you fix will be fine. I'll look forward to seeing you."

Ed hung up and leaned back in his chair An unfamiliar feeling swept over him. It was kind of a tingling sensation, not so much physical as emotional. *It's been almost two years now since Sally died,* he thought. *There's nothing wrong with having lunch with Fanny, or any other woman. Why does it feel like I'm being disloyal to Sally? I've got to get over that.* He knew that grief could do strange things to people and it made him hesitant and uncertain.

Pulling up behind Fanny's Lexus in the driveway of the massive old Victorian house he suddenly felt self-conscious, like he didn't quite belong there. The house had a fresh coat of paint, the lawn was immaculate, and the gardens Annabelle Jauswell had loved showed an exciting resurrection. Ed pushed his uncertain feelings aside and walked up to the house. Even before he could ring the bell, Fanny opened the door and invited him inside with a broad smile and an embrace.

"Hi, Ed. I'm so glad you could come." Fanny looked striking in a bright green knit top, khaki skirt, white sandals and a stylish costume jewelry necklace with matching earrings. Her silver hair now had a reddish blonde tint to it and was brushed back with a flair. Ed had noticed before that she seemed more trim than he remembered. Fanny presented a smart contrast to the old days when she had been Harper's housekeeper.

"Thanks for the invitation," Ed said as he stepped inside." He was immediately struck by the changes in the house. Gone was the museum-like quality from Harper's day, along with the antiques.

"You have quite a flair for decorating," he said. "I love the changes you've made—the stylish furniture and the colorful walls. Wow! It makes you feel alive just stepping in here."

"Oh, you're exaggeratin'," Fanny said, but he could tell she appreciated the compliment.

Fanny had accomplished a feeling of warmth by scattering colorful carpets around the hardwood floors. A variety of bright, colorful artwork adorned the walls. Two paintings of local scenes jumped out at him. "Aren't those paintings by Stan Grayson?" he said.

"They sure are! I think he's a great artist. In fact, I think he's a great person," Fanny said. Ed detected a warmth of emotion behind her words.

"I agree with you on both points," he said as Fanny motioned him toward the dining room where she had set the table for lunch.

"I don't mean to rush you into lunch if you'd rather sit and talk a bit first," Fanny said, becoming more animated and pausing at the dining room door.

"Oh that's fine, I don't feel like I'm being rushed. We can talk while we eat, and besides, I'm sure you have other things to do today."

"Actually, I don't have a lot to do," she said. "Isn't it strange that I was the housekeeper here for so long, and now I have a housekeeper! What do you think of that?" she added with a laugh.

"That must leave you with some time on your hands."

"Well, it does—in fact, that's one reason I thought about talking with you because I wonder how you handle the emptiness that used to be filled by having another person in your life. Until I married Leonard I had always felt like being alone was sort of natural—except for that short time when CJ and I were dating each other. Then after he ran off and all the things that followed that, I just sorta fell back into being a loner. But once Leonard and I married I got used to having someone else in my life and I've been surprised how hard it's been to get used to bein' alone again."

"I understand what you're saying. Yes, I have my moments when what I call the "aloneness" gets to me. But after nearly two years I'm beginning to feel comfortable with that."

"Maybe I will, too," Fanny replied with a sigh. "You mentioned Stan Grayson's paintings. I have bought one of his pieces each of the last two years at the Art Extravaganza. Since his wife was killed in that awful wreck I know he has to be feeling the pain and loneliness, and sometimes I feel like I want to talk to him about that. But he seems so preoccupied and busy, I just never have felt like I could talk with him."

"Maybe you need to just take things in hand and give it a try—you know, just tell him you'd like to talk and see what happens," Ed said. "I've known Stan a long time and I can see that he's still going through his grief. He might cover that up with busyness, but underneath that he's very approachable. You probably just need to get his attention."

Ed felt uncomfortable with the direction their conversation was taking. He didn't want to get involved with either Stan's or Fanny's personal life. As a pastor he'd had to deal with such dilemmas many times, but this felt a little different. Then a thought crossed his mind.

"You know Stan's looking for some volunteers for the Art Extravaganza right now. It's just a thought, but if you give him a call maybe you can work with him and Molly over the next few weeks. You never know—you might both find an opportunity to talk and share some of your experiences."

"Oh, that's a good idea!" Fanny said, excitedly. "I didn't know they needed more volunteers. I'll call him later."

That having been established, Ed and Fanny settled into the story about the strange catch on Saturday, and his retirement, and some of her interests, and after nearly two hours they realized how late it was getting.

"Look at the time," Fanny said. "I didn't mean to take up so much of your day, but I really have enjoyed having you come by for lunch. Maybe we can do it again sometime."

"I've enjoyed it, too, Fanny. It's hard to move back after so many years and pick up with old relationships, so I really am glad you called. I'll keep you in my prayers, and I'd appreciate it if you'd do the same for me."

Agreeing to this they went to the door, said goodbye with an embrace, and Ed drove back to his apartment.

❧

Stan and Molly were at the gallery immersed in art festival details. They were both making phone calls dealing with things like the awards for the artists on Saturday night, and the arrangements for the meal they would serve them. Unexpectedly a new problem arose when the person who had been organizing the hospitality volunteers called.

"I feel terrible dropping this on you at the last minute, but I have to leave town and I won't be here for the show. My daughter in Ohio is sick and she needs me to look after the kids for her. I'm leaving tomorrow morning."

Organizing and managing the hospitality volunteers was a huge responsibility. These were the people who manned the registration tent, showed people to their spaces and answered their questions about the mechanics of the show. They also carried around snacks and water for the artists, and sat in for them while they left their tents for lunch or breaks. It took a lot of people to do all this and a lot of time to plan and manage it.

"I'm so sorry to hear that," Stan said. "You're doing the right thing, and don't you worry about the hospitality volunteers. We just appreciate all you've already done. If it would help, I could come by and pick up the materials and go over where things are with you. We'll find someone to take your place."

As he told Molly about the call Stan had a sudden thought. "You know, Ed told me he wanted to do something to help now that he's retired. He certainly wouldn't have any problem managing people since he spent his life as a pastor. I wonder if he might handle this committee for us. Actually, most of the work is already done, we just need supervision and coordination."

"That's a good thought," Molly replied. "I don't know much about running churches, but I imagine it's not too different since it involves working with volunteers."

"That's kind of what I was thinking," Stan said. "I'll ask him."

"I'm good with that," Molly said. "What's next?"

"Maybe it should be lunch," Stan suggested. "How did it get to be after one o'clock already?"

"You know the old saying: 'Time flies when you're having fun,'" Molly said, laughing. "Are we having fun yet?"

Stan gave her a sarcastic look and then said, "Are you game for the Seafood Pavilion? I think I'm ready for a crab cake sandwich, and they have the best. Treat's on me."

Molly laughed. "That's an offer I can't resist."

They closed the shop and walked over to the restaurant where they were ushered to a window booth. While waiting for their food Stan said, "I can't tell you how much I appreciate the way you take care of the details that Lillie used to handle. If it was up to me alone this whole art show would probably have fallen apart by now—if not the whole gallery."

"Oh, you're doing okay with things, but I know what you mean. It takes a team of people to manage the teamwork of everybody else. We seem to be a pretty good team."

Their food was served and they had just settled into eating when Stan's cell phone rang. It was a reporter for the *Dinkel Island Sentinel*, the town's weekly newspaper.

"Mr. Grayson, I hear you had a strange catch off Lighthouse Point when you were out fishing Saturday. It sounds like a fascinating story. I understand there's some money involved and the police are trying to find who it belongs to. Maybe an article in the paper will stir up some results, so I'd like to come by and talk with you this afternoon. Is that possible?"

That was just what Stan did not want in the midst of everything else, but he knew there really wouldn't be a good time for this, so he agreed. "I can spare you five minutes," he said. "We're really stacked up with preps for the extravaganza right now—in fact, we're just on a late lunch break. Can you drop by around three o'clock?"

"Yeah, I can do that," the reporter said. "See you at three."

By mid-afternoon Sarah Jones had spread the word all over town about the mysterious money pulled out of Tranquility Bay on Saturday. "I hope you're not in the middle of anything," she would say, "because there's something really strange going on in town, and we all need to be on the lookout." When people asked what she was talking about she would say, "that money they found out at Lighthouse Point. You heard about that, didn't you?" If they said "no," it gave her a chance to embellish the story.

"I heard it was Stan Grayson who found it when he and Ed Heygood pulled up some old bag of some sort when they was fishin'," Sarah informed everybody. "Just think, Ed Heygood's just moved back into town and already he's stirred up something big."

As Sarah continued calling around town peoples' attention turned away from who found the money to the amount involved. It kept getting exaggerated until Sarah called Cheryl Drew who listened beneath the surface. She called Kate Sheppard.

"Hi Kate. This is Cheryl. I hate to bother you with this, but I have a concern about Sarah Jones and I thought I should pass it along to you."

"What's going on with Sarah?" Kate said.

"She's been on the phone all day about that money they found in Tranquility Bay last Saturday. She's really getting stirred up over this, trying to make it into something scary. I called to ask you to pray for her because with her heart condition and that stroke she had last year, she could do herself in over something like this."

"Let's back up a minute," Kate said. "I've been at the hospital in Potomac City all day and I just came in. What money are you talking about?"

"All I know is Stan and Ed were out fishing on Saturday and they pulled in some kind of container that had a lot of money in it, and the police are trying to find who it belongs to."

"Ah—so this is something Sarah has worked up into a big deal."

"That's right. I've been praying for Sarah to let go of this before she works herself up into another stroke or something. She seems to listen to you, so I wondered if you might be willing to check on her."

"Of course, I will," Kate said. "Why is this mysterious money such a big deal, anyway?"

"I really don't think it would have been such a big thing if it hadn't gotten stirred up on the grapevine. Anyway, I'm concerned about Sarah."

"So am I," Kate said. "Thanks for letting me know."

Kate fixed herself a quick supper, then called Sarah and arranged to go by and visit with her briefly. *I must say,* she muttered to herself as she went out the door, *the craziest things get stirred up in this town!*

5

A New Chapter

Joe Truvine arrived at the gallery right on time. Stan led the way to his small office where he motioned the reporter toward a chair while he sat on the corner of the desk.

"What do you need to know?" Stan asked.

"Everything, basically," Joe said. "Chief Draper gave me a copy of his report on the incident and let me photograph the backpack and money. I also have a lot of 'I don't knows' from him in response to some of my questions, so maybe I'll get further with you."

"Maybe," Stan said with a chuckle. "I guess that depends on what you ask."

Joe shot him an exasperated look and said, "Can you tell me who was with you, where you were, and how you happened to find the money?"

"Well it wasn't any big deal. My buddy Ed Heygood and I were coming back after fishing unsuccessfully most of Saturday when I saw some activity on the fish finder over off Lighthouse Point, and—."

"That's a good stretch along there," Joe interrupted. "Where were you exactly—could you find the spot again?"

"Well, like I told the police, we were just off the cliff that obscures the lighthouse from close-in. There is a narrow creek with thick brush and trees on each side located a little to the right of the cliff. You could actually miss it if you didn't know it was there. I guess that could be a landmark."

"I'll look for that. I want to photograph the area where the money was found," Joe said. "Now tell me exactly what happened."

"Well, we got into some croakers and spot and actually had a pretty good catch. We were about to call it a day when Ed thought he had a hard bite on his line. I thought it might have been a large bluefish or a skate because it seemed to pull, then go slack. Finally we got it close enough to the boat to see that it was a backpack."

"Why didn't you just cut your line and get rid of it?"

"I don't know, we just got curious, I guess, so we brought it on board. There was a lot of crud in it and the backpack itself was slimy, so we knew it had been there a long time. Inside we found this plastic bag with a zipper and we could tell there was something inside of that so we cut it open. We were shocked to find all that money."

"What did you think might be in the bag before you opened it?"

"We had no idea—the money was inside one of those refrigerator sandwich boxes you can press to seal tight. It was damp, of course, but we were able to pull the bills apart enough to get an idea how much it was. That's when I called Chief Draper and he met us at the dock. From there on things have been in his hands."

"Any thoughts on how it got there?" Joe asked.

"I guess there are as many thoughts as people thinkin' em," Stan answered, "but I wouldn't hazard a guess about that. I'm sure Archie will get to the bottom of it."

"Would you mind running out there and letting me photograph you at the spot?"

Stan's voice revealed his growing irritation as he reached for the door and said, "I'm sorry, this is not a good time for me right now. With Dinkel Days and the Art Extravaganza just a couple of weeks away I'm kind of strapped here. I'm sure you can understand that I really don't have time to do that."

"Of course, I wasn't thinking about all of that," Joe said. "Thanks for your time. Let's hope the person who lost the money comes forward, or somebody who knows about it."

"Yeah," Stan said. "That's what bugs everybody—the amount of money. Losing a few dollars might be one thing, but this is a lot more than that. You'd think there'd be a record of that much money turning up missing. Archie said he'd look into it and I haven't heard any more from him. Like I said, it's out of my hands now."

"You'd probably like for it to be 'in' your hands," Joe said, laughing. "You could do a lot with five grand."

"Oh," Stan said, "I wouldn't keep it, and neither would Ed. We already talked about what we would do if no owner for the money can be found. We'll donate it to the rescue squad. Make it do some good in the community."

"Well, aren't you guys good-hearted! Wish we had more people who thought that way," Joe said.

"There probably are more," Stan said, "we just don't have occasions where we become aware of them."

∿

As Ed came into the gallery Molly looked up from her work. "Hey, Ed. If you're looking for Stan, he's back in the office, but I wouldn't advise bothering him."

"Oh?" Ed said. "Must be something big going on."

"No, it's just that reporter from *The Sentinel* askin' Stan a lot of questions about that money you guys found out in Tranquility Bay."

Just then the office door opened and the two men came out. Stan said, "Come on back and let's talk about the Beach Art

47

Extravaganza. We've got some terrific talent coming in here, plus some good local folks, and we'd like to talk it up."

"I'll probably do that first of next week," Joe said, and then noticed Ed standing at the counter talking to Molly.

Stan said, "Here's my partner in crime, Ed Heygood. He's the guy who caught that big bad money bag Saturday."

"Oh, glad to meet a celebrity," Joe said.

"What did you say your name is?" Ed asked Joe.

"Joe Truvine—you've probably seen my byline in *The Sentinel*."

"Well, I probably would have," Ed replied, "but I just moved back to Dinkel Island the other week and I haven't gotten into reading the local paper yet. I remember *The Sentinel* back when I was pastor here nearly thirty years ago."

"Oh, that makes an even sweeter story," Joe said. "Maybe I should get your take on things while I'm here."

"No need," Ed said, "I'm sure Stan told you the whole thing. Whatever he said I second."

The phone rang and Molly answered, then said, "Stan, it's for you."

"Okay"—Stan said—"who is it?"

"Hey, you've got things to do," Joe said as Molly told Stan it was Fanny. "I'll just be on my way. Thanks for the story."

Stan picked up the phone. "Hi, Fanny. To what do I owe the pleasure of this call?"

"I wondered if I might come by and talk to you," Fanny said. "I understand you need some more volunteers and I might be able to help you out. Is it too late to drop by now?"

Stan was taken aback for a moment, then said, "Well, sure, come on by."

"Okay, see you shortly," Fanny said and hung up.

Ed turned to Stan, "I was just coming to tell you I had lunch with Fanny today and mentioned that you might need a volunteer."

"Apparently she heard you," Stan said. "We just had a big problem surface this morning when the head of our hospitality committee called in and resigned because of some family problems. We were kind of left hanging on that one—we even thought about asking you to take that on, old buddy."

"Well, I appreciate the thought," Ed said, "and I'd be willing to help out wherever you need me, but I just retired from being in charge of stuff so I don't want that wrinkle in it. If it's hospitality, Fanny's probably just right for the job."

They talked on a few more minutes, then Ed went upstairs to his apartment, and Molly said she needed to leave a little early, so Stan was by himself at 4:30 when Fanny walked in.

"Fanny!" Stan said greeting her at the front door, "I'm glad to see you. So you want to volunteer to help with the Beach Art Extravaganza?"

"Yes, I seem to have a lot of time on my hands these days, and I heard you still needed volunteers so I thought I'd see if there was somethin' I could help with. I'm not a secretary or clerk or anything like that—until a few years ago all I ever did was keep Harper's house. But I'm willing to learn, if you need me."

Stan motioned toward a couple of chairs and said, "Why don't we sit down and let me tell you what we need. We have just lost one of our key people who had to drop out due to family issues. She was in charge of our hospitality committee."

Fanny nodded, "So what would I need to do—I assume you're asking me to take her place?"

Stan spelled out all the details. "So you can see it is a big responsibility—I wouldn't tell you differently—but it's also true that with all that has been done so far it will basically involve pulling things together. You'll need to be here most of the time during the festival, to oversee the hospitality folks. If that's more than you want to tackle, I can understand. But if you're interested, I can sure use your help."

At first Fanny felt overwhelmed as Stan talked. It was very complex, but then she did what she had learned when dealing with Harper's estate. She began to listen between the lines, to hear more than words. She began to see herself fitting in. She knew it would be a lot to learn, but that would be good for her, too.

"Yes!" Fanny said.

"Yes?" Stan said, not sure what he was hearing."

"Yes, I'll do it. When do I start?"

"Well, thank you. I guess I thought you'd have to think about it or something. This is wonderful. You can start tomorrow, if you want."

"I'll be here in the morning," Fanny said. Then a thought struck her.

"Stan," she said, "I'll bet you've been so busy around here that you've hardly been takin' time to eat. Maybe you and me could go down to the dinin' room at the Grande Hotel and I'll treat us both to a scrumptious meal. What do you say?"

Again, Stan was taken aback by the unexpected. He was seeing something in Fanny he'd never really noticed, some depth that he liked, and she was certainly right that he hadn't made any plans for supper.

"You know, Fanny, I think I'll take you up on that, but I want it to be my treat—that's the least I can do for somebody who's volunteering for a big job."

"Don't be ridiculous," Fanny said. "I'm not expectin' to get anything but satisfaction from volunteerin'. Besides, I've got enough money to do almost anything I want, and I can certainly afford to treat you."

Stan closed up the shop and he and Fanny walked into a new chapter in their lives.

6

Reactions

On Thursday morning the featured article in the weekly issue of *The Island Sentinel* read:

Preacher Finds Mystery Money
By Joe Truvine, Reporter

While fishing last Saturday afternoon off Lighthouse Point, Rev. Edward Heygood thought he had caught a skate. When he got it to the boat, however, it turned out to be an old backpack containing an estimated $5,000 in cash.

Heygood, who has just moved back to Dinkel Island after retiring from the ministry, was fishing with local artist, Stan Grayson, aboard the Lillie Plume. Grayson said the catch came as a total surprise, and he immediately turned the money over to Dinkel Island Police Chief Archie Draper, who says an investigation is under way.

The mysterious money has created an active buzz at Pappy's Place, and throughout Dinkel Island. For Heygood, who pastored the Dinkel Island Wesleyan

Brethren Church from 1983 to 1988, creating a buzz is nothing new. In 1984 he and his church hosted an event at the campground that featured a parachute preacher, and launched church activities that stirred up the whole town.

Chief Draper says so far no one has come forth with information about the money, and he has no solid leads as to its source. He asks anyone who might have information to contact him at the Dinkel Island Police Department. If no one comes forth to claim it, Grayson says he and Heygood will donate it to the Dinkel Island Rescue Squad.

The article was accompanied by a large photo showing the cliffs at Lighthouse Point with a small photo inset showing the money and the plastic bag in which it had been found.

Reactions to the newspaper article were instant and electric, catapulting the gossip up several levels from grapevine whispers to full-fledged conversation. The lunch counter at Dinkel Drugs was abuzz from the morning coffee crowd until it closed at three o'clock. As was his custom, Bob Drew, the owner of the drug store and pharmacist, took a few minutes to sit down with Doc Patcher, Jimmy Charles and Darrell Tellerson. The foursome met for coffee at 8:30 every Tuesday and Thursday to keep up some camaraderie, and try to find a time when they could get together for a round of golf. They became known around town as "The Old Geezers."

Doc Patcher said, "Looks like that preacher who moved back into town has stirred himself up a cauldron of gossip, from what I see in the paper. I expect he'll be takin' some heat around town."

"You mean Ed Heygood?" Bob asked, and Doc nodded. "Heck, Ed's a good guy. He was pastor at the Wesleyan Brethren Church when Cheryl and I joined. He handled some rough stuff back in those days; I'm sure he can take the heat."

"Well, there really shouldn't be any heat," Darrell said. "All he did was pull up something out of the water, and turn it over to the police so they can find where it came from. That's just good citizenship."

"Oh, I didn't mean 'heat' in the sense of 'trouble,' just in the gossip that something like that stirs up," Bob said. "Cheryl and I hear it in here all the time."

"Yeah," Jimmy said, "it probably would have been nice to move in and get settled without all the attention he's getting, but, hey, it'll pass in a day or so. I wonder if he's a golfer," he said with a twinkle, "maybe we could get him out and win some of that new-found money off of him!"

"I know Ed," Bob said. "I think he does play golf, but I'll eat my hat if he ever plays for money. That's not his style. He'd just play for fellowship and fun."

"Can't argue with that," Doc said. "So what else is new in town. This thing will die out just as soon as they find who the money belongs to."

"You can't count on that," Darrell said. "It all depends on why it was even out there, apparently for a long time. This old fish tale smells a little rotten to me, and I believe it still has some mileage left in it. I'll guarantee it!."

They all laughed, turned to the subject of baseball and then set a time for golf on Saturday afternoon.

❧

Chief Archie Draper sat down at his desk and opened the *Sentinel*, saw the feature article, and read it quickly. Then he took the paper and went out into the office where he said to his dispatcher, Hank, "Did you see this?"

Hank glanced his way and said, "Oh, you mean about the mysterious money. Yeah, I saw it."

"It must take a special breed of folks to be reporters," Archie said. "Joe got the facts right, but then he added in some twist about the guy who found it being a preacher who stirs things up. Where'd that come from?"

"You know yourself, you gotta watch every syllable of every word you say to a reporter. I expect either Heygood or Grayson—whichever one Joe talked to—said something that led to that little twist in the story."

"I'm sure you're right, Hank. We know all too well how things get twisted or carried to extremes. By the way, we haven't gotten anything in from our inquiries about that money have we?"

"Not a thing. If that was honest money there would have been a record of it disappearing somewhere back over the last few years, but there's nothing. I went back in the logbook twenty years and there was nothing about missing money in an amount like that. So I'd guess it was dirty money to begin with."

"You got a point there," Archie replied. "We'll keep up the inquiries for a while, but my guess is somebody running drugs lost that out in the bay somewhere and got roasted for losing it. It could have been bouncing along on the bottom for quite a while."

With that Archie and Hank turned their attention to more current affairs in the life of Dinkel Island.

When Kate Sheppard read the article about the mystery money she felt a strange sensation. It seemed to touch something in her own life, which seemed strange since she didn't fish and she certainly hadn't lost any money in Tranquility Bay. It had bothered her how upset Sarah Jones seemed to be over this mysterious money. Sarah seemed to have an entrenched fear that something bad was going on around town. Kate had prayed with her and tried to relieve some of her anxiety but she wasn't sure Sarah had let go very much.

"Oh, my," Kate said aloud, "the way this article tells the story it's sure to charge Sarah up even more." She thought about Stan, Ed and the strange money. She prayed that there would be healing and release from any evil that might be involved. Then she got her things together and went on to church to her office.

Her secretary, Margie, was already at her desk. "Good morning," she said as Kate walked in. "Looks like another beautiful summer day."

"Yes, it sure does," Kate answered. "Have we had any calls this morning? I really need to work on Wednesday's Bible study notes, so I hope we don't have any new illnesses in the flock."

"Well, there have been a couple. Did you read that story in *The Sentinel* about some mysterious money? I'd already heard about it from Sarah Jones a couple of days ago, but seeing it in print makes it more real."

"Yes, I saw it. I'm sure it's something simple, although it does seem someone would have reported that much money missing somewhere along the way. Anyway, the police will straighten it out."

"Yeah, but we'll probably have to straighten out Sarah Jones the way she's been going on about this."

"I know," Kate said. "I talked to her about it the other day and she really is holding onto this thing. All we can do is pray for her, I guess—unless she opens the door for us to help in some other way."

"It really does touch our church, too," Margie continued. "I mean, with Stan Grayson and that retired preacher who was at church with him Sunday involved, it seems like it really touches all of us."

Kate and Margie talked a few more minutes about some congregational issues, then Kate went into her office and closed the door. She sat down at her desk, closed her eyes, and began to drift in a meditative mood. Suddenly she heard voices from the past—her parents talking about a cousin she hardly knew having disappeared—*what was her name?* Kate tried to pull it up from her memory. The girl was only a teenager, one of several children of her mother's sister who had married some oysterman in Maryland somewhere, and sort of pulled away from the family.

Cybil! Kate opened her eyes and at up straight. *That girl's name was Cybil. I think they decided that she and some boy she ran away with, died in a boating accident during a storm.* Kate sat back, closed her eyes, and tried to recall more.

I knew it was a mistake for Morene to marry that waterman. Kate remembered her mother's words. *I never liked the look in his eyes, and he was always ill-at-ease, shifting his feet when he talked to you.* It was as though her mother was right there in the room.

Her dad's voice came into her mind next. *Your read on people is usually right on target* he had told her mother. *Morene ran off with that guy and until all this happened with Cybil we never heard from her again.*

Most people didn't, her mother had said. *She did call me a time or two early on, but then she stopped and when I tried to reach her the phone was out. That husband of hers probably cut the phone line.*

That was back in 1989, Kate thought. She remembered a newspaper story. *Two kids ran off without a trace and were never found. It was assumed they met with tragedy because of the condition of the old boat they were using. The boy—what was his name?* She couldn't remember—*he was twice as old as Cybil.* It was claimed that he had abducted her. *What a tragedy! Somehow Morene always was involved in things that bordered on tragedy.*

Kate's thoughts went on a bit, then she suddenly sat straight up, and said to herself, *Enough of this, Kate! That stuff was a long time ago and it has nothing to do with this mysterious money.* With that she settled herself to the task of preparing for her Wednesday Bible study class.

7

---◆---

In the Dark of Night

The early October night air was chilly and Cybil Froster shivered inside her wool sweater and windbreaker. A sudden crackling noise behind her made her jump with a startled gasp. "Who's that?" she spat out in a half-whisper as she twirled around in her tracks.

"Hey, I'm sorry. I didn't mean to startle you." The voice belonged to Tom Brewster, a young crew hand her daddy, Tumble Froster, had recently hired on his workboat.

Cybil had seen him around. He was the only one of her daddy's crew who didn't try to push himself on her. *Oh, oh! Trouble!* "Get away from me! Why ain't you back there with them other guys drinkin' and carryin' on?"

Tom stepped out of the shadowy trees along the seashore path and made a gesture with his hands, opening them, palms up, and spreading them out. "You don't need t' be afraid o' me. I ain't after ya."

Cybil kept her guard up. She had learned to handle herself around watermen who wanted to take advantage of her. She wasn't sure about Tom. "You stay back there! You ain't answered my question."

Tom stepped back, lifting his arms, palms open. "Okay, okay. Don't get excited. I ain't back there partyin' 'cause I don't wanna be. Ain't no sense in all that drinkin' and yellin' an' such. Way I see it, life's more fun sober than drunk."

What's this? I ain't never heard nobody talk like that. "And I'm s'posed to believe that?"

"I guess you don't gotta believe me. Don't know if I'd believe me if I was in your shoes."

"What's that s'posed to mean?"

"It means I just want to make yer acquaintance—maybe be yer friend."

"Why, so's you can get your way with me?"

"No! No! Look, if I meant ya harm I'd have jest jumped all over ya—but I didn't. I was jest walkin' along behind ya to see where ya was goin'. You're different from your sisters and them other gals at the packin' house. I bet ain't nobody ever had his way with you."

"Ain't gonna, neither, lessen I invite 'em. Up to now I ain't seen nobody I'd care to invite."

Tom stretched out his hand. "Let's jest shake hands an' be friends. Okay?"

Cybil let her guard down. Tom seemed okay, and she had noticed he was different from the others. She shook his hand and halfway smiled at him, "I was just takin' a walk, tryin' to git away from all that mess back there."

"Is it okay if I walk along with ya?" Tom said.

"Well, maybe—how come you're so different?"

"Oh, I've had my times, but I learned that I didn't like myself very much when I done some of them things. So I don't do 'em."

They started walking back toward the packing house. "Ain't too much farther ya can go out this way," Cybil said. "We might's well go back."

Cybil studied Tom's features in the moonlight as they walked. His sandy hair blew across his forehead and he brushed it away. He wasn't wearing a greasy old cap like most of the men in her world. *He's actually kinda cute* she thought. Suddenly she felt a long-suppressed restlessness swell up inside her.

"Does your daddy always throw them wild parties?" Tom said.

"Sometimes, when he gets a really good haul of oysters from the tongers. I got tired of that mess a long time ago," Cybil said. She was surprised how comfortable it felt talking with Tom. "Sometimes I dream of gittin' outa here," she said. "That's what I think about when I walk away from things on nights like this." *Now why'd I go and say that,* she thought.

Tom stopped and looked her square in the eyes. "Are you serious?"

Cybil turned away from him. *If only he knew—but I don't know him. Why am I talkin' to him like this?* She turned back and looked him in the eyes. "Yes I am!"

Tom seemed thoughtful for a moment, like maybe he was sizing something up in his mind. "We could do it together," he said.

They had walked back to the boat house. The sound of Tumble's party seemed to grow louder as the wind shifted. Tom stooped down next to the pier, motioning for her to get down, too.

"I was plannin' to leave tonight myself," he said. "That's the real reason I wasn't hangin' around the party. Then I seen you walkin' by yerself when I come down here to git in my boat, so I decided to see what ya was up to."

"I was up to wishin', not doin'. But right now doin' suddenly feels like a pretty good idea. If I go back up there one of them guys is gonna try to mess with me, an' I'm gonna git mad and cuss at 'im and Daddy's just gonna stand there and laugh at it all. I just decided—I ain't gonna do that no more. So you got a way outa here, I'm ready."

It had all just spilled out and when she saw how surprised Tom looked, she thought about what he'd said about leaving.

"You tellin' me you just gonna walk away from yer job?" she said.

"I don't stay long around most of these guys runnin' the buy boats. They treat ya' bad and try to steal yer money back once ya earn it. I hate to say it, but yer daddy ain't no different from the rest."

"He is my daddy, but he ain't been nice to me or my sisters. I'm the one that fights back and he ain't been as hard on me. I hate to leave Mama, but she'll understand. She ran away from her daddy when she was eighteen like me—only she ended up just as bad off. I ain't gonna end up that way."

Tom caught her age. "So you're eighteen! Tumble can't make ya stay here if ya don't wanna. You're an adult at eighteen."

"Well, almost eighteen. My birthday's next month. But it's close enough. So where's this boat of yours?"

"Out at the end of the pier," Tom said. They moved stealthily out along the pier and there it was, a small, rough looking old pleasure boat that had seen better days.

"This?" Cybil said. "Looks like it'll sink if you git it away from the dock."

"Yeah, don't look like much, does it? But it runs good and it's safe."

Cybil quickly decided to take Tom at his word. They jumped aboard, cast off the lines, and the two of them paddled the boat out from the pier a bit before starting the motor. The quarter moon cast just enough light to pick things out in the shadows, but not enough to really illuminate them. Tom had no running lights, which was illegal, but it made him relatively inconspicuous. The boat creaked and groaned, and she could hear water sloshing in the bilge, but it stayed afloat. He started the motor and idled along through the channel.

After a while Tom said, "You want somethin' to drink? I got some Pepsi down in the cooler."

"Maybe. What else ya got?"

"I ain't got no beer or nothin'—got some water down there. Jest go on down in the cabin and git what ya want."

The cabin was dirty and smelled of grease and fish, but it had a bunk on one side and on the other some built-in cabinets and a shelf with dirty rags on it. The cooler was under the shelf, so she got out a Pepsi then sat down on the bunk to drink it. There was a small lantern hanging from the ceiling that produced a dim light, and soon Cybil laid back on the bunk and dozed off.

After a while she felt the engine pick up to a higher speed and the boat began to pitch and roll, which told her they were now in the Chesapeake Bay. She didn't feel alarmed. For the first time in her life she was doing something on her own. She really didn't care where they went or how long she stayed there. She fell asleep for a couple of hours, awakening when the sea became calmer and the sound of the engine changed so that she knew they were in some creek or cove. She decided to go up to the cockpit and talk to Tom.

She found him steering the boat slowly through a cove with dark foliage on each side. In spite of the cold night air, he was standing there in his t-shirt and jeans without a jacket. She wasn't sure how old he was, but she thought he might be in his thirties, which made him seem old compared to her. The moonlight was gone now and he handled the boat skillfully. She wondered how he kept from running aground.

"Where are we?" she asked.

"Oh jest up in a little creek on the Virginia side that nobody uses much. Good thing the tide's up or I'd hafta cut the motor and pole the boat up in here," he said, then looking at her he asked, "You ain't scared, are ya?"

"Not if you ain't," she answered.

"I got a little place up this creek where I sometimes hang out when I want to get away from ever'body else. Thought maybe we could go there and kinda get to know each other."

Cybil began to realize that she had taken a bold step, and a moment of panic struck her. *What am I getting' into? What if I don't wanna be here? What if it's just as bad as back home?* "Think we can get back by mornin' light?" she said.

Tom gave her a puzzled look. "Do we hafta?"

"Not 'specially, I s'pose. Depends on if I like where we're goin'."

"I hope you will"—Tom paused a moment—"I guess I moved too fast. Maybe you needed time to think about this. Sorry, but I guess it's done now." Tom shifted his feet. "Don't be mad at me. And please don't cry—I can't stand to see people cry."

"I'm not mad, and why should I cry? You ain't hurtin' me," she said. Then the fire flew in her eyes and she added, "You ain't plannin' to hurt me are ya?"

Tom looked at her and it was like *he* was hurt. "No!" he barked. And that was the end of their talking because he cut the engine off and secured the boat in among the trees, jumped out onto a path and pulled her up to him.

"This way," he said, and they began to walk up through some thick woods. It wasn't a long walk, and suddenly she saw the shadowy shape of a small cabin right in front of her.

"This is it," Tom said. "You wait here."

He opened a creaky door and stepped inside, and she saw the glow of a lantern begin to shine, and then he came back out. Taking her hand he helped her up onto the small porch and they went inside and closed the door. It smelled musty and it was dirty, but it was not trashy. She saw an old wood-burning cook stove with a pipe up to the chimney, and a sink with a hand pump for water. There were two cabinets over the sink, and one under the shelf beside it, plus an old table and two rickety chairs. Under the table was an old rag rug. On the other side of the room a full-sized bed had pillows and a nice handmade quilt on it. Some clothing hung on hooks along the front wall, next to the door.

"This ain't too bad," Cybil said as she walked around, poking at things.

"You sound surprised," Tom said. She studied his sandy hair, blue eyes and deep tan. The more she was around him the more she liked him.

"Well I guess I am, I mean, how did I know what things was gonna be like where we ended up. I'll tell ya in the morning what I think of it when there's some daylight. I know one thing, it sure needs t' be cleaned."

"Yeah, I guess it does," Tom replied. There was a fireplace on one wall and some wood stacked beside it which he used to build a fire to take the chill off the room. Then he started undressing, and she felt a wave of fear, which he seemed to sense.

"I ain't goin' to hurt ya. You don't gotta do nothin' with me you don't wanna do. But it's late and we both gotta sleep. Might's well git your clothes off and git in this bed. We had us a long trip and daylight ain't too far away."

That was how the strange abduction of Cybil Froster came about. Tom slept in the buff under the covers, but Cybil kept her clothes on, covered herself with a coat from one of the hooks on the wall, and slept on top of the quilt. He never tried to touch her or bother her, and by morning she felt as though a new door had opened in her life.

When Mo Froster found out her daughter was gone she said, "Well ain't this a fine can of worms. That girl's done run off, but she'll be back—ain't got enough sense to take care of herself." After that she never mentioned it again.

With Tumble it was different. He knew that Tom Brewster, at least that's what he said his name was, had run off during the night. He put two and two together and fired up his pickup truck. That boy ain't gonna git away with stealin' my daughter," he yelled back in Mo's direction as he tore off toward town. When he reached the sheriff's office he skidded to a halt, jumped out of his truck and stormed into the building.

The deputy on duty was used to Tumble's theatrics, so he casually looked up and said, "Well, look who's here. Somebody steal some of your ersters, Tumble?"

"I got bigger trouble than that and I need help," Tumble said. "Some no good drifter I had workin' fer me done run off with m'girl, Cybil."

"How'd he go and do that," the deputy asked. "I can't imagine anybody gettin' past you to lay a hand on your kin 'lest you give 'em permission."

Tumble ignored the deputy's comment. "His name's Tom Brewster, at least that's what he told me. I never seen him write it down. Don't know where he's from. Came in a few weeks ago in an old cabin cruiser that looked like it would sink afore it reached th' dock."

"You mean you didn't keep no paper work on him? You know better than that!"

"Now hold on, he was jest temporary day labor, contractin' on his own. I didn't need no paperwork. Just paid him off for his last week and while we was celebratin' a good month he sneaked around an' stole my little Cybil."

"How old is Cybil?"

"Reckon she's seventeen now—be eighteen before long."

"So how old is this Tom fella?"

"I don't know, but he's older'n that. He done abducted her."

"Okay," the deputy said. "He might have, and he might not have. I know how you party out at your place sometimes. She might have used the confusion to just run off on her own. It's been known to happen. Why don't you check with some of your relatives or friends of hers and I'll bet you'll find her."

"We ain't close to no relatives," Tumble said, "and she ain't got no friends outside of family and people who live close by us."

"Okay, and you think this Tom fella has left the area, is that right?"

"Well that old boat weren't there this mornin', but like I say, I don't think it would git too far the condition it looked to be in."

The deputy had been filling in some papers while Tumble and he talked. He had Tumble sign a complaint and said he'd look into it. That was the best Tumble could do, so he turned around and went back home.

∼◡∽

Two of Tumble's regular watermen, Mike and Jud, picked up on what was happening as soon as they got to work Monday morning. Tumble was downright mean, no tolerance for joking around or anything else. Mike had seen Cybil walk out onto the pier with Tom Brewster and get into his boat during the partying Friday night. He'd seen them head out of the harbor. All the guys fantasized about Cybil, and everybody knew one day somebody was going to get her pregnant and that would be the end of the fun. It didn't take much to figure out what might be going on with Tumble.

"What's the boss man got up his behind today, anyway," Jud asked as he and Mike were getting the gear ready on the boat.

"I expect somebody done got to one of his little gals, and he's loadin' up the shotgun," Mike said. "I seen that new guy, Tom, takin' her out to his boat Friday night. They sneaked outa the harbor, too. Come to think of it, I ain't seen him around here today."

"Don't that beat all!" Jud said. "Man, I wish that'd been me."

"Well, what'd Tumble expect, keepin' that girl around here with us when we get to partyin'. He didn't mind us playin' with her, but Tom done more than play around with 'er, that's what I think. That's about th' only thing that would make Tumble mean like he is today."

"What you girls talkin' about out there," Tumble yelled at Mike and Jud from the pilot house door. "You git them side boards secured or go find yourself some other place to hang out, you got that? I'm lookin' to buy a lotta ersters today and I don't wanna lose none of 'em over the side."

"Yeah, boss," Mike yelled back. "We just about ready."

They did have a good day buying oysters from the tongers and brought in a full load. It was late when they finished offloading at the packing house. Tumble had eased off during the long day's work, and by evening he was his usual self—that is, until the deputy came rolling up onto the lot in his cruiser. Tumble got fired up immediately.

"You done found my little Cybil already?" he said. "I don't see nobody with ya. What you doing out here?"

"No, we haven't found 'em. But I do think we have a lead on where them two went."

"So why ain't ya pickin' 'em up?"

"Not so fast. I said a lead, I didn't say we know where to put our hands on 'em."

"What kinda lead?"

"Somebody out toward the mouth of the creek, right there where that sand bar runs out into the channel—somebody who lives back in there heard a boat but couldn't see no lights. There ain't many reasons to run through there without lights unless you don't want to be noticed, and the boat was going slow, holding down its wake and motor noise."

"So they went out the creek," Tumble replied. "They sure didn't come back in, so where'd they go?"

"We think they might have crossed over to Virginia. A couple of watermen we know said this kid, Tom Brewster, has been hiring out with different crews off and on, and said he told them he was from over on the Virginia side."

"So what do we do now?" Tumble asked. "I want that girl back here and I'm gonna square this with that no good scoundrel."

The deputy said, "'*We*' ain't gonna do nothin', you got that? You stay out of this and we'll go through our connections with police along the bay and we'll find 'em. It might take a while, though. Just thought you'd like to know where things are."

Tumble cooled off. "Okay—I guess I should say 'thanks' fer what your doin'. You find them as fast as you can, y'hear?"

"I understand how you feel, Tumble, and yes, we'll do our best to find 'em as soon as possible."

With that the deputy left, and Tumble told everybody except the women to go home and get back early in the morning. The women would be busy half the night culling the oysters.

As Mike and Jud were leaving, Mike said, "I know some guys that work over in Virginia, some little place called Dinkel Island. Went there once, but it was too quiet fer me. I'm gonna call one of them boys and see if he knows anything."

Mike did call his Virginia buddy, a guy named Ben Wartman, who said he'd check around. That was the last anybody heard about Cybil and Tom for about a month. Then in November Mike got a call from Ben.

"Y'all still looking for that Brewster guy and the girl he run off with?"

"Sure are," Mike said. "Have you found 'em over there?"

"Oh, yeah," Ben said. "But that ole boy's into lots more than running off with a girl. He's a thief. I seen him steal money real slick like right in a busy store. And that ain't all. I heard he was out begging for money to buy gas for that wreck of a boat he's got"

"If he's that open about it, seems to me somebody woulda turned him in by now."

"Maybe they have. I wouldn't know about that. I just know what I seen and heard about him. Your boss man willin' to pay for some more information?"

"I can't speak for him," Mike said. "But it seems like he might, but I ain't heard about no reward for findin' the girl."

"Well you tell your boss I got a good idea where them two is stayin' an' I'll be glad to follow 'em and tell him where they are if they's a reward in it fer me."

"I got a better idea," Mike said. "You just go tell the police where they are and stay out of it, man. You gonna git y'self messed up with some trouble if you go takin' things into your own hands."

They batted that back and forth a minute and then Ben said, "Okay, I'll stay out of it. I just thought you wanted to find 'em. If they is a reward and you change your mind, just let me know, y'hear?"

Mike agreed and then hung up. He decided it didn't matter to him one way or the other, so he just let it go. He never said a thing about it to Tumble.

8

Two Journeys

*F*or the next few weeks Cybil lived in the most comfortable world she had ever known. Tom went off working with oyster crews and whatever else he did to bring home money that he added to the collection in the vinyl bag under the house. They went shopping in Dinkel Island every week, and took walks in the woods. Once they went to the remnant of an old lighthouse near their cabin that had obviously burned and been abandoned years earlier.

They found a grassy field where they romped and played and rolled around like young puppies. Cybil read avidly and began to imagine a story about her new world that she would write someday. It bothered her that Tom had no appreciation for what she was doing. An old book of nautical charts was the only thing written on paper that he cared to read. That surfaced as a confusing issue one day when he came in and found her writing with papers scattered over the table.

"What are ya doin'?" he said as he walked in the door. Cybil realized she had let the time slip away and he was looking for supper. She could read irritation in his expression.

"What's it look like?" she said, feeling offended by his attitude. This was the first time they had clashed about anything she did.

Tom's face was red and he took a couple of steps toward her, waving his arms wildly. "Looks to me like yer wastin time," he said. "I don't see no supper gettin' cooked."

Instinctively Cybil winced in fear and turned her face aside. *I thought he was different from Daddy!* When he made no further move toward her she decided to stand her ground. "Y'know, you go outa here every day and I ain't got no idea what yer doin'—and I don't care cause it ain't none of my business. And it ain't no concern of yours what I do when you leave me here alone all day."

Tom looked wounded and reached toward her. "I'm sorry, Cybil, that was wrong of me to say that. It's jest that I don't see no use in writin' stuff down. I'm sorry."

Cybil's angst softened and she let him draw her to himself. She looked up into his face and caught a tear starting down his cheek. He brushed her face with his hand, and they kissed, then stepped apart. Cybil began gathering her papers. "I'll fix us somethin' to eat. Won't take long."

"What's on all them papers?" Tom said.

"Being with you is jest about the best thing ever happened to me," she said. "I been writin' down what we been doing together and how it all feels." She handed him the papers and said, "Here, you read 'em if ya want."

Tom look flustered again, and then looked her in the eye. "Can't read 'em. I never went to school much. Don't read much except them charts I use in the boat. My daddy taught me to read them." He handed the papers back to her.

This was the first time she'd heard him mention his family. All he'd told her was that he'd been alone most of his life. She had decided he'd tell her more when it suited him. "You ain't never mentioned your daddy. Was he a waterman, too?"

"Yeah," Tom said. "We moved around a lot, kinda like I do now, so I never stayed anyplace long enough to go to school. Then when I was 12 he got arrested for somethin' and went to jail. Momma jest went out one day and never came back. So I learned how to get along on my own."

Cybil felt such a warm surge of affection that she held him close and said, "I didn't know—I'm sorry. Let's jest forget this all happened."

～～

On a cold day in mid-November they were lying wrapped in blankets before a blazing fire, talking about their dreams of things they would do in the spring. A storm had been building up all day with periodic rain squalls, strong wind gusts, thunder and lightning. Tom said it was probably a nor'easter blowing in, and Cybil agreed, having been through such storms herself.

"It might git bad enough to knock down some trees," Tom said. "Me and you need to use our emergency plan—I'll move the bed off the trap door." He was referring to a plan he had worked out and shared with Cybil just to be prepared if someone came snooping around because her daddy had figured out where they were. Increasingly Tom was concerned about the frequency of their trips in and out of the creek. It was easy to slip in and out unnoticed when you only did it occasionally and usually at night, but lately he'd been going and coming much more frequently.

They were pulling on heavier clothes—jeans, sweat shirts, and boots when Cybil noticed a different kind of noise outside—a crunching sound, like someone or something thrashing around in the woods. "I hear somethin' besides the storm outside," she said, and they both strained to hear, but the sound had ceased.

"Naw—that's jest them big ole rain drops, and the wind in the trees," Tom said. "Don't go gettin' spooked now. If you hear a loud crash, it'll mean trees is startin' to fall and we need to get on outa here in case that happens."

Cybil heard the noise again. It wasn't just the wind, and it wasn't like thunder or a tree falling. "I hear it again, Tom. I've got the backpack—I think we better get down outa here fast."

"Here, put on this coat and pull this cap down over your hair and ears. It's gonna be cold and wet, probably for quite a spell," Tom said, tossing the items to her. He pulled the bed away from the trap door, opened the hatch, and motioned for her to go down first. She heard him lock the hatch as he followed behind her. With the help of a small flashlight they scurried along the dirt. "Wait!" he said. She saw him retrieve the money bag from under the cinderblock and stow it in the backpack. They caught their breath and froze in place for a moment when a voice yelled, "Hey, in the cabin! We know you're in there, you yellow-bellied slime ball."

Then another voice boomed, "We know you stole that girl out of Maryland and we come to get her. You get yourself out here or we'll burn the cabin."

"How many are there?" Cybil said.

"I don't know," Tom said. "Just keep going—don't look back."

Cybil reached the end of the house where the brush was thickest and slid quickly out and then scurried down through the sloping, thickly wooded terrain. She could hear the frightening sound of an ax chopping away at the cabin door, and then nearly jumped out of her skin at the sound of a shotgun blast. Tom yelled and she stopped and looked back. She saw him fall into the brush back closer to the cabin. She could tell he was in pain and yelled "Tom!" She started to move toward him.

"No!" he yelled. "No—leave—get outta here. Go!"

Tears exploded from her eyes and her anger flared as she caught sight of one of the attackers coming around into the brush. Another shotgun blast showered the trees above her with pellets. She got up and ran as fast as she could, cutting a zig-zag path as branches tore at her hair and skin. She cut back and came out right where the boat was moored. With strength she hadn't known she had Cybil cast off the lines, grabbed the pole and began pushing the boat out through the creek. She could hear thrashing and shouting in the woods as someone tried to find her, then she saw a frightening glow in the sky as the intruders set fire to the cabin. She knew her paradise was gone, and Tom with it, and it stabbed at her heart like a knife.

When she reached water that was more open she started the engine. The propeller bit into the water and she threw the pole back toward the stern. Glancing back she saw that she had dropped the backpack when she jumped onto the boat. She had forgotten all about it! The pole had pushed it down into a well Tom had built inside the transom to hold his gas cans. Cybil wanted to reach for it but she couldn't leave the helm. She decided it would be safe wedged in with the cans.

It seemed to take forever to reach the mouth of the creek, and then she realized that she faced an even bigger battle with the three foot surf pounding in toward her. The rain was so heavy that she had a hard time watching for hazards in the water. *I've never been out in such a storm,* she thought, almost in a panic. *I can do it,* she told herself. *I can handle this boat.* Her daddy had taught her to steer through a storm and his words came back to her. *Take the swells with a rolling motion—stay out of the troughs. Take them on an angle.*

Cybil put all her energy into the wheel but the outboard motor lacked enough power to maintain a course. The wind howled and whistled with hard rain pounding down all around her. "Oh!" she cried as the windshield wiper broke, impeding her vision even more. A swell caught the boat head on and the wind whipped it around, tossing it violently. "No!" she screamed as old weathered wood splintered under the water's impact. The bow plunged into the trough behind the swell with a slamming sound, rotating the boat so that it rolled broadside into the trough.

Water splashed around Cybil's ankles and all at once a loose piling that was being whipped by the sea came up under the boat, smashed into the bottom, breaking the structural framework and ramming itself up into the cabin. The boat began to break apart and the life jackets Tom had stowed in the ceiling of the cockpit suddenly broke loose as the roof supports failed. Cybil grabbed one of them just before she was violently thrown out of the sinking boat. Panic hit her, then subsided. She looped her left arm into one part of the life jacket and kicked her legs, trying to maneuver herself toward land. *Don't panic! Swim! One stroke at a time.* The boots and heavy clothing made it hard going, but she knew she had to deal with it. In that brief, traumatic moment all of her newly discovered dreams and contentment were lost and her only thought was of survival.

Cybil hung onto the life vest and kept twisting, turning and kicking until she found herself being carried in toward shore. When she finally got a foot hold and dragged herself out of the water, she was exhausted, grief-stricken, cold and wet. She realized the storm had washed her to land just a bit south of the Lighthouse Point cliffs. She crawled into the woods and collapsed, unconscious, while the storm raged. She awakened at sunrise the next day, remembered her ordeal, and decided on a plan.

I won't go back to Maryland under any circumstances, she told herself. *I've got to find a place to hide. Gotta dry out and find a way to get away from here.* She knew Tom was dead, and the cabin had been burned. She had lost the money bag. All she had was herself now. *O God, help me!* Until that moment she hadn't known whether she really believed in God or not. Suddenly pleading to God for help made sense

She found her way through the woods and moved inland cautiously. The sun began to warm the air and dry things out. Even though she was dirty and rumpled, her clothes dried. Pulling off her coat she discovered there was an inside pocket with a buttoned flap. *What's this?* She opened the flap and found a batch of soaked bills. The money was too wet to count, but she pulled a few bills apart carefully. *There must be several hundred dollars here! Oh, Tom!* She broke into tears. *Always thinking ahead—always planning for the unexpected.* It was as though Tom was there with her.

Cybil laid on the ground, exhausted and grief stricken for a time, then got up and began following a nearby road. *Florida!* she thought. *I'll go to Florida. They ain't nobody who knows me or my kin in Florida. Gotta head south.* When she came to a small gas station with a convenience store where she bought some food, used the restroom to try to improve her appearance, and then struck out walking again. As the sun faded into evening shadows she felt chilled. Then she spotted an old barn that looked abandoned about thirty feet back from the sparsely traveled road.

Careful! Cybil told herself as she explored around the barn to determine whether anyone had been there recently. *Nobody's been here for quite a spell, I'd say.* She walked around the building again, looking more closely. *Aha! A door!* It was hanging there nearly off its hinges. She cautiously went inside. The barn smelled like mildew and mold and she sneezed. It was dark inside now and she felt her way. *What's this? A ladder!* Carefully she climbed up to discover a loft with hay bales. *A good place to sleep!* She went back down and explored some more, finding two musty old blankets with straw matted into the fabric. She shook out as much mildew and straw as she could, then took them up to the loft where she wrapped them around herself.

After fashioning a meal from the bread and other food items she had purchased at the gas station, she settled herself to sleep. She felt a strange restlessness and then did something she'd never done before. She closed her eyes and said a prayer. *God, if you're there, if you hear me, then please help me. If you saved me from that boat wreck, then I'm thankful, and I wanna do somethin' back to make it right. Help me find a way, if you're there, God. Thanks.* It was nearly noon when she awoke. She ate some bread and drank some water, and then set out on her journey.

I don't know how I'll do it, Cybil thought, *but with your help, God, I know I will. Help me find my way south. Lead me to food and safety and a new life.* One thing she had always had was determination. Her daddy always said she was stubborn. Now she had something else along with it, something nobody in her world had ever had so far as she knew—she had faith in God. God made sense to her now. When people survived terrible things it had to be because God was looking out for them. She found deep comfort in that thought. That morning she began two journeys, one with her life and one with her faith, and she felt both of them would carry her into a future where there was something beyond the suffering and hardship she had known too well in her eighteen years.

9

Bad Choices

Ben Wartman had no idea what the guy looked like that his friend Mike wanted him to find. A drifter himself, Ben rarely got to know many people as he moved from place to place. Dinkel Island was different. He liked its lazy lifestyle and it had a large packing house and he had found a job crewing on one of the dredge boats. He had begun to hang out at Pappy's Place with some of the watermen after work so he decided to start there in his effort to find Tom Brewster.

"Gimme a couple more beers," he said as he stood at the counter in Pappy's Place and invited a couple of guys he worked with to sit down and shoot the breeze. "It's my turn to buy."

They sat down and told a few jokes and some gossip and then Ben said, "Hey, I got a buddy up in Maryland who said to look up a friend of his who works around here, but I ain't never been able to find him."

"What's his name? Maybe I know him," one of the guys said.

"Tom Brewster."

They thought about it a minute and one man said, "I worked with him once. He don't stay on one crew very long. Seems to drift all over the place. Ain't seen him for a while."

"Oh, yeah," the other man said. "Ain't he that guy that goes around in that floating piece of junk he calls a boat. That thing looks like it would sink if you kicked the hull."

"That's right. I seen him a couple days ago. He had some hot babe with him. They was over at the town pier."

"The town pier," Ben said. "Maybe that's the guy. I'll have to hang over there and see if I can spot him. My buddy said he had a message for him but didn't know how to reach him."

"Lotsa luck on that. I don't think he comes around regular like, but you might catch him over there. I ain't never seen him hang around with the other guys in town—I think he's a loner."

On Saturday morning Ben went around to the town pier. It was used mostly by pleasure boaters and tourists because it had easy access to the Food Lion and some other shops on Commerce Street. He sat down at a picnic table with a cup of coffee and sausage biscuit he'd brought with him and pretended to read a newspaper.

By noon Ben began to feel like he was wasting his time. Several other people hanging out nearby left so Ben decided it was time for him to leave. That's when he noticed an old cabin cruiser that looked like it would sink any minute tie up about 30 yards from him. He sat back down and lit a cigarette while he watched a guy who looked to be in his thirties help a very attractive young woman from the boat and then walk with her up toward the Food Lion.

That's him, Ben thought. He glanced around to see if anyone he knew was in the area and saw no one. *I wonder where them two is livin'? Maybe I better follow 'em.* He lit another cigarette and walked up Commerce Street far enough behind Tom and Cybil to keep them in sight. They went right to the Food Lion, so Ben went into a Rite Aid across the street where he bought some cigarettes and pretended to read the sale ads by the front window. After a time Brewster and the girl came out loaded down with bags and walked back toward the pier. *I'll bet they come in here every Saturday to buy stuff. Next week I'll be ready for 'em.*

The next week Ben rented a runabout to do some fishing. He came around Dinkel Island toward the town pier at about the same time he had seen Tom and Cybil come in with their boat the week before. He dropped his anchor and threw out a line. After a while the old weathered boat appeared. *Bingo!* Ben thought. He moved his location slightly and went back to fishing again. About an hour later he saw the old boat coming back out so he pulled in his line and fell in some distance behind Tom's boat. He watched as Tom cut across Tranquility Bay toward the Lighthouse Point cliffs and they disappeared into a narrow creek he probably would have missed for the thick brush that seemed to hide it. *How 'bout that. That boy's got hisself a hidin' place up that creek! Bet I can find a way in there by land.*

His spying done, Ben went back to Pappy's Place, turned in the boat, and drove to his apartment. The next couple of evenings he did some exploring out around the old lighthouse and stumbled across a cabin deep in the woods. Being careful to stay hidden, he watched until he saw Cybil step outside to toss out a pail of water. *Got 'em,* he thought, and went home to figure out his next move.

The next day Ben noticed two guys he hadn't seen before hanging out at Pappy's Place. He sat at a table behind them and listened to their conversation, then turned to them and said, "Don't think I've seen you guys before. I'm Ben Wartman."

The two men turned toward Ben. "I'm Roland and this here's Bubba. You ain't seen us 'cause we jest got here."

"Where you from?"

"All over," Roland said. "We jest heard about this place and thought we'd check it out."

"I move around some myself," Ben said. "If you guys lookin' to make some easy money I might know how ya can do it."

Roland and Bubba looked at each other, then Roland said, "What kinda easy money?"

"I'm working on a plan that could pay off pretty good, and I need a couple of guys who can keep their mouths shut, follow instructions, and know how to handle themselves in a tight spot."

Roland said, "What exactly are you talkin' about, man?"

"A friend over in Maryland told me about a girl that was abducted and carried over here a few weeks back, and I've been snoopin' around some. I know who's got her and I wanna pull a surprise visit and git her back. They's a reward in it, and we can all split it. This thing is quick, quiet and sure to pay off. Think ya might be interested?"

Bubba said, "I don't know, man, how we know we can trust you?"

"You don't," Ben replied. "Neither do I know if I can trust you, but I'm pretty good at readin' people and I believe you two are okay."

Roland wrinkled his forehead and stared hard at Ben. "How come you commin' to us? If you from around here why don't you git some local guys to help you?"

"Don't take no rocket scientist to figger that out," Ben replied. "Too much risk of the word getting' out and havin' to share the reward with a bunch of people who gonna claim they helped find her. Besides, if things get out of hand and there's some kinda 'accident' I don't want nobody to know I was involved. You two guys don't have no roots here so you can jest move on. Way I figure it, we do the job, take the reward, and go our separate ways. Who's the wiser?"

Roland and Bubba whispered to each other for a couple of minutes, then asked, "You say if somethin' goes wrong—what kinda 'wrong' you talkin' about?".

"Like if we had to beat the guy up a little, maybe send him outa town with a fear of them Maryland guys bein' hot on his trail," Ben said. "Somethin' like that."

The answer seemed to satisfy Bubba who asked, "How much money you talkin' about?"

Ben lied. He figured he'd get the job done first, and then put them off about how long it took to get through the red tape for the actual money.

"I heard the reward was $15,000," he said, pulling the figure out of the air. "That's five grand for each one of us—plus I have reason to believe this guy has been stealin' money and who knows how much of that we might be able to split up? You in?"

Roland and Bubba looked at each other, and then said, "Yeah, we're in. When does this come down?"

"Tomorrow afternoon," Ben said. "You just meet me here. There's a road that crosses through the salt marsh and then up to where this guy is hidin. I been up there and scouted it out. There's an old burned out lighthouse up there, then a brushy field, and they're in a cabin in the woods past there. We'll park at the lighthouse and sneak up on the cabin."

"How do you know he'll be there?" Bubba asked.

"Easy answer," Ben said. "He might not be there hisself, but he always leaves that girl there, so we just rescue her and grab any loot he's got, then we'll git outa there."

Roland and Bubba thought about this a minute, then said they were in. The next afternoon when they met, the storm was beginning to move in, and they weren't sure it was safe with the squalls and wind.

"Shows you boys ain't from around here," Ben said. "This storm's to our advantage. You just get in my truck and we'll go do this thing. The storm will cover any sound we might make that would ruin the surprise."

When they got to the lighthouse, Ben backed the truck up next to an old shed, then got out a can of kerosene and a 12-gauge, doubled-barreled shotgun.

"Hold on," Bubba said. "I don't like the gun—and what you plannin' to do, set the place on fire?"

"The gun's jest in case he has one and tries to use it; and yes, I do plan to burn that old shack down. It'll get rid of any evidence if somebody comes snoopin' around, and it'll look like somethin' that happened during the storm. Stuff like that happens 'round here all the time."

Bubba carried the kerosene, and Roland walked next to Ben, who carried the gun.

"What kinda shot you got in that thing?" Roland asked.

"Bird shot, that's all," Ben replied. "Might not kill somebody but it'll sure give 'em somethin' to think about for a while." He wasn't about to tell them he really had buckshot in the breech.

They all laughed at that and crossed through the field and then entered the woods. It was very dense, and sometimes they had to break branches to get through. The rain made it harder, and cut down what little visibility they had. Suddenly the cabin was right there in front of them. They had planned what to say, and Ben was first to call out toward the cabin, followed by Roland. Bubba set down the kerosene and grabbed an ax he saw on the ground, and when there was no answer, Ben motioned for him to go break the door in.

Roland went with Bubba while Ben moved around toward a brushy side of the building. That's when he saw Tom who suddenly stood up and looked back toward the cabin. Ben raised the shotgun and fired, and Tom went down; Roland and Bubba turned toward Ben and Roland yelled, "What'd ya do that fer?"

"He stood up like he was gonna shoot at me," Ben said, "I jest fired first." That's when Cybil screamed and they saw how far down she was in the sloping woods. Ben fired the other barrel, and yelled to Bubba, "Go get that girl!"

"Come on," Ben said to Roland, "Let's finish that door and grab whatever money he's got in there." Once inside they started ripping through things looking for money and saw the trap door, which they couldn't open, so they broke through it with the ax. Ben went down and when he saw that it was just an escape passage under the building, he was furious.

"Go out there and check that dude to see if he's got the money on him," Ben said. "If he moves, hit him with somethin'." Roland went out reluctantly, and then came back after a couple of minutes.

"That guy's hurt bad," Roland said, "but he ain't dead. He was makin' some noise so I hit him in the head with a piece of log, and then searched him. He ain't got no money as I can see."

"That girl's probably got whatever money they had," Ben said. At that point any rationality that might have been present in Ben's mind departed, and he opened the breech of the shotgun, took out the two spent shells and put them in his pocket, and then shoved two more into the barrel, spun around and aimed it at Roland.

"We're gonna put him in that cabin and set it on fire," he said. "Nobody will know he was shot when they find him—if they find him. It'll look like somethin' that happened in the storm. That's how that old lighthouse got burned down years ago—it was struck by lightning."

"Look man, that's murder," Roland pleaded, frantic in the face of the shotgun aimed at his head. "We didn't sign on for no killin. You said this was quick 'an easy, just git the girl back and take whatever money might be layin' 'round."

"So things change," Ben spat back at him, shoving the shotgun barrel at Roland for emphasis. "We don't got no choice now. Things done changed."

"He might die on his own without us helpin' it along no more than we have already, the way I see it. Why don't we just drag him down away from the cabin, cover him up with a bunch of brush and let nature take its course. At least we won't of killed him direct like."

Ben's temper flared, and he was about to pull the trigger when something inside him said maybe this wasn't such a bad idea. He held up and thought a minute. *What if a fire investigation found evidence Tom had been shot? What if someone actually would remember seeing the three of them driving up there during the storm?* He decided Roland's idea might not be so bad. Chances were that nobody would find the body, but he decided he could listen to news reports and if they did find it, he could get out of town fast.

"Okay, maybe you got a point there," Ben said, lowering the shotgun. "Come on, let's git him away from here." The rain was coming down harder now, and the wind was gusting stronger than ever. Lightning struck nearby and startled both of them. "Grab his other foot," Ben said, and pointed to a less encumbered area through the trees. They had pulled him about twenty yards when they saw a large tree that had been knocked down, leaving a huge root ball with a cavity under it.

"Let's shove him down in there," Ben said, indicating the cavity. It took some effort, but they managed to push Tom far enough that they could cover him with leaves and brush. They were soaked from the effort, and went back up to the cabin where they splashed kerosene around and then let it ignite from the fire that was still burning in the fireplace. The whole building began to burn rapidly as they ran from the scene.

"Come on, let's find Bubba," Ben said as he and Roland took off through the woods. They met Bubba coming back up, without the girl. "Where's that girl?" Ben demanded.

"She jumped on a boat she had down there and got away before I could catch up with her," Bubba said, "but this storm will slow her down."

"Don't count on it," Ben said. "Come on, let's go up on the cliff and see if we can spot her." They climbed up to the cliff face where they could look out on the raging sea below.

"She ain't goin' to git noplace in that," Ben said, and Roland and Bubba turned to see him aiming the shotgun at them. "And you ain't goin' no farther, neither."

"What's wrong with you, man. We ain't done nothin' to you. You done shot one guy already, ain't that enough for one day?"

"Wouldn't have shot nobody if it hadn't been for you two idiots botching things up. Can't leave no evidence walkin' around. You ain't got no life anyway—jest driftin' around."

"We is leavin'" Bubba stuttered, "you ain't got nothin' to fear from us."

"Tell you what," Ben said. "I'll give you a chance. This here cliff is high but they's a lot of water comin' in down there with the storm. Take your choice: you can jump off the cliff into the water, or I can shoot you here and now."

Bubba and Roland looked at each other and at the water below, and then at the shotgun and the look in Ben's eyes, and without another word jumped, hoping to fare better in the stormy water than where they were. Unfortunately, even with the storm surge the water at that spot was shallow. Ben looked over and saw them floating in the surf, being carried out from shore, so he threw the shotgun and the spent shells into the water, then ran up past the burning cabin and out of the woods, across the field toward his truck.

A county sheriff's deputy and emergency crews arrived at the lighthouse shed just as Ben arrived at his truck. He ran toward them, frantically waving his arms. "I'm glad you guys got here," he said, out of breath. "I think lightning hit somethin' up there in the woods. I was getting' ready to look in this old shed for stuff I might be able to fix up and sell when—."

The deputy interrupted, "You outa your mind doin' that in a storm like this? What could be valuable enough to look for it in a storm?"

"All kinds of stuff man," Ben said, "places like this is gold mines for old tools and stuff."

"Who gave you permission to go into that shed?" the deputy persisted.

"Well, nobody—I mean, it's abandoned. I seen it ain't locked. Just some old abandoned shed."

"That's trespassing if you went in there without permission," the deputy replied.

"Didn't have no time to actually go in," Ben answered. "Like I was sayin', I just got here when I seen them flames up there"— he said, pointing toward the fire—"and I ran up to see what was burnin. That's when I heard you guys comin', so I ran back down here."

The deputy studied Ben, who was obviously soaked and looked distraught from the ordeal, and really didn't come across as being too bright. He checked Ben's driver's license and checked his address and phone number, then told him he'd better go home and get some dry clothes on, and not to leave in case he needed to talk to him again later.

The ground was too wet to take the tanker truck up to the fire, so they had to let it burn itself out. To prevent the wind-driven flames from igniting the woods around the cabin, the fire fighters cut away some of the trees and brush and pulled them away, creating a fire break. The heat of the fire was intense and soon the entire building was consumed.

The next day, after the storm had passed, the sheriff went to the burned out cabin with an investigation team from the firehouse. They searched through the charred rubble looking for clues to determine whether the fire had been accidental or a case of arson. It was obvious that someone had been living there, apparently a squatter who must have run off when the fire started. Damage from the storm along with the brush the firefighters had piled up erased any clues that Tom's body had been dragged through the woods.

"If we got a team of folks in here we could search these woods to see if anybody's hidin' in there, but I expect that was some derelict staying in the cabin and he'd be long gone by now," the chief inspector said. "It seems clear the guy had a fire going in the fireplace, and we found a couple of oil lanterns in the rubble, along with a kerosene can. Most likely whoever was in there panicked, maybe dropped a lamp that set it off, or tipped over the kerosene. There doesn't seem to be any reason for someone to set fire to the place—doesn't look like there was anything worth stealing."

The deputy nodded. "I'm going to follow up with that guy who was up here when we arrived." He found out that Ben was a waterman who had been around town for a while, but there was no record of any complaints against him. It was concluded that a derelict staying in the house had a bad moment when the storm hit and accidentally set fire to the house, then ran off.

When the remnants of a wood boat began to drift ashore at Dinkel Island after the storm, Chief Draper called the Maryland police.

"I think we might have found the boat you've been looking for," he said. "Since the storm several people have found debris that appears to be from a boat washing up on shore. We had some boats damaged, but nobody around here lost one."

The deputy was cautiously encouraged. "What about the couple who were on the boat that we're looking for—let's see—a guy in his thirties and a teenage girl? Any signs of them?"

"No," the chief said. "We wondered about that, but no human remains have surfaced. I'll tell you, from the looks of it this was a violent crack-up, maybe a collision with something else in the water during the storm. It's likely whoever was on that boat was killed when it broke up."

It soon became a cold case and was mostly forgotten in the presence of more immediate concerns. The bodies of Roland and Bubba were never found, and since they were drifters anyway, nobody thought anything when they weren't seen around town anymore. After a few weeks Ben decided it was time for him to move on and he was soon out of sight and out of mind at Dinkel Island.

10

<hr>

Ain't God Somethin'!

*T*here had been many storms at Dinkel Island over the years since 1989. Each one left its own unique memories, but as Stan went to bed on Sunday night his focus was not on storms. It was on celebrations. Dinkel Days and the Beach Art Extravaganza were seminal events in this town. The only storms he could imagine would occur if the massive preparations were to suddenly unravel. Reflecting on the last few weeks, he was thankful for Fanny Grant whose cheerful spirit and tireless energy had helped bring all the loose ends into place.

A deep restlessness persisted within him, however, as the night wore on. He found himself experiencing again one of those nocturnal visits that he could never consciously recall. Without warning he felt Lillie's presence beside him, her fingers gently stroking his arm. He turned toward her and she pushed back the covers, beckoned him to hold onto her hand, and then they soared up and out of the room. The night was swallowed up by a refreshing glow that cast a surreal aura over Dinkel Island. They soared above the trees until they reached the Grayson/Plume Gallery, and then floated inside and hovered there.

"Oh!" Lillie exclaimed, pointing toward one of the featured paintings on display. "I love that!"

"That's Arnie Jackson's latest piece," Stan responded. "Notice the rich intensity in his use of color that spawns an abstract quality his earlier work lacked. Arnie has a studio here, and I see such emerging freshness in his work that I gave him a featured spot here in the gallery."

"I know," Lillie responded warmly. "It looks like you've got things under control now for the Art Extravaganza. I'm so glad you let Fanny help you."

Stan felt an inward stab of pain when Lillie mentioned Fanny. He had discovered a quality he really liked within her that he had never seen before. That set up dissonant emotions within him so that he tried to distance himself from her at the same time that he felt drawn toward her. Fanny seemed not to notice. In fact, she seemed to warm toward him a little more each time they were together, which amplified Stan's emotional struggle.

"Fanny's been a help," Stan said, "but it feels so strange having her around. This place, this show, everything that she and I are dealing with belongs to you."

"No," Lillie replied, pulling him closer and wrapping her presence around him. "No, it doesn't belong to me. It never did. It doesn't belong to you. It belongs to some small part of the whole universe."

Feeling buoyant with her increased presence, Stan floated up to the ceiling and hovered. "What if Fanny falls in love with me. What will I do? I get confused. I love you, Lil, but I also need to break away somehow."

"Yes, you do need to make a break. Why do you think she's in your life now? She's there to make that break possible. You can't be with me anymore. You've got to let go. Set yourself free—give yourself permission to experience something new. Go with your feelings."

Stan was perplexed. Here was Lillie telling him it was okay to have feelings toward Fanny, and she was even embracing the relationship. "How can I let go, Lil?"

"Stop holding onto me so tightly. You've done a great job taking hold of things. The extravaganza is in great shape. Molly has kept you on track, but she isn't there for you in a deeper way. Fanny wants to be at the center of a shared life with you. I know what's in her heart and it's pure."

"I don't know how I feel about Fanny," Stan admitted. "I try not to think about it too much, because it drives me crazy."

Lillie pulled away, but kept his hand in hers and they rose above the gallery, breathed in the freedom of the outdoors, zooming around the town, almost at a dizzying pace.

"Lil, what's going on? Why are we moving so fast?" Stan implored.

"It's not fast, it just seems that way. Time is in your perspective, and you have to get in step with it. We're spinning away to new levels of being," Lillie said.

"But I don't want to"—Stan started to say as Lillie swooshed in close to him, putting her hand against his lips to stop his words.

"It's time, darling. It's time to say goodbye. I'll always be in your spirit, but not always in your mind. You're free now. Go! Embrace what's real in the here and now and stop looking back. Do you remember how we found God in such fresh ways during the early days of our marriage? Go back to that level of trust in God and ask him to heal you of your grief now. That's how you can let go of me."

Her hand slipped from his as she spoke, and her image swirled around like a cyclone, dispersing energy, releasing her connection to time and place, and then with an intense surge, she was gone.

Stan was shaken by emotions that rapidly subsided. Strangely, unexpectedly, he felt free.

He awoke! It was only four o'clock. He still had a couple of hours before daybreak. He sat up, shook his head as though to clear an inner cloudiness, and took a deep breath.

"Wow!" he exclaimed. An immense sense of peace flooded over him, and all of a sudden he felt more content and satisfied than he could remember for some time. Fanny suddenly came to his mind. *I wonder how she is—what is she feeling?* His thoughts felt awkward. *Who is she? Who is Fanny?*

He looked at the phone on the bedside table. *Call her!* an inner voice said. He hesitated. *I can't do that—it's too early. She'll resent being awakened.* He turned over and tried to go back to sleep, but his legs became restless and he couldn't keep them still. He tossed and turned and argued with himself. *I need to call Fanny—but I can't.* He prayed. *Lord, what's happening to me? Please help me to settle down and sleep. Comfort me with your Spirit so I can sleep.*

Sleep eluded him! He turned on the light, reached over and took the phone—paused—then put it back down. He struggled like this a couple of times then spoke to himself, *Okay, Grayson, you're a 65-year-old grown man, and you can handle this. Call the woman and if she resents it, apologize. If your relationship can't stand that, then you need to drop it.*

Stan picked up the phone and dialed. Fanny answered on the first ring. "Hello?"—she said softly, then paused and Stan started to speak, but she said, "Stan?"

"Hi Fanny—how did you know it was me? I apologize for the hour, but I had this strong urge to call you. Are you all right?"

"Yes, I'm fine—in fact, better now that you called. I really needed to hear your voice."

Stan paused, feeling buffeted between the opposing emotions of joy and guilt, then he suddenly felt a deep release and heard himself saying, "I needed to hear yours, too."

"I don't know what's come over me," Fanny continued. "Working with you has been so excitin' and refreshin' that I guess I'm just sort of floatin' on air. I feel almost like a teenager," she added, laughing.

Floating! Stan felt a sudden charge of energy in that word. "I feel the same way—in fact, that's why I called—to tell you that."

Fanny was silent for a moment, then in an emotive whisper said, "Thanks! I'll see you in the morning. Go back to sleep. Oh! Why don't you come by here and we'll have breakfast together before we go to work? I'd love to fix you breakfast."

Stan felt a sudden emotional escalation. "I'd love to have breakfast with you, Fanny. We have so much to learn about each other."

"Then I'll see you at, say, eight o'clock—is that okay?"

"Sure, see you then," Stan said as they hung up and he rolled over, feeling relaxed with a deep inner fullness, and dropped into a deep, peaceful sleep.

∾∽

Stan arrived right on time with a jittery kind of nervousness in his stomach. Fanny opened the door before he could even ring the bell. Her fresh, smiling warmth took his breath away.

"Good mornin'," she said, reaching for his hands and pulling him across the threshold. "I'm so glad you're here." She let go of his right hand and pushed the door closed, and then suddenly they both seemed to merge together in an embrace. They kissed deeply, and Stan found himself embracing her firmly with his left arm while stroking her hair with his right.

"Whooh!" Fanny exclaimed as she broke from the kiss and stepped back. "I—" she started to say, but their lips came together again—"I need to come up for air!" She laughed and tossed her head. "I'll bet you didn't expect a kiss like that for breakfast." Her eyes sparkled as she said, "come on, the rest of breakfast is in the kitchen."

Stan felt rattled by the suddenness and extent of the intimacy they'd just shared. "I didn't mean to come on so strong," he said. Fanny reached out and touched his lips exactly as Lillie used to. His words died on his tongue. He took in her appearance—a light blue sweater, khaki skirt, sandals, and seashell earrings with a matching necklace. Her face was radiant, and Stan felt captivated by her. *She's beautiful! Why haven't I seen her this way before?*

"It's been so long," he said, still being apologetic. "I guess I got a little carried away." He paused, and then said warmly, "You look beautiful today."

"So do you! And it's okay if we both got carried away 'cause I think that's what we both needed."

The aroma from the kitchen stimulated Stan's senses. "Can I help with something?" he asked.

"Not this time. This time is special. I made this just for you and I want to serve it to you. You can help me clean up later!" She tossed him one of her entrancing smiles.

"Okay," he said. "What a treat this is!"

In her characteristic, teasing manner Fanny said, "Well, I wouldn't do this for just anybody, you know."

They settled down to a delicious breakfast and talked about their phone conversation in the early morning hours, and began exploring how they had been drawing closer together over the last few weeks. Suddenly they realized it was getting late, so they piled the dishes in the sink and Stan said he'd come back with her and help clean everything up later.

"You'd better," she said. "I'll be expectin' you around here a lot more, you know."

❧

At that moment Stan's cell phone rang. "Stan Grayson," he answered.

"Good morning, Stan—what are you doing, sleeping in?" It was Ed Heygood.

"No, just on my way in to the studio. What's up?"

"There's a woman here who says she knows you and wants to talk to you about being in the art show. Says her name's Lucy Mac."

"Lucy Mac!" Stan exclaimed with puzzlement. "I don't know anybody by that name."

There was a pause and Stan heard Ed talking in the background. "She says she did some shows with you a few years ago. Says her full name is Lucille McCall."

"Oh!" Stan said as he felt his brain searching through his memory files. "That name rings a bell. You say she wants to exhibit in our show?"

"That's what she says. She drove up in a large van and says she has everything she needs with her."

"Okay—Fanny and I had breakfast together and we're on our way in now. Tell her to bring in some of her work so I can take a look at it. We'll be there in a few minutes."

Stan hung up and saw Fanny had been trying to piece the conversation together from what she could hear of it. "Was that Ed?" she asked.

"Yeah," Stan answered, "We are a little late. Since I gave Molly the day off, Ed offered to open up and he says an artist I used to know from my show days is there and wants to be in the Extravaganza."

"Really! Ain't it cool how God provides," Fanny said. "We were short a couple of artists so that's another fee to help with expenses and support for the Community Art Fund. What's her name?"

"Get this—its 'Lucy Mac'—a strange name and I'm beginning to recall her a little. I think she does some very different kind of paintings."

"Diversity is cool," Fanny replied. "Let's go see this lady and find out what she's up to."

When Stan and Fanny entered the gallery they found Lucy Mac explaining to Ed the features of a large abstract painting she had leaning against the sales counter. Several other smaller canvases were leaning against one of the display walls. She was a large-framed woman who appeared to be in her mid-fifties. Her dark eyes and eyebrows were framed by spiked blond hair with dark roots showing near the scalp. Her wide lips smiled, although her eyes seemed intense. She had on denim shorts, a tie-dyed top with a straw hat that sported a well-worn brim perched back on her head. Before Stan could say anything, Lucy Mac lunged toward him enthusiastically with her hands outstretched.

"Stan!" she said loudly. "I'd know you anywhere. Gosh, it's been a long time since I saw you—at least twenty years—in that awful show at Resort City."

Stan sidestepped her advance slightly, shook her hand and said, "Lucy Mac! It has been a long time, hasn't it. Let me introduce you to Fanny."

"Hello," Lucy Mac said, distantly, exchanging a brief handshake with Fanny. "Stan and I used to do shows together."

"Yes," Stan said, "we were in a few of the same shows back along the way." He put his arm around Fanny, pulling her closer to him, looked Lucy Mac in the eye and said, "I think it was the Resort City show. I haven't thought about that place in a long time."

"You remember," Lucy Mac said, putting her hands on her hips. "That stinkin' hot weather—we almost suffocated under that walkway where we had to set up. Nobody even knew the show was there until old Dutch had that plane fly over the beach pulling that sign advertisin' where we were."

"Yeah," Stan replied as the memory returned. "Dutch—what was his name? Oh, yeah—Carlson. That guy was so laid back we all had to fend for ourselves. I never did another show with him. Gosh, I haven't thought about that in years."

Fanny was looking back and forth between them wondering what they were talking about. Stan recalled a few more details and she could imagine the frustration they must have experienced. She began to catch the humor of it all.

Stan turned back to Lucy Mac. "So, you'd like to exhibit in the Art Extravaganza. We sent out publicity back in the spring looking for artists and we have a pretty good bunch of folks coming in. This is a little late to be taking on someone new. How'd you hear about the show?"

"Oh, sorry, I forgot to tell you. It was recommended to me by a preacher up in Potomac City who saw my stuff in a small show I did there last week. When he told me you were running the show, those memories from Resort City came back, and I just had to come see if I could get in. I travel around doing shows full-time now."

"Really! That's quite an undertaking. How are the shows going for you?"

"You know how it is," Lucy Mac replied. "Sometimes it's great, sometimes not. But it's a life I love."

"And you say a preacher told you about the show and me." Stan glanced at Ed and then Fanny, and they both nodded as he said, "Wouldn't be a guy named CJ Crumbold, would it?"

"Yeah, that's his name. Strange name, hard to forget. Anyway he bought one of my paintings and said he was gonna use it in his office. Said he works with some kind of jail ministry."

"Yep, that's CJ," Ed said. "I didn't say it, but I'm a retired pastor and I've known CJ for a long time. He's pastor of the Wesleyan Brethren Church up there, and he's well known for his prison ministry. I can see where one of these paintings would appeal to him."

The paintings were very colorful abstracts done by splashing or throwing paint onto a canvas and allowing a pattern of color and essence to emerge in the process. Stan remembered now that she had won a top award in a judged show in Northern Virginia that he and Lillie had attended together, and they had talked with Lucy Mac about her process.

As if reading his thoughts, Lucy Mac said, "Somehow I thought you were married to another artist, uh, what was her name"—Lucy Mac stopped, glanced at Fanny and seemed to feel awkward about her comment.

"Yes," Stan replied. "Lillie Plume. Lillie and I opened this gallery when we got married and did some shows for a few years until things here began to take all of our time and energy." Seeing Lucy Mac's dis-ease, he added, "Lillie died a few years ago. She's the one who built the Beach Art Extravaganza into a top-billed show. I still run the gallery along with Fanny." He spoke with an affection for Fanny that Ed noticed and a slight grin crossed his face.

"I guess I come on a little strong," Lucy Mac said after a moment of awkwardness. "But I really do want to be in your show if you have room and will accept my work. I know I should have applied earlier and been juried in."

"Actually, we have a vacancy from an artist who couldn't attend at the last minute," Fanny said, looking at Stan to be sure she wasn't overstepping her role.

"That's right," Stan said, smiling. "Sure, your work is fine. We don't have anyone working in this same style, but Fanny's right, we have a vacant space. If you want it, the entry fee is $200." He proceeded to tell her the set-up time, show hours, and how things worked. "Judging will be Friday afternoon, and we'll have a supper for the artists after the show closes Friday night, at the Wesleyan Brethren fellowship hall. That's where we'll award the prizes."

After telling about the prize levels and answering some questions, Stan said, "I expect you'll know some of the artists working with us. If you need a place to stay, we have a special rate at the Grande Hotel that I can get for you."

"No," Lucy said, "I pull a small trailer with me, so I'm staying out at the campground." She wrote a check and Stan and Ed helped her put her paintings back into her van.

"See you Friday," Stan said, and Lucy drove off.

Back inside the gallery Ed and Fanny started to speak at the same time, and then broke into laughter, each telling the other, "You first."

Stan said, "I think I can read your mind, Ed."

"Yeah," Ed said, looking back and forth between Stan and Fanny. "I think you two have become what my kids used to call "an item" back in their high school days. When did this happen?"

Stan and Fanny looked at each other, and she said, "I think maybe it's been there for a long time, and we just found out about it working together the last few weeks."

"You know, that's an answer to a prayer of mine. I couldn't be happier!" Ed said.

"That's not the only prayer that's been answered, Fanny said. I've been prayin' for some other artist who really needed a show to come and take at least one of those empty places, and here she is. Ain't God somethin'!"

11

A Volatile Incident

"How'd you like the parade last night?" Fanny asked one of her workers who was helping in the registration tent. The first day of the Art Extravaganza had finally arrived and artists were flooding in to get their space assignments and set up their displays. The Dinkel Days Parade had been held the night before.

"I didn't think it was as good this year."

"Really?" Fanny said. "I love a parade. Every parade is fun to me."

Molly walked up with some additional packets. "Everything goin' okay?" Fanny went over the progress so far and Molly said, "One thing's sure—you couldn't ask for a better day. Weather's supposed to be ideal all weekend." She busied herself a few minutes with various details and then said, "Let me know when you need a break, Fanny. We don't want to wear you out."

"Oh, I'll be fine. But if I need help I'll let ya know."

A country music band began playing down the street at the Town Park Gazebo. Entertainment was scheduled throughout each day of the event, giving local talent a chance to shine. "At least we know the sound system's working," one of the workers said. "As loud as that music is here, I'd hate to be set up in a booth right in front of the park." They all laughed.

Stan said, "How are things going?" as he and Ed walked up to the tent.

"I'm amazed how smoothly it has all gone," Fanny said.

"Me, too," Molly said. "Remember last year—" she said to Stan—"that guy who didn't have a tent and wanted special permission to bring his truck into the street each morning and evening to do set up and take down. Boy, he was a rough one!"

"Yeah, I found a tent we could bring in for him to rent, and we were even willing to help him do his set-up, but he didn't want to pay the rent and refused to do it. He got belligerent with me and I finally had to call in Chief Draper to eject him from the show site."

"No kidding," Ed said. "That could have gotten dangerous. Did you have any trouble with him after the show?"

"That's the strange part. No! He never got back to us, and didn't apply this year. But you never can be sure something like that won't happen again."

"Well, it couldn't have been smoother this year!" Fanny exclaimed.

"That's because of you," Stan said, "you set everything up so clearly and your volunteers were so helpful nobody would dare cause a ripple."

"No—come on, now," Fanny said, laughing. "Seriously, God has blessed us with things working out, so let's not take the credit away from him."

"Right on!" Ed said.

The show went without incident all day and after everything had been secured for the night Stan, Fanny, Ed and Molly went to the Seafood Pavilion for a late supper. They got so involved talking that they lost awareness of the time. When the restaurant closed at ten o'clock they all went home. Stan escorted Fanny to her house, and when they got to the porch she said, "Are you in a hurry to leave?"

"No," Stan said, "it's not too late, although I really do want to get some sleep. We have to get started early again tomorrow morning."

"I know—maybe we can sit on the swing for a few minutes," Fanny said, referring to a wood swing hanging from hooks in the porch ceiling that was screened from the street by the tall boxwoods in front of the railing. She often sat out there on summer evenings.

"Sounds pretty romantic," Stan said. "I'd love to."

The air had cooled into the upper 70's after a hot afternoon, and a gentle breeze was rustling tree leaves, bringing the sounds of tree frogs into an orchestration of nature that caressed their ears with a soothing serenity. Stan put his arm around Fanny and she laid her head over against him as they swung back and forth in silent contentment for some time.

"I ain't felt this good in such a long time," Fanny said. They had spent some time each evening talking and exploring their relationship. She turned her face up toward Stan's and said in a whisper, "I love you, darlin'."

Stan felt a warm sensation of total well-being swell up within him. "I love you, too, Fanny." They came together in an embrace, and began to caress and kiss each other with growing affection. Deeper urges began to move within him but Stan didn't want to give in to that, yet he wanted to hold onto his feelings in that moment.

Fanny seemed to sense his emotions and said softly "It seems things are happening fast between us. I like being with you so much that I'd like nothin' better than to have you just move in here with me, but we both know that's not the way to do it. We'll know when the time is right to make a commitment to each other."

Stan hugged her warmly and they kissed. "Yes, we'll know," he said. "I'm so thankful for finding you in my life. It's like some blissful completeness has suddenly returned after a long absence. Thanks for being you."

"Thanks," Fanny said. "I feel the same way."

"You know, we could have a great time after this week is over just taking a day and going out in my boat," Stan said. "Would you like that?"

"I forgot you had a boat. I've never seen it. Yeah, that'd be great."

"You know, when you get out there you sort of leave the whole world back on the shore. You're in your own world, and it's a terrific feeling."

"I can't wait," Fanny said. "I've always wanted to go out on a boat. Can you believe I've lived in Dinkel Island all my life, with boats all over the place, and I've never gone out on one?"

Stan laughed. "Yeah, I can believe it. It's like tourists who visit a place and are impressed with what they find there while the locals are so used to all of it that they never even see it."

"Yeah," Fanny said. "It's kinda like that, ain't it? I'll tell you what, we both need to get some sleep so we'll be ready for things tomorrow." They kissed again, Stan walked her around to the door where they said goodnight and he went back to his condo. As he unlocked the door and turned on the lights, the place felt empty, but he felt full.

Bliss, he said to himself. *Bliss is returning in my life*. His warm inner feeling prompted a soft prayer thought, *O Lord, I thought I would never feel this way again. Thank you for Fanny*. He went to bed and slept soundly.

Friday morning, while Stan, Ed, Fanny and Molly were getting the show off on its start for the day, the Old Geezers were gathering at the drug store with the excitement of Dinkel Days engaging their conversation.

"What'd you think of the parade Wednesday night?" Darrell Tellerson asked as the usual foursome modified their coffee with cream and sugar to match their respective tastes.

"Same old, same old," Jimmy Charles replied. "You see one, you've seen 'em all. I mean, the whole town's held hostage to some juvenile football rivalry. It's okay, but I'd love to see something different at least once."

"Like what?" Bob Drew asked.

"I don't know. If I did maybe I could tell those guys over at the town hall how to change it."

"Its tradition!" exclaimed Doc Patcher, setting down the creamer with a sharp noise. "Every town's gotta have its traditions. That's what keeps folks coming back each year."

"Well, maybe," Jimmy replied with resignation. "Even this art show that's supposed to be such a big deal is just the same old thing every year."

"Sounds like you got up on the wrong side of the bed this morning," Doc said.

"Yeah, his wife gave him the cold shoulder this morning, that's what happened," Darrell said. "That'll set him off every time."

"Okay, wise guys. Maybe I'll just keep my wisdom to myself," Jimmy said. "Oh, changing the subject...."

"Sure," Doc interrupted, "let's change the subject." Everybody laughed. "So what words of wisdom do you have to break the monotony of the great traditional Dinkel Days?" he asked.

Bob broke in, "I don't know about words of wisdom, but I have some friends in Richmond who said the story about our mystery money was carried in the Times-Dispatch last weekend. My friend called to ask me what that was all about."

"That doesn't surprise me," Darrell said. "The way ole Joe Truvine wrote that story it sounds like we have a preacher in town who's a real trouble maker. That kind of publicity draws attention to a town, but it's not the kind of attention you want."

"I hear what you're saying," Bob went on, "and I know that article seemed to make some innuendos about Ed Heygood, but that's just not true. I knew Ed when he was pastor here and he's a solid guy."

Reaching for another donut to dunk in his coffee, Jimmy said, "Well, it's that kind of stuff that could bring the wrong people to the art show. Archie needs to have his guys keep a sharp lookout for unsavory types."

"Now how you gonna do that at an art show?" Darrell asked. "Sometimes artists themselves can look unsavory. Sometimes their art raises questions, too."

"Hey, I'm just shootin' the breeze here with some off-the-cuff remarks. No need to get stirred up over it."

"Yeah, we know you, Jimmy. The only thing you hit straight is a golf ball, and even that hooks into the woods sometimes," Doc said, and everybody laughed. "I have to get to work—some of us have to make a living, you know. I'll be walking through the art show this evening. Maybe I'll see you guys there."

Everybody said goodbye to Doc, and then got ready to leave. "I do wish Archie could get this thing about the mystery money settled," Bob said. "I thought it had been lost in the background up until now. Maybe it really *is* in the background. You guys have a good day. I've got to get back in the pharmacy and get things moving. Take it easy, guys."

"You, too!" Darrell and Jimmy exclaimed, and they both left the shop.

∾∾

It was 3:15 Friday afternoon when the atmosphere was rocked by a sudden explosion. The sound came from the Community Art

Center where smoke and flames suddenly appeared around the roof and the rear of the building. Stan was in the gallery at the time, and the explosion shook the walls, knocked paintings askew and sent some sculpture pieces tumbling.

"What the heck!" Stan exclaimed, and he immediately jumped into action, charging through the door into the main exhibit and class space in the art center building. Paintings were a-kilter and there was some debris scattered about. Smoke seeped into the room from the hallway into the artists' studio area. Stan hit 911 on his cell phone and told the dispatcher that there had been an explosion of unknown origin in the art center.

"So far I don't see anyone injured. I didn't think anyone was in here with the show going on outside.

"Fire and rescue is on the way, and Chief Draper has been called," the dispatcher said. "Where are you now?"

"I'm in the community room, just heading back into the studio area where I think this came from."

"Don't go back there alone, Mr. Grayson. It might not be safe. Please make sure no one else goes in there until help arrives."

"I can't just stand here," Stan protested. "I want to find out what's going on."

"Please hold off," the dispatcher said again. "Wait for Chief Draper." Stan knew the dispatcher was right. He could hear the sirens approaching and wondered how all of this must appear to the people at the art show.

"I'm going out front to keep people calm," he told the dispatcher. "We have a lot of folks out there and I don't want any panic."

"That's a good idea. Chief Draper will be there any moment," the dispatcher said and the call ended.

Out in front a crowd gathered quickly. The emergency responders began to take control, cordoning off the scene and holding people back. *Where's Fanny?* Stan wondered. As Chief

Archie Draper came up to Stan a boy who looked to be around 12 years old broke from the crowd and ran up to them.

"I seen him," the boy said. "I seen a man run out from behind the building."

"Where did he go?" Chief Draper asked.

"He ran across the street and into the woods headed toward the town pier, I guess," the boy said excitedly.

"What did he look like? Can you describe him?"

"Looked about like everybody else but I did notice he had a beard and red hair. His hair was kinda messy and it stuck out under a dirty cap he had turned around backwards."

"That's a big help," the chief said, kneeling now as he spoke with the boy. He got his name and then stood up and spoke to his parents as they were allowed through the police cordon. "Can you remember anything else? This is important," the chief said.

"He had on an orange t-shirt, and tan shorts. His clothes looked dirty, just like his cap."

After talking briefly with the parents and getting their address, Chief Draper turned back toward Stan, got on his radio and made a report back to the station, and then called two officers over. The firemen were inside the building, on top, and around the side and back hosing down everything. The smoke was becoming less intense.

"What's in the back of the building," Archie asked Stan.

"There is an emergency door that is locked on the outside, but can be opened with a panic bar from the inside. There's another door to our maintenance and storage area back there, and it's also kept locked."

"Who has the key to those doors?"

"Well, I do, and Molly does—and we have another set in the key cabinet in the office. Oh—the boy who cuts the grass and does the yard work has a key to the maintenance room. In fact, when we were out in the registration booth this morning I heard him running the lawn mower in the back. He was supposed to do the grass yesterday."

"We'll check him out, and check out the storage area as soon as we're able," the chief said.

"Honey, are you okay? What's happening?" Fanny called out as she came running up to Stan, concern in her expression and voice.

Stan embraced her. "Sure, I'm okay—but I'm not sure about the art center. Something exploded in the back. We're not sure what it was or exactly where it happened. Some kid saw somebody running away from the back of the building into those woods over there," Stan said, pointing in the direction the man had run.

"That's awful! Do you think he caused the explosion?"

"I have no idea. It doesn't make any sense, I mean, why would anyone want to damage the art center? We haven't had any threats of any kind. I think it was something purely accidental."

"I hope you're right about that. I guess they'll be going over things trying to find out. What a shame for all of this to happen in the middle of the Art Extravaganza," Fanny said.

Stan replied, "I told you I had those fears, ever since the trouble with that artist last year. Now I guess I know why."

"That's nonsense," Fanny said. She touched his lips. "Don't let fear get the upper hand, honey. Don't let it rule you."

Stan felt a sudden twinge. Those words were almost the same as Lillie had said to him. "You sound just like Lillie," he said to Fanny. "She always said fear and faith can't live in the same space, so push the fear aside and keep the faith."

"Wise woman!" Fanny said. "See—you need wise women in your life. That's why I'm here."

Without another word Stan drew Fanny to himself and kissed her. It was the first time they'd shown affection in public.

"Whoa! Maybe I'd better come back later," Ed Heygood said as he happened to walk up on them at that moment.

Startled, then self-conscious, but keeping balance, Stan and Fanny pulled apart, turned toward Ed, and Stan said, "No need to leave. You'll probably see a lot of this if you stick around us."

Ed put his arms around both of their shoulders and they walked back into the gallery to recoup and try to get the show back into a normal state. "Chief Draper said the fire chief would have an investigation team in the first of next week," Stan said, "after the extravaganza is over, and they'll try to figure out what happened. Meanwhile he said he would get out an alert for a man that might match the description given by the witness.

"Just because the boy saw him run from behind the art center doesn't mean he had anything to do with the explosion," the chief had said. "He might have been startled and simply run away in fear. We'll find him, I'm sure."

As quickly as possible the firemen and their equipment were removed from the scene, the affected area cordoned off, and people began to get back to the art show.

"After we finish tonight," Fanny said, "I'm treatin' us to the best seafood dinner you've had in a long time, at the Yacht and Supper Club."

Stan looked at her with a depth of love and amazement he hadn't felt in years.

"Okay," he said. "We can both use a break after all of this!"

❧

When the explosion occurred, Lucy Mac was talking with a customer in her tent at the far end of the show. The woman had been looking closely at a large painting with a prism of colors that created an impassioned visual expression that apparently appealed to her.

Lucy Mac approached her. "I've noticed that you seem drawn to that painting. I'm the artist," she said with a smile, extending her hand.

The woman had on a fashionable wide-brimmed white straw hat, a sleeveless top with a low v-shaped neck, a long, sweeping flowered skirt, and white sandals with a modest, solid heal. She looked like someone who could afford the painting.

"Happy to meet you," the woman said, extending her hand. "I'm Elaine Longstreet—from Newport News. I drove out today just to see what the show might offer that would complement my collection. I must say, I haven't seen anything really extraordinary up until now, but this piece fascinates me."

Lucy Mac went on to discuss the painting with her, answering questions about her painting techniques, and about her motives in creating it.

"I don't see a price," Elaine said. "How much are you asking?"

"This piece is $1800," Lucy Mac said.

"Oh!" Elaine responded. "It's certainly worth every penny of that"—she paused, cocked her head to the side, and then said, "Do you mind if I touch it?"

"Not at all. You won't hurt the painting by touching it. I know sometimes touch communicates as much as visual appearance."

"Yes, it does!" Elaine said, smiling, and after exploring it briefly, said "I don't have a problem with your price except that's more than I am prepared to spend today. Could you take it outside the tent where I can see it in the full light?"

"Of course," Lucy Mac said. She took the painting out and stood it against the plain back wall of the tent. That's when the explosion happened, and it stopped everything around them.

"Whatever was that?" the customer remarked.

"I have no idea," Lucy Mac replied. "It seems like it came from down at the other end of the show."

As they heard sirens and people began running in that direction the customer turned back to Lucy Mac and said, "Okay! I'll give you $1500, for the painting. I really like it and I need to get on my way home before traffic gets tied up from whatever is happening."

They completed the sale and Lucy Mac had one of the hospitality volunteers help carry the painting out to the woman's car for her. Her work was so different from other art in the show that this was actually her first sale of the day, and she felt relieved that her expenses were covered and she hoped to make more sales. Suddenly she was startled by a noise. She looked up to see a familiar face peek around the side of the tent.

"You!" she exclaimed. "What are you doing here! You get away from me."

Lucy Mac jumped up and the fire flew from her expression as she put her hands on her hips, took one step forward, then pointed directly at the intruder and said, "You leave me alone or I'll call the police."

"Now, now, Lucy babe, take it easy," the man said in a soft, almost pleading tone as he stepped more completely into view. His graying reddish beard and hair were as unkempt as she'd ever seen them, and he had on an awful orange t-shirt with some kind of dirt smeared on it and a couple of tears in it. He looked like he might have been on a binge.

"What do you mean following me here. How'd you find me?" she asked.

"That weren't hard," he replied, a sly grin trying to paint itself on his grimy face. "You got all chummy with that preacher that bought one o' your paintin's in Potomac City, and I was right outside your tent when he told you about this show. So I knowed you was comin' here, and I knowed you was after that artist that runs this place. I heard what you said. I came here to protect my interests."

"You ain't got no interests, you idiot. I couldn't stand livin' with you and when I left I told you if you tried to follow me or interfere in my life I'd turn you in," Lucy Mac said as she reached behind her pedestal and grasped a steel rod she kept for just such an emergency. She was bigger and stronger than he was, which he had found out the hard way on more than one occasion. She had her I-phone in the other hand as she took another step toward the man and said "I'm calling the police now, so you better make tracks."

"That won't do you no good. They's busy down there with all that confusion. But I'm leavin', babe. Ciao!" With that he disappeared as quickly and silently as he had appeared. She loathed the day she had ever gotten hooked up with Ben Wartman!

12

Attempted Reprise

$\mathcal{T}$he rest of the art show went off without incident. A crew of volunteers cleaned up behind the departing artists, and by Saturday morning the Beach Art Extravaganza was but a memory to be shelved until the next year. Several days later the police and fire officials met with Stan and Molly at the gallery. Chief Draper took the lead, explaining what they had found in their investigation.

"We found the remains of a propane tank with the valve open, along with remnants of what appears to be burnt twine on the ground outside the storage room. Inside we found traces of turpentine, kerosene, gasoline, and remnants of some old utility rags. We think the perpetrator was an opportunist who found the storage room door unlocked, and then quickly devised a way to cause an explosion. We think whoever did this was the same person seen running from the building, perhaps to a car that had been left on one of the nearby streets, or perhaps the town pier parking lot."

"So, it was arson," Stan said, pacing around, "but we don't know who did it or why." He looked directly at Chief Draper and said, "That's just crazy—it doesn't make any sense. We've all been wracking our brains trying to recall someone angry enough to do this, and we just can't come up with anyone."

Chief Draper said, "I understand what you're saying. We think robbery could have been the original motive. I mean, it makes sense. The show had everyone's attention pulled away from the building. Whoever did it may have figured they could come in the back way, but found the fire door was locked. Then let's say they noticed the unlocked maintenance door and tried that way in. Perhaps they underestimated what the propane explosion would trigger and when it blew with such force and started a fire, they got scared and ran off."

"Yeah, I follow that," Stan said, "but there are two problems. First, why would anyone want to rob the art center? Maybe they thought we had a lot of money from the art show in there, but the artists sell their own work and collect for it. Common sense would suggest that we do our business in advance of the show and don't hold a large amount of cash. Second, why would anyone be stupid enough to think they could blow a hole in a wall and not draw a lot of attention, even if it didn't cause a fire?"

"The robbery angle really doesn't play well, as you say," Chief Draper said. "Then again there was something in the Richmond papers recently about that money you and Ed found in Tranquility Bay. Who knows? Maybe somebody thought you had it here in the building and took advantage of your attention being drawn away for the art show. Who knows what goes on in peoples' minds?"

"I think there was something else going on," Stan said.

The chief nodded. "Could be. We've looked at the idea of the explosion as a diversion but that doesn't play out any better than the robbery idea with the facts at hand. For instance, if it was a diversion, what was it supposed to divert our attention away from? There were no other crimes reported during that time. Nothing has surfaced to support the idea of a diversionary tactic. Yet it looks as though it was intentionally done."

What about somebody who's a little whacko? Stan thought. "Maybe somebody just wanted to stir up some excitement. Maybe there was no other real purpose than that. That sounds far-fetched, but this whole thing is far-fetched when you come down to it."

"Who knows?" the chief said. "We could guess about this all day long and never hit on the right motive. Right now we can't rule anything out. There's even the possibility that this person is a serial arsonist. We're checking around for other similar situations, but so far nothing has come in."

"Well, I appreciate what you're doing," Stan said, shaking hands with the police and fire chiefs as they started to leave. "You know, if he wanted to break into my office, why didn't he break into the back door of the gallery instead of the art center?" Stan asked. Then he answered his own question, "Of course, if he didn't know the buildings were connected by an inside door, or where the office is located, he might not have known to try that entrance."

Chief Draper paused, turned back toward Stan and asked, "You have someone living in an apartment above the gallery, don't you?"

"Yes, Ed Heygood. But Ed wasn't around at the time because he was working with us out at the art show."

"I'm not suggesting anything, Stan"—the chief said—"just trying to fill in all the blanks. Right now we're looking for small details that might reveal something. At any rate, we know it was arson and the robbery motive is also possible. The case is open and we're continuing to investigate."

Molly, who seemed to be on top of every situation, had been listening to the conversation. She seemed to be nervous. "It doesn't make me feel safe getting to work early," she said. "What if the robber does think that money Stan and Ed found is in the building and he comes back for another try? What if he's around here watching, figures out who I am, and tries to force me to let him in?"

Stan said, "I understand your fears, but Ed is right upstairs over the gallery. Why don't you tell him when you plan to arrive and have him meet you at the door. I think this person is rather cowardly, and I doubt if he'd approach you if Ed is with you."

"Oh!" Molly said with apparent relief. "I hadn't thought of that."

Stan said, "I'll talk with Ed if you wish."

"Oh, that's okay," Molly said. "Ed and I have gotten to be friends. I'll talk to him. I'm sure he'll help me out."

♋

With the completion of the report and an official status to the continuing investigation, the insurance company worked out a settlement with Stan and they began cleaning up and repairing things the following week. Josh, the lawn boy, was remorseful over his negligence when Stan talked to him.

"Son, what were you thinking? Did you have something else on your mind?"

"I got in a hurry to make up for not cutting the grass when I was supposed to," Josh said. "Then after I finished I forgot where I put the padlock. With the art show and everything going on you weren't around. I waited for a while and then I just closed the door and left. I meant to come back later and tell you I had lost the lock, but I got busy and forgot about that, too—until the explosion." The boy was obviously nervous. "I'm sorry," he said in a pleading tone. "I don't blame you if you get somebody else to cut the grass."

"Putting your equipment away and locking the door were your responsibilities. Sometimes things like this happen, and usually there are some kind of consequences. I hope you've learned something from all of this."

Josh looked up at Stan with a penitent expression. "I know—I'm sorry."

Stan put a hand on Josh's shoulder. "Let's put it this way," he said. "The first time you make a mistake that creates a problem, I have to take it as my responsibility because it means I haven't trained you well enough to avoid the problem. Now, if you make the same mistake again, I'll see that as your fault, and we'll deal with it differently. Okay?"

"Okay," Josh said with a relieved expression on his face. "Thanks, Mr. Grayson. I won't let you down again."

"I'm counting on you, Josh. You're still my grass cutter."

Right after his encounter with Lucy Mac, Ben Wartman left Dinkel Island. The place made him nervous. It was reading about the mystery money in the newspaper that had brought him back. Even though he had raided that cabin looking for the girl from Maryland and her boyfriend over twenty years earlier, he still woke up sometimes with nightmares about it. When he read about a lot of money in a backpack that had been in the water a long time, he remembered that the girl who got away that night had been carrying a backpack. *I just know that's the same money that girl ran away with,* he had told himself. *I gotta go git my hands on that money.*

Then his efforts failed again, just like with the raid on the cabin. He knew he had to leave town fast. *At least I found Lucy Mac again!* He wanted her, and he was going to get her back. *Gotta keep her in sight—gotta wait fer jest the right time to move on 'er.* He knew she could be scrappy, but he also knew she liked hooking up with him no matter what she said. He'd never found anybody else he would rather hang with.

Ben's thoughts went back to the raid on the old shack. *Wish I hadn't been such a hot head. Wish I hadn't killed Brewster—shoulda jest scared the stuffing out of 'im.* He thought back to Roland and Bubba—to everything that had gone on. *Wish I hadn't burned that old shack. I could use someplace like that right 'bout now. All that's water over the dam. Jest gotta make the best of things.*

When he reached Richmond, Ben got a room in a cheap hotel. He hadn't worked for a few weeks and was running low on money. If he'd just been able to get into that art center—he knew that mystery money was in there. *I got a right to that money,* Ben told himself. *After all the trouble I went to findin' it in the first place, I got a right to have it now. I need that money, and them guys ain't got no need fer it. It's my duty to take it.* At least that's how he rationalized the whole thing.

Ben slept fitfully and the next morning he knew he had to go back to Dinkel Island. He shaved off his beard, trimmed his hair, and then colored it with some black hair dye. When he finished, he studied himself in the mirror. *By durn, even my own mama wouldn't know me—if she was livin'.* He was satisfied with his efforts. *Maybe Lucy Mac will warm up to me now!*

When Ben got back to Dinkel Island he tried to be low key. He had followed Lucy Mac's movements and knew she had a trailer and was staying at the campground. He figured she would stay around for a while since she seemed to be chasing after that Grayson guy who owned the art center. *She won't quit 'til she gits what she wants—Lucy Mac always gits what she wants! The trick is to make her want what I want her to want!* That was his task now.

Ben drove out to the campground with mixed emotions. *Maybe I better give her a little more time,* he thought as he was about to turn in, so he kept going up toward Lighthouse Point.

Durn, what's this? He said to himself. There was a locked gate across the road. Ben got out of his truck and tried the gate It was old and both it and the lock hasp were rusted. He got an axe out of his truck and after a few whacks the rusty lock broke and the gate came open. *Hot dang!* he said as he drove through and then closed the gate behind him. He hadn't been up to the scene of his crime in all these years. *So why'm I goin' up here now?* he argued with himself. *Reckon it won't hurt none to find out what's changed, and what ain't.*

Just like twenty-two years earlier, he parked at the shed near the lighthouse, and then walked up through the overgrown field and into the thickly wooded area. He found the charred remains of the cabin, but everything was grown over with scrubby trees and vines. He thought about the root ball cavity where they had stuffed Brewster's body. *Wonder where that root ball is? There oughta at least be some bones.* But the tree and its root ball had rotted and other trees had fallen so he couldn't be sure where to look. After thrashing around for a while he decided there were no remains left.

That's good, he told himself. *We done that thing right, at least.*

Ben went back to his truck and returned to Dinkel Island with a strange unsettled feeling inside. *What if there ain't no remains 'cause that guy somehow survived? But that's impossible. He was shot and next to death when we stuffed him down into that cavity and covered him up.* Ben was feeling paranoid. He didn't want to go back through the nightmarish trauma again, but the haunting feeling remained. On the way out he stopped and re-set the gate to look like it was locked. *Wish I'd never gone back up there,* he said to himself.

Ben rented a small trailer back a dirt lane along Lighthouse Point Road—remote enough not to be readily noticed, but convenient to everything that mattered to him. He found a job doing clean-up work at the local Wal-Mart. It didn't pay much, but it was a job. *I'll hit Lucy Mac up for some money. She'll come through. She ain't never turned me in.*

Lucy Mac knew what Ben had done. He had been shocked when she told him what he'd said years ago when he had been high on drugs. They had been lovers then and lived in a cottage up in Monterrey, in the Alleghany Mountains. It had all started when he met her in a bar during a weekend of folk arts, crafts and merriment to welcome in the fall season.

He remembered that time with her fondly. *Man, she was somethin'!* After several drinks they had gone to her hotel room where they drank some more and then caroused until the alcohol and exhaustion overcame them. *Whooh!* Ben thought. *I ain't never had a hangover like that one!* Their relationship lasted through a long, cold winter of traveling and cavorting together. She did shows, and he worked the crowds with a variety of con schemes. They drank and played and traveled from place to place.

Wish I'd never of gotten into them drugs, Ben thought. *She was smart. She wouldn't do 'em.* He could still hear her screaming at him when he finally sobered up.

"You're a rotten snake," she had yelled, looking as if the devil himself had gotten into her. "You're slime. You're a criminal. I ought to turn you in," she had yelled at him. "Now get out of my life and don't you ever come around me. If I ever see you again I'll go straight to the police and tell them."

I let her scare me, he thought. *I shouldn't have done that. Shoulda stayed with her no matter what. She ain't never gone to the police, and she never will. That's why I gotta git her back, so's we can have a life together again. We belong together.*

∿∾

Stan was alone in his office. Molly had the week off after the extra time she had worked during the Art Extravaganza, and Fanny had gone to Food Lion to pick up some groceries for the supper she was going to fix for herself and Stan that evening. Stan heard the bells over the front door tingle and someone called, "Hello! Anybody here?" He didn't recognize the voice, so he thought it might be a customer.

"Be right there," he called out, and quickly closed down his computer, and then went out to the gallery. As he walked in through the door, he caught Lucy Mac in his peripheral vision. She seemed to lunge toward him.

"Hey, Stan," she said wearing a huge smile and her usual overbearing attitude.

"Lucy Mac," Stan said as he sidestepped her advance. "I thought you had gone on to your next show—what are you still doing in town?"

"Why Stan, I couldn't leave without having a chance to see you again. You know, I came here to do the show, true, but I also came because I heard you were here. I've missed you."

Stan scrutinized her as he said, "Lucy Mac, I don't know what you're talking about. I only met you once in my life that I can recall."

"Why, Stanny, baby, how could you say that? Don't you like me?" she said, taking on a seductive manner. "You and me, we're the same kind of people, we're artists. We're free spirits. We could have some fun together." She puckered up her lips and started to move in closer.

Stan stepped around behind the sales counter and said, "Lucy Mac, you and I have nothing in common, really. No disrespect to you, but I have someone in my life already—you've met her—Fanny, who worked with me on the art show."

"So, are you two engaged?" Lucy Mac persisted.

"That's immaterial. I'm not interested in any other relationships," Stan said with a tone that indicated that was to be the end of the conversation.

Lucy Mac started to go around the counter saying, "Come on, Stanny—just give me a chance."

At that moment Ed Heygood walked in the back door and, hearing Lucy Mac's voice, sensed that something was not quite right. He made no effort to muffle his footsteps, but walked straight through the back room, calling out, "Hey, Stan, where are ya, buddy?"

Lucy Mac was startled by the sound. She flinched and backed off. "Who's that?"

Stan didn't answer her, but called to Ed, "In here, old buddy. I was just having a very strange conversation with Lucy Mac—you remember—one of the artists."

Ed entered the room. "Sure," he said, taking in the situation. "I met you that day you came by and wanted to get into the art show."

"Yeah," Lucy Mac said with scorn, "I remember. So what, do you work here regular or something?"

"No," Ed said. "I live here. I thought all the artists had gone home after the show. Did you forget something?"

"Oh, she forgot something all right," Stan said, keeping eye contact with Lucy Mac. "She forgot to go home. She seems to think she and I should have some sort of relationship together. I was just telling her that ain't the way things are."

Ed caught on quickly. "So, this lady's out of line, would you say?"

"Oh, yeah, big time," Stan said. He looked Lucy Mac straight in the eye again and added, "Lucy Mac, I'm sorry you've talked yourself into some idea that you and I should have some kind of relationship, but that would have to be a two-way deal, and it ain't gonna happen from my end. I think it's time for you to leave."

"But, you run a gallery, and I want to leave some paintings on consignment." Lucy Mac pouted in a whining tone. "You can't turn down a business relationship."

Losing patience Stan said, "I only exhibit work that I select for the gallery, and I don't believe yours will fit into our context here. I'm sorry, but I can't take any of your work."

Lucy Mac was a large woman, and she momentarily looked like she might try to challenge Stan physically, but then her expression changed to one of hurt, and she spat out, "Don't worry, I wouldn't lower myself to put my paintings in a sleazy place like this. And you can count on this—I'll tell everybody I know what you and this gallery are really like." With that she stomped out.

"What got into her?" Ed asked.

"You know, I think she thought since Lillie is dead that I must be vulnerable and she wanted to 'catch me,' as the saying might go. I'm as dumbfounded as you over this. Anyway, I'm glad you happened to come in when you did."

When Fanny came back from the store, Stan and Ed told her about the strange events of the afternoon. After they got over the shock of the whole thing, they found the humor in it and laughed their heads off at the expense of Lucy Mac.

13

Gracie Love

*T*he rest of August passed uneventfully and on the day after Labor Day an unexpected opportunity arose for Kate Sheppard. While sorting through a back-up of mail a colorful flyer dropped onto her desk. "Gracie Love Sings God's Praise" it said, and gave details of a coming gospel music concert at a church in Richmond. Kate had heard of Gracie Love. She was the featured female vocalist with a gospel music group called *Joyful Morning* from Sarasota, Florida, and with her first CD out, she was rumored to be a rising star in the gospel music world.

"Hmmm, Kate said to herself as she checked the date for the concert. *That sure would be worth attending, but I'd have to move some things around to do it. I wonder what it would cost to bring her to Dinkel Island while she's in the state?* She called Margie in and asked her if she had noticed the flyer.

"I did," Margie said. "It caught my attention because my sister in Georgia heard her sing and said she is really good. If you're going to the concert in Richmond, maybe we could get a group together from the church."

"Better yet, why don't we see if she could come do a concert here sometime—we could invite the other churches and have a great celebration. What do you think?"

"Oh, that's a great idea—but you'd better talk with the Baptists first. You know Mammoth Baptist always arranges the community gospel music programs."

Kate rolled her eyes. "I know! We've crossed them a couple of times before, but I don't think they 'own' gospel music programs at Dinkel Island. No, I think we'll check this out, get the details, talk with some of our own folks first, and then bring the Baptists into it after we have things together."

"It's your funeral," Margie said, laughing.

"Oh, I don't think Baptist opposition is that bad!" Kate said, handing the flyer to Margie. "Would you mind making some calls to check on this—find out the cost and get some details together?"

"Sure," Margie said. "I'll work on it this morning."

Margie went back into her office, and Kate decided to check the idea out with Herb Melloman, so she called his office.

"Melloman here," the pleasant baritone voice announced as Herb answered the phone himself.

"Oh," Kate said, startled—"I thought I'd get your administrative assistant, Herb. This is Kate at church."

"Hi Kate—did you want to talk to Peggy?"

"No, I wanted to talk to you, I just didn't expect you to answer the phone yourself."

"That's okay—it always confuses people when I answer the phone. What can I do for you this fine day?"

"You're familiar with some of the leading gospel music groups," Kate said, "have you heard of a group called *Joyful Morning*?"

"Well, yes, I have," Herb said. "They grew out of an all male gospel quartet called the *Son Shiners* who sang mostly in Florida, and then took on some female background singers and changed their whole approach. Why do you ask?"

"I'll get to that in a minute—what do you know about Gracie Love? I've heard a recording by her and she has a terrific voice, and apparently a powerful story about her faith, from what I've heard."

Herb filled her in a little more. "Gracie Love was apparently a waitress in Orlando, Florida who sang in a local church group a few years ago. When the *Son Shiners* wanted to add some female voices and expand their group, they held auditions there for background singers, and Gracie Love was one of those they hired. I don't know too much beyond that, except that the group did expand, changed their name to *Joyful Morning*, and now includes the male quartet, both male and female soloists, and a male/female duet that I hear is really good."

"That's fascinating," Kate said. "Now, my question: do you think it would be a good idea to try and get *Joyful Morning* here in Dinkel Island?"

"Yes, absolutely—*if* you can get them. I understand they're touring Virginia and North Carolina this fall, but I think we're too small for their kind of group. I'm sure their price is high."

"I got a flyer in the mail today about Gracie Love singing at a concert in Richmond," Kate said, "and I got to thinking, wouldn't it be a great idea if our church could bring her and her group in for a concert—but maybe that's not practical."

"Well, yes, that would be fantastic if you could do it," Herb said, "but it's usually the Baptists who arrange all the gospel music events, and we'd certainly have to do it as a community. The folks at Mammoth Baptist usually set up these things—why don't you ask them about this idea?"

"That's what Margie said," Kate replied. "Actually, I'm not sure why, but I want to take the lead on this, check it out and see if it's at all practical, and if it is we could invite the Baptists to participate with us. Surely this isn't about which church is into gospel music, or who has the power to bring in something big. It should be about inviting people into a fresh spiritual experience, no matter which church takes the lead."

"Uh-huh"—Herb said pensively. "Actually, I don't think this needs to be a win-lose situation with the Baptists. It can be a win-win situation for everybody. Why don't you contact Mammoth Baptist and see if the two churches can work together to bring this in, and if not, then we could do it simply as a program in our own congregation if we wished."

Kate thought about that. "Okay, I think you're right, Herb, only I think it will work better if it's done through the lay people, not the pastors. Would you be willing to make the contact for me?"

Herb said, "I'm okay with that. Can you e-mail me the information for *Joyful Morning* and Gracie Love? What dates do they have available and how much will it cost? What kind of equipment and other arrangements do they require?"

"Hold on—not so fast, Herb. Margie's trying to reach them now."

"Okay," Herb said. "Call me when you have the details and I'll be glad to make the contact."

Kate thanked Herb and hung up. She looked through the flyer and then called Margie and told her that she had changed her mind and wanted to make the call herself. She found the group's contact number and dialed it. The phone was answered in Sarasota, Florida with a recorded track from one of the groups featured numbers, and then a live voice came in, "Greetings in Christ whose name we praise. This is Annie. How can I help you?"

Kate identified herself and then told Annie what she and Herb had discussed. Annie said, "I will pass this on to Mark, our tour manager. He checks email all the time when he's out on tour. The group has just left for Virginia and North Carolina on an extended trip—did you say you're in Virginia?"

"Yes, but you've probably never heard of our town. We're a small place on the Chesapeake Bay called Dinkel Island. As I said, I'm pastor of the Wesleyan Brethren Church here."

"Dinkel Island—no, I don't think I've heard of that. But our group plays in large towns, small towns, cities—wherever the Lord leads us. I'll tell you what, I'll e-mail Mark that you called, and I'll give you his e-mail address so you can contact him yourself. How would that work?"

"That's wonderful," Kate said, not really sure if she was being put off, or if this really was the way to go. Annie gave her the email address and after she hung up Kate sent Mark a message giving her e-mail, and her cell phone number for his response. She wondered how long she would have to wait to hear back from him.

She didn't have to wait long. After lunch Kate made some pastoral visits in the community, and when she returned to her office about three o'clock and checked her e-mail, there was Mark's response. He said the group was starting their tour in Roanoke the coming weekend, and they had concerts every few days through October. It happened, however, that he had a cancellation at Fredericksburg on the last day of September, which was a Friday night. Kate wasn't sure that would give them enough time to prepare. She got the rest of the information Herb needed and called him back.

When Herb answered the phone, Kate said, "Good news/ bad news, Herb. They are on tour through Virginia and North Carolina, and they have a cancellation in our part of the state—but here's the bad news—its right around the corner, on September 30th. And, they are expensive. I'm not sure we have a large enough space for them, either, although they do sing in local churches a lot. We might be able to use our community center for this."

"Let me see how some folks at both the Baptist church and our church feel about this," Herb said, "and then we can decide whether or not to proceed. We have done some big things on short notice before, so we could probably pull this off. Let me check it out."

They agreed to that, and Kate decided it was probably just a fantasy idea on her part, and she began to let go of it. The next day she had a call that shook her up—it was from Gracie Love herself.

"Rev. Sheppard?" Gracie said as Margie transferred the call to her desk. "This is Gracie Love with *Joyful Morning*. I understand you called wanting to know if we could do a concert at your church this fall, and I believe Mark e-mailed you that we do have an unexpected opening on September 30."

"Yes," Kate responded. "We are interested in doing that, and I'm glad you have a date available, but now I'm not sure we can raise sufficient funds for your expenses on such short notice."

"That's why I called," Gracie said. "My husband's father lives there in Dinkel Island—my husband sings baritone in our quartet, so we travel together, and he thinks it would be great to sing there. He hasn't seen his dad in quite a while, so we have a personal interest in doing this."

"Oh, really!" Kate exclaimed. "Who is your father-in-law?"

"He's an artist—you might know him—Stan Grayson."

"Oh, my, yes! Stan is an active member of our church, and he runs a gallery and an art center that does a lot for the community. I didn't know his son was a gospel singer! I'll have to get on him about keeping such a secret."

"Well," Gracie said hesitantly, "he probably doesn't know it. You see, Marty, my husband, and his dad haven't been close for many years. It's a long story, but after Marty and I talked about this possibility of singing there, we both thought maybe God could use our presence to mend some fences between the two of them."

Kate was surprised with all of this. She hadn't really known much about Stan's background except he had told her he moved to

Dinkel Island after his divorce nearly thirty years ago. He hadn't mentioned his son, which told Kate the split was pretty deep.

"Thanks for your openness about that," Kate said to Gracie. "I believe the Lord uses many resources for healing and restoration amidst brokenness. The only question I have is about the cost of bringing your group in—."

Gracie interrupted, "Please," she said, "don't let that be a factor. We've talked it over in our group and we're willing to come on a love offering basis. You let us present our music ministry and offer our CDs for sale, receive a love offering for us, and we'll trust God to provide for our needs. Does that work for you?"

"Well, yes," Kate said, overwhelmed. "It certainly does. Now— we will be advertising this to the community and another church in town frequently brings in gospel music, so we'll invite them to participate with us. This is wonderful!"

"I'm so excited!" Gracie said. "This is an answer to prayer. God does so much when we step back and trust him to show us the way."

"Yes, I see that every day in the parish. Blessings to you and your group. We'll look forward to meeting all of you, and praising God through your music."

"One other thing," Gracie said. "There are six of us in the traveling group—we don't bring the entire entourage with us on the road—four men and two women, that is to say, two married couples plus two men. We have two large RV's and we'll need space for them. Can you handle that?"

"I think so," Kate replied. "We have a large parking lot, and there is also a campground in the community, if that helps."

"I'm sure we can work that out, then," Gracie said. They exchanged a few more thoughts and concluded their conversation.

Kate called Herb right away.

"Herb," she said when Peggy transferred the call to him, "Great news! *Joyful Morning* travels with a small entourage of six people in two RV's, and they're excited about coming to Dinkel

Island. They will come for a love offering—no other fees. Isn't that fantastic?"

"That's wonderful," Herb responded. "That will help. Cost is the sticky issue with the Baptists. They actually didn't take offense that we were trying to set this up."

Kate went on to explain to Herb that one of the men in the group was related to someone in their congregation without going into details. Herb felt that was a good selling point, and Kate cautioned him not to go into that until she checked out some things about that relationship. He agreed, and they hung up.

"Margie," Kate said as she went into the outer office. "Margie! Wonderful news—not only can *Joyful Morning* come to do a concert with us, but they'll do it for a love offering! I really do see the hand of God working in this. Hallelujah!"

Kate filled Margie in on the relationship between Marty and Stan and the role that relationship was probably playing in getting the concert. "Let's just keep that quiet for a bit," she said to Margie, "because I need to talk to Stan about this and see where he is with it all. It's strange he never mentioned his son is a gospel singer."

"That's news to me, too," Margie said. "I remember he mentioned that his son lives in Sarasota and that he's a graphic artist there. This is the first I've heard about him singing."

"Well, it sounds like some healing is needed here, and God is at work. It'll be exciting to see how all of this comes about."

14

A Surprise Call

Stan and Fanny found a chance to go out on his boat sooner than they had expected when Molly said on Wednesday that she thought Stan needed a break, and she could handle the gallery and the art center for the day. If she needed help she could call on Ed, who had been helping out a lot anyway since the Art Extravaganza. He told her that working in the gallery gave him a positive focus in his retirement. Molly was growing fond of him, so that suited her just fine.

After breakfast the next morning, Stan and Fanny drove to Pappy's Place, parked the car and carried some food, drinks, and bait out to the boat.

"Oh!" Fanny said, "it's so big."

Stan laughed, took her hand to help her step aboard, and said, "what were you expecting, a rowboat?"

"Well, that would be romantic, but I just can't see you rowin' me around Tranquility Bay."

"Oh, I wouldn't do all the work alone," Stan said. "You'd have to row, too."

"I don't mind work, and I'll do my share with a lot of things, but rowin' boats ain't one of 'em," Fanny said, squinting her face in the bright sunlight as she spoke. "Seriously, I knew the boat had a motor, but I just couldn't picture it bein' this large."

"I know," Stan said, grinning back at her, "I never thought I'd have a boat this large or this nice. I bought it used a few years ago—in fact, I bought it right here at Pappy's Place."

"They sell boats here?" Fanny said.

"Yeah, they buy up old boats that are in good shape and then refurbish and re-sell them. They don't do all of that here—they have a boat house for that. And they only do a couple at a time. I think they did a great job on this one and I've been happy with it—except when I hit the gas pump."

Stan gave Fanny the grand tour of the boat, then he showed her how to cast off the lines as they backed out of the slip and headed out into Tranquility Bay.

"Have you ever fished at all, Fanny?" Stan asked.

"No, never. But I want to learn. Is it hard?"

Stan answered, "Naw, the fish do all the work once they bite into the bait, get hooked and try to fight their way off your line all the way to the boat." Fanny playfully wrinkled her nose, and then Stan added, "now I'll teach you how to cut bait."

Fanny liked to kid around, but she wasn't squeamish, and in fact she learned very quickly. They were off of the Lighthouse Point cliffs near where Stan and Ed had found the mysterious money. They cast out their lines and then sat down to wait for the fish to bite. Stan knew this day wasn't really about fishing as much as it was about Fanny and him bonding. Since the water at this spot was calmer than farther out in the Bay, it was a perfect place to relax, talk, and leave all the distractions back on shore.

They stayed there for a couple of hours, occasionally catching a fish that they threw back, exploring their similarities and differences, and finding points where they enriched each other. They weren't talking about engagement, but each was thinking about it. Finally Fanny said she'd like to ride out around Dinkel Island and see the town from the water, so they stowed their tackle, pulled up the anchor, and set out for a sight-seeing jaunt. About one o'clock they pulled in to the town pier and tied up, then ate lunch on board before pulling out and traveling farther up the shoreline toward the mouth of the Potomac River. It was during their return that Stan's cell phone rang.

"Hope that's not some problem at the gallery," Stan said as he answered. It wasn't. It was his son, Marty.

"Marty!" Stan said, "I've been thinking about you lately. Glad you called."

"Hi Dad," Marty said, then paused. "Have you got a few minutes? I think we need to talk."

"Is something wrong?"

"No, but there are some things we need to talk about. I should have called you long ago, but you and I have been distant from each other for so long, I just didn't do it."

"Hang on a minute, Son," Stan said, and then he explained to Fanny who had called. He had been teaching her to run the boat and she learned fast, so he cut back the speed to reduce engine noise, gave Fanny a course to follow, and then stepped back.

"We're out on the boat, so the motor's a little noisy—can you hear me okay?"

"Yeah," Marty said, "I can hear you okay. Can you hear me?"

"Sure can," Stan said. "What's up—I take it you have something on your mind."

"You say 'we' are out on the boat—are you sure you don't want me to call back later?"

"No, its okay. Fanny Grant is with me. I've been teaching her to fish. Fanny and I have known each other for a long time and this summer we began dating. I'd love for you to have a chance to meet her."

"Okay," Marty said, "we just might get to do that—that's what I called to talk about. Now, hold onto your hat—I got married back in May, and my wife is a gospel singer—."

"You—you got married? That's wonderful! Why didn't you let your old man know?"

"I wanted to, but I've had a lot of feelings from way back when you and Mom were divorced that I had never worked out, and that prevented me. I know that's a lame excuse, but that's how it was."

"That's not a lame excuse, Son. You had every right to feel that way and I always knew some day you would work things out to where you and I could get back on an even keel. That's why I haven't pushed you. I'm happy for you."

"I'm glad to hear that," Marty said. "I worked with a counselor for quite a while a couple of years ago, after I first met Gracie. He helped me discover some feelings that were affecting me that I had been pushing down inside. I guess falling in love with someone truly different and special motivated me to get a better perspective on things. But that's too much to go into right now. I just want to make sure you and I are open to each other."

"Son, you have no idea how I've prayed for you to have that kind of experience. I see no reason why we can't get on more positive terms with each other. I look forward to it."

"Well, that's good," Marty replied, "because Gracie and I both sing in a gospel group and in a couple of weeks our touring group will be at your church there in Dinkel Island."

"Really? My church?" Stan replied. "When did this come about?"

"It was very sudden. Actually, we had a cancellation and then your pastor called us to see if we could come there, and it all just fit together. All of this has just come about in the last couple of days, so I wanted to get in touch with you right away."

"I'm sort of shocked—not in a bad way—but shocked that I'm so out of touch that I didn't know about it on this end. Hey! This is great—and I look forward to meeting your wife."

"Gracie's right here with me—would you like to speak to her?" Marty asked.

"Sure," Stan replied. A moment passed, then Gracie spoke.

"Hello, Mr. Grayson. I'm so glad Marty called you. He's a wonderful man, and I'm looking forward to meeting you."

"Hi, Gracie. Just from hearing your voice I feel like I know you already," Stan said. "I understand you're my new daughter-in-law, and I look forward to meeting you. When did you say you will be in Dinkel Island?"

"In a couple of weeks—September 30," Gracie said. "You know, I just had a thought—we're singing in Richmond on September 25. Why don't I arrange a pass for you to come and hear the concert, and then we can get together afterwards."

"Oh, that's a great idea. Can you make that two passes? I have a very special lady in my life that I want you to meet and she'll be with me—hold on, let me make sure about that, she's right here—."

Stan turned to Fanny and explained what was going on, and she said, "Well of course I'll go with you. I can't wait to meet your son and his wife. In fact, let me talk to her now, we'll just get acquainted." Stan handed Fanny the phone.

"Hello," she said. "Gracie, is it? Hi—I'm Fanny Grant. Stan and I have found a great companionship together and I'll be glad to come along with him to meet you and Marty in Richmond on the twenty-fifth."

"Hi, Fanny. Oh, is it okay for me to call you by your first name?"

"Well, you sure better!" Fanny said. "We're all family, or close to it."

"I'm so happy to meet you, even if it is by phone, and I'll look forward to seeing you all on the twenty-fifth."

Fanny handed the phone back to Stan who talked with Gracie and Marty a few more minutes, and then hung up.

"Wow! What a surprise," Stan said. His face showed the deep joy and relief he felt about all that had transpired. We need to get this boat back home and then I'd like to take you out to dinner at the Seafood Pavilion, and over a good meal and a glass of wine, I'll fill you in on Marty—okay?"

"Sure, honey," Fanny said. "I remember meetin' Marty when he was younger and came to visit you. Remember, you brought him to church. You didn't know I had an eye for you way back then, did you?"

"No—I didn't know many people in Dinkel Island back then," Stan said. He took the helm and pushed the throttle up until the boat planed out and they skimmed across the slight chop in the sea until they reached Tranquility Bay. It seemed to Fanny like it took no time at all. The sudden pick up in speed caused her to lose her balance and she sat down hard in a deck chair. "Wow," she said, "this boat's got some get-up-and-go, don't it?"

"I'm sorry—are you okay?" She laughed and nodded that she was. "I should have warned you,' Stan said, "I'll be more careful."

❧

When Marty hung up the phone, Gracie said, "I like your dad—and Fanny. She sounds like she'd be a lot of fun. Do you know her well?"

"I don't know her at all," Marty replied. "Until now I didn't even know she existed. The last time I saw my dad he and Lillie were married—and then I saw him after she was killed in that accident—when I went to the funeral. It's been several years now since she died. The two of them being together is probably a good thing."

"You mean, kind of like the two of us?" Gracie said softly. They were alone in the RV and didn't expect anyone to interrupt them anytime soon. They drew together and caressed each other, shut the bedroom door and spent the next hour making love.

When they emerged from the RV they were dressed to go out for supper. The rest of the group members were gathered around a charcoal grill, cooking hamburgers.

"Well, well," Mark said, "you two really get dressed up for a picnic, don't you?"

Marty and Gracie laughed. "We're running out on you tonight," Marty said. "It's not the company, we just want a good restaurant meal—you understand."

"That's what we get for traveling with newlyweds," Mark said. "Oh well, guess we can get along without you two. Just be careful."

The group towed a small Hyundai sedan behind the smaller of the two RVs so they would have personal transportation during their layovers between concerts. Gracie and Marty used the car to find a Red Lobster restaurant where they asked for a booth in the back where it was a little quieter and they could talk while they ate.

"Would you like to talk about your dad, Marty?" Gracie asked. "You've told me about the divorce and your anger at him. How are you feeling now that you've gotten in touch with him again?"

"I really blamed him for everything when I was young, but it wasn't all his fault. Once I saw him and Lillie together, I realized what had been lacking between him and my mom. I never saw a woman bring out a man like she did with my dad. He just blossomed once they were married."

"It's so sad that she died before they could grow old together," Gracie said.

Marty nodded. "You know," he said, "I went to her funeral and kept in touch for a while after that, but I still hadn't resolved my anger, so I cut him off again. I feel so guilty about that. I've prayed for forgiveness, and I know God has forgiven both him and me for our hardness of heart toward each other."

Gracie reached across the table and folded his hands between hers, looked him in the eye with a warmth and connection that always stroked his spirit, and said, "God loves you, I love you, and your dad loves you—all those sins of the past are forgiven and no longer have power over you, or him, or us. We're free, and I love how you reached out to your dad today."

"Thanks, sweetheart," Marty whispered across the table. "You know dad bought some old boat and named it for Lillie a couple of years ago. He just couldn't seem to break away from her to get past his grief. That's what I felt going on with him the last time we spoke—before today—grief! Deep grief! I know he is a man of faith who trusts the Lord, but he just didn't seem able to overcome her loss—that is, until today. That's what I sensed in him. He's free! I think his grief is being healed! Praise God for that, honey. I think Fanny is part of his healing."

"Oh, darling," Gracie said. "I had that same feeling. I've never met or spoken to your dad until today, but from what you'd told me I sensed a healing process going on. I liked Fanny. I can't wait to meet them both."

The waitress came to their table and they declined desert, so she brought them their check, they paid the cashier, and then left the restaurant and returned to the campground. It was dark and apparently the others had gone to bed, so Marty and Gracie slipped quietly into their room and fell into a peaceful, restful sleep.

∿

After Stan and Fanny cleaned up the boat and secured it at the dock, they went to the Seafood Pavilion, ordered their drinks and a cobb salad for each of them, and then discussed their entrees.

"If we had kept those spot we caught out there today, I would have wanted to bread them and fry them," Fanny said, "so that's what I think I'll order."

"Hmmm—not a bad idea, except I think I'll have fried flounder—and some French fries, too."

The waitress took their orders when she came back with their salads, and they settled down to talk about the surprising phone call and all the thoughts it had opened up for them.

"Are you all right, honey?" Fanny said, reaching across the table and taking his hand in hers. "If you feel like talking about Marty, I'd love to listen."

"Yeah, I'm all right," Stan said pensively, "the phone call just brought up a bunch of stuff that probably rattles around in the back of my brain all the time, but I don't really think about it very often." He looked into Fanny's eyes and read her compassion and love, and his spirits sparkled as he added excitedly, "I sure do like Gracie, though, and I feel a deep satisfaction that they are married."

Fanny said, "I'll bet you feel like a heavy weight has been lifted off of you now."

"I guess that's a good way to put it," Stan responded.

A server came to the table with their food. "Now, who gets the flounder," he asked.

"That will be me," Stan answered.

The server set their plates down. "Your waitress will be checking with you in a moment if you need anything else. Enjoy!"

Fanny said, "Do you mind if I offer our prayer?"

"Please do," Stan said, and they both closed their eyes.

"Lord, we are so thankful for your goodness that touches the sad parts of us and makes joy possible at just the right times. Thank you for giving Stan and Marty the joy of your healing spirit today. Help us all to grow closer to each other as we share our closeness with you. Thank you for this food and every blessing you supply. In Jesus's name. Amen."

"Thanks, honey," Stan said, and they settled down to eating in an appreciative silence for a few minutes, and then resumed their conversation.

"I remember Marty back when he first visited you here at Dinkel Island," Fanny said, "I could tell he was angry, but I could also feel his love for you—and I guess his confusion. I don't know what it was like before the divorce, but from what I've seen, kids usually have a tough time accepting things like that."

"So do parents, really," Stan said. "The way I see it, divorce doesn't solve all the problems, it just creates new ones. Sure, some things change for the better—two people who never should have married to begin with get away from each other, but when kids are involved, they always feel the pain—and a lot of guilt. They think it's their fault."

"So they get mad at their parents," Fanny said, "and mad at themselves because they think they caused it all."

"You got it. It's tough to live with for everybody."

"Well, it looks like both you and Marty carried that guilt and anger around a long time, and you both have a chance to get rid of it now," Fanny said. "I'm gonna pray that you can do it."

"Thanks, honey..." Stan said as the waitress arrived with their check. "This was a good dinner, but not as good as what you cook."

Fanny thanked him for the compliment as they paid their bill and walked back to her house. They had their arms around each other's waist and seemed to move almost rhythmically. Fanny said, "I don't know what happened in your first marriage, but you sure made up for it in your second. I'm so sorry you had to lose Lillie."

Stan stopped and turned to her, took her in his arms and said, "Sweetheart, Lillie taught me so much about myself, and we grew in our faith together, and yes, we were a very tight couple. And God has taken her home, now"—he paused—"and he has brought you and me together—and I think we're pretty 'tight', too."

"I love you so much," Fanny said as they kissed and walked on to the house. At the door she said, "maybe this is the time."

Stan knew what she meant. He felt his heart racing, and he kissed her again and then said, "I'd love to stay with you tonight, darling, but you remember what you said not long ago—we aren't ready to make the commitment needed to do that?"

"Yes," she whispered, holding onto him.

"I want to make that commitment to you right now, Fanny. I don't want to live my life without you. Will you marry me?"

Fanny broke into tears of joy, stepped back and looked intently into his eyes. "Absolutely! Yes I will. When?"

They embraced and kissed again, and he said, "just as soon as we get through with this visit from Marty and Gracie. Let's choose a date for the wedding at breakfast, okay?"

"Okay, darlin'—I can't wait."

15

———◆———

Blissful Beginnings

*D*uring worship on Sunday morning Kate Sheppard made two special announcements. "We have an exciting opportunity coming up in just a few weeks"—she told the congregation— "to host the gospel group *Joyful Morning* from Sarasota, Florida. Herb Melloman can tell you more about it."

Herb stepped up to the lectern wearing his dark Sunday suit with the red tie, and his ever-present smile. "I've checked all the details on this myself," he said, "and I am convinced this is a chance to share our faith effectively with the Dinkel Island community. After going over the details, the official board has authorized us to proceed. The group is only asking for a love offering—no fees—and they will have their CD's for sale, of course. We've talked with Mammoth Baptist Church and they are participating with us. It should be a memorable evening of inspiration and blessings."

There was applause, and after Herb stepped away, Kate said, "That leads me to the second announcement, which actually has two parts. First, all of this is possible because the lead female vocalist with *Joyful Morning*—Gracie Love—is the daughter-in-law of one of our members—Stan Grayson, whose son, Marty, also sings with the group."

There were exclamations of surprise and joy throughout the congregation as Kate paused, then continued: "Now for the even bigger news—Stan and Fanny Grant have given me permission to announce their engagement—."

Before Kate could continue, a great applause and shouts of congratulations, arose throughout the sanctuary. "They're talking about a November wedding," Kate went on. "I'm sure we'll hear more about that soon. Blessings to you both," she said with her hand outstretched toward them. Stan and Fanny stood and exchanged waves with the congregation, then when the service was over, people flocked up to them with expressions of love and support.

"Oh, Stan," Cheryl Drew said, "Bob and I are so glad to hear this wonderful news—and Fanny, you and I have to get to know one another better. I noticed you two working together during the art show last month, and you both seem so suited to each other—and Stan, your son singing with *Joyful Morning*—and married to Gracie Love! Wow!"

"I remember your son, Marty, from years ago," Jenny Tyrone said, "when he used to come visit you. You've been keeping secrets from us—we had no idea he was a gospel singer."

"Actually, I didn't either," Stan said. "He's been working as a graphic artist with an advertising agency in Sarasota and doing some singing on the side. Fanny and I are looking forward to getting to know Gracie and him as a couple."

"You kind of pulled off a grandstand play there, old man," Ed said to Stan as they left church and headed toward the Seafood Pavilion for lunch.

"I guess so," Stan said, "unintentionally, that is. I didn't know it would cause such a fuss."

After church as Stan, Fanny, Ed and Molly walked to the Seafood Pavilion for lunch, Molly seemed almost to have a glow about her. Stan thought, *I've known her for quite a while now and something's happening in her life. I wonder if this has anything to do with Ed?* He recalled her reaction when he had said a friend of his who was a retired preacher would be living in the apartment above the gallery and might sometimes help out in the shop.

"A retired preacher?" Molly had said in dismay. "That's just what we need around here—some stuffy, boring, self-righteous old man who hasn't got anything better to do than hang around."

Stan had been taken aback by her reply. He had often found Molly to be outspoken, but she usually couched her thoughts in some sort of humor—but not this time. Stan had just laughed. "Tell you what"—he had said—"wait 'til you meet Ed and then you'll eat those words! He's not like that at all. You'll like him—just wait and see."

Stan had been right. It didn't take long before she said to him, "Have you got any ketchup? I guess I'll need it when I eat those words I said about Ed Heygood. He's not at all like I had pictured in my mind. He's okay—down to earth and fun to be with—in fact, I like him."

∾↶

At the restaurant the four of them sat down and placed their orders. Almost immediately Stan and Fanny began to be swamped by well-wishers from church who stopped by. Sitting across from them, Ed and Molly began talking to each other. He had felt a growing closeness toward her, yet a reluctance to express his feelings. He surprised himself as he said to her, "I'm so glad you agreed to come to lunch today. I've been wanting to ask you out for supper some time, but I didn't want to seem too forward."

Molly smiled, and after a moment she said, "I would have said 'yes' if you'd asked. Maybe you will sometime!"

Feeling a leap of joy in his spirit, Ed reached over and took her hand. "That makes me very happy. So I'll ask—what about Thursday night? We could do it up big and go to the Yacht & Supper Club."

Molly's smile answered before her words. "Sounds great to me," she said, squeezing his hand. Ed lost himself in the aura of her presence for a moment. *She is gorgeous!* he thought. Her honey-colored bangs were parted at the forehead with her straight hair tapering in a slight wave toward the back of her neck. On the left side her hair was brushed slightly behind the ear so that her small gold-loop earring stood out. Her full, rich lips curled into a captivating smile. Ed soaked in the moment of delight at being with her.

All of a sudden they became aware that people who had stopped to talk with Stan and Fanny were getting in on a budding romance on the other side of the table. They smiled sheepishly, and then their food arrived, so the attention of well-wishers subsided.

After lunch, Ed and Molly walked back to the church where she had left her car. "Would you like to come by my house later?" Molly asked. She lived just outside Dinkel Island proper, in Crabber's Creek estates, and Ed had never been to her house.

"You know, I'd like that," Ed responded. "What time?"

"Tell you what—you treated me to lunch today, so why don't you come around five o'clock, and I'll treat you to a salad and sandwich?"

"Sounds wonderful," Ed said with tenderness. "Can I bring something?"

"Just yourself!"—Molly said—"and an appetite."

When he got home Ed felt uncertain what to do with himself until he went to Molly's. He felt drawn to a closet and a box of old photographs he hadn't looked at for some time. He felt himself floundering emotionally. He knew he had to get in touch with whatever lingering grief he had over Sally's death. It was something he'd been putting off.

The box contained photo's from Billy's and Angie's childhood years—Christmases, little league baseball games, family trips, lots of pictures of everyday moments that Sally managed to capture on film. There were pictures of the different churches they had served, and the parsonages they had lived in, and pictures of the different people the children had brought home to test the waters of acceptance or rejection during their teenage dating years. And there were so many pictures of Sally—from her childhood, her college years, early motherhood, the early years in the pastorate at Dinkel Island, and some of her girl friends with whom she had stayed in touch all her life. Then there were the photo's taken of Ed and Sally together on so many different occasions.

Closing his eyes, Ed began to feel a deep sadness swell up from within his chest. Suddenly Sally became so real that he heard her voice—her laugh. He felt an overwhelming desire to pull her back through the veil of death, to cancel the impact of the last two years, to resume their life together and do the things they'd wanted to do as they grew older. Then the deep gulf of reality swallowed him in one huge gulp, and he cried in great sobs and throes of remorse. "Sally," he cried out. "Sally, come here—come back!"

The sound of his own voice hung heavily in the air as he opened his tear-drenched eyes. He knew! He had always known! Sally was absolutely gone. He felt drained and limp and time seemed to stand still. Then, ever so gradually, he felt a warm certainty swell up within him—a sense of the "now" and the "tomorrow," breaking down the sense of "yesterday" so that it could claim its proper place of respectful existence. A huge sigh swelled up as he said to himself, *It was all so good—and it's so gone—but it all still lives as it should.*

A prayer he had often used as a pastor came into his mind, and he claimed ownership. *Thank you, God, for all you have given me, all you have taken from me, and all you have left me; for I know that it is in the full circle of your grace that all of these things create wholeness. Amen.* A sense of blissful inner peace ensued and he felt unbroken.

Putting the box of photos back into its storage place Ed realized he had sweated profusely during his emotional ordeal, so he went to freshen himself before going to Molly's. Deep joy filled his spirit as he showered and he began to sing words from Elisha Hoffman's hymn. "What a fellowship, what a joy divine, leaning on the everlasting arms—." He sang through all the stanzas that he could recall, ending with, "What have I to dread, what have I to fear, leaning on the everlasting arms."

Gazing into the mirror as he combed his hair, he saw in his reflection a timeless "Ed"—unscarred by loss and suffering, refreshed by faith, embracing the moment. As he stood before the mirror he imagined Molly standing beside him, saw her smile and her hair just as she'd worn it today. He blinked, turned out the light, and walked into the living room where he got a light jacket from the closet. *Yes, it's time,* he thought; *it's time to step into the next chapter. I have nothing to fear. I'm leaning on you, Lord.*

When Ed reached Molly's house he felt almost as though he was walking on air. He couldn't remember the last time he had felt so free, so completely happy. He waltzed right up and opened the unlocked storm door, poked his head inside and called, "I'm here, Molly."

It was a two story brick home with a central hallway going back to the kitchen and family room, and a stairway to the upstairs bedrooms. As he stuck his head inside he saw Molly coming down the stairs, her beauty and brightness as engaging as they had been earlier.

"Come in," she said. "I just took a little nap this afternoon." They embraced and then she said, "Come on, let's fix supper together."

Ed was surprised by the openness and warmth of the kitchen as they entered. He took in a large box window in a breakfast nook with a table and chairs that were set off from the rest of the kitchen by a serving counter. The box window had a built-in, attractively cushioned bench seat positioned beneath twelve-inch-square glass panes framed by yellow, swept-back sheer curtains, against a background of medium-blue walls with white glossy trim. The window overlooked a vast, shaded and landscaped back yard featuring bird houses and feeders, and a small fountain with a poi fish pond. Somehow the place just seemed to have "Molly" written all over it.

"How do you like it?" Molly said

"It's beautiful, and really unique!" Ed exclaimed. "This room is so warm and inviting that you could almost live totally right here in this space."

"Thanks," Molly said as she went to the refrigerator and began getting out the makings for salads and sandwiches. "You'll find some luncheon plates up in that cabinet," she said, pointing the direction. "What would you like to drink? I could offer you a glass of ginger ale, or—."

"Ginger ale will be fine," Ed said.

Molly told him where to find place mats, silverware and napkins, then she set the table and they sat down to eat lunch. "What kind of dressing would you like," she asked. Ed selected Thousand Island, and they busied themselves eating.

"I didn't know anybody could make a salad taste this good," Ed remarked.

"Oh, go on"—Molly said, brushing his words aside—
"there's nothing special about making a salad. But, thanks for
the compliment."

After they had finished eating they went into the family room
where they sat on a vinyl couch in front of a picture window
overlooking the back yard landscape. Ed also noticed a large Stan
Grayson painting on the wall opposite the couch.

"I see you have a piece of the boss's work," he said.

Molly chuckled, "Doesn't everybody in town? Seriously, I like
his work and bought this when we first moved in."

"You have so many talents—cooking, decorating, designing,
and I'll bet you even made the beautiful quilt draped over that
chair," he said.

"No, my mother made that one—but I do enjoy quilting and,
in fact, I belong to the quilting group that meets at church during
the fall and winter months. We're just about to resume our work
in two weeks."

Ed felt relaxed and drawn to Molly as a bonding fabric began
to weave itself between them at a soulful level. "I see so many
things about you that I really appreciate," he said, reaching for
her hands.

Molly blushed slightly, looked him in the eye and said, "It's
been a long time since anyone said things like that to me, Ed.
Thanks for your compliments. You're a pretty special person too,
you know." As she drew closer to him he saw tears in the corner
of her eyes.

He suddenly felt self-conscious. "I've noticed at the gallery
how you always keep your sense of humor, no matter what's
going on. I admire that."

"I wasn't always like that," Molly said, reaching for a tissue.
She wiped her eyes, then said, "When I worked with the insurance company up in D.C., it was a high pressure world. I learned
very soon that if I took to heart everything that came my way, I
would soon fall apart."

Ed could feel the tension in her words. "So I learned to do my job well," she went on; "to be observant, keep my eyes open to learn new things, and to mind my own business. I got along very well until my late husband Carl decided it was time to retire and we had this house built. Then I retired, too, so we could move in here"—tears began to flow again—"It's so sad that we never really got a chance to enjoy the retirement we longed for. Carl didn't learn how to disengage from stress, and it killed him."

"I know that feeling of incompleteness from losing Sally to cancer before we even had a chance to retire. Sometimes when I least expect it I will suddenly feel afresh the pain of helplessness and incredible grief that came to mark our relationship toward the end. So much changed as I became her caretaker, and that role always left me feeling emotionally orphaned during her times of deepest need. Sometimes I would call my friend, Stan, and he would pray with me and help me to hang on.

They moved closer to each other, still holding hands, looking into each other's eyes. A tear and short cough caught in her throat as Molly said, "Thanks for being here today." She wiped away another tear. "I think you and I are good for each other. I think we need each other."

Tears came to Ed's eyes, too, and he pulled out his handkerchief to dab at them. They looked each other in the eyes and began to laugh. It was a laugh of release with a potential for healing. They hugged each other for a couple of minutes, then broke apart, and leaned back against the cushions.

"We do need each other," Ed said. "We've both suffered deep losses, and we know how hard it is to let go of the pain."

Molly leaned against Ed's shoulder and he put his arm around her. "I never thought I could feel this way again," she said softly. "Maybe I've been holding onto what's gone so much that I couldn't see what's here now."

Ed stroked the side of Molly's face and said, I didn't mean to get so—.

"Molly interrupted, touching his lips. "I know! Neither did I—and it's okay. We both wanted this to happen."

They kissed. "I think I'm falling in love with you," Ed whispered.

"I feel the same way," she whispered back. "I'm glad!"

❧

Kate Sheppard's announcement of their engagement spurred Stan and Fanny to spend the afternoon talking over all the pieces of their lives that were about to get reshuffled.

"It's so different from when I married Leonard," Fanny said. "He was ten years older than me, and I had seen him a few times when he came to visit Harper—I didn't know it then but I found out later that Harper had managed some investments for him that paid off really good. It was a while after Harper died and I moved into the house that Leonard came to see me. He seemed nice, like he knew now alone I was feelin', and we kept in touch, and went out to dinner a few times. When he asked me to marry him it was kinda out of the blue. We weren't in love the way you and me are, but we loved each other in a different way. We lived in Richmond, came here lots of weekends, and I felt safe. We had five years together—but just like Harper, Leonard had a heart attack, only he didn't get over it and died a few weeks later. Oh," she said, suddenly embarrassed, "I'm sorry. Don't know why I went off on all that."

"No, that's okay," Stan responded. "That's what we need to do. We need to share our lives that are past so we can be free to go forward. Our past marriages are part of who we are now, and the worst thing we can do is try to push them aside, because then we can't really be with each other completely."

Fanny mused over that and then said, "I guess you're right. I hadn't thought about it. So, how have you managed to get over losing Lillie?"

"You know," Stan said, "I only just managed to do that since I've been with you. I had never really let myself be with anyone until you came along, but then whatever barriers I had in my mind just broke apart and I was suddenly able to admit to myself the feelings I have for you. It's hard to explain—it was like a spiritual struggle. Then that morning when I called you and came over for breakfast it was like all the struggle dissolved. I've felt free and complete with you ever since."

The weather was overcast but mild, and they were sitting on the porch swing, holding hands as they talked. Now they turned toward each other and embraced.

"Let's go inside," Fanny said. "I feel kinda exposed out here, and I just wanta be alone with you this afternoon."

Stan looked deeply into her eyes, saw tears glistening and sensed the depth of her feelings. "Yeah," he said, "let's do that."

Inside they sat on the couch. "Here," she said, "stretch out and put your head in my lap." He did, and then closed his eyes. "You comfy," she said.

"Yep—and you?"

"I love this closeness with you. I've never felt like this with anyone." The aura of their blending lives took hold and after a while Fanny said, "I hope you don't mind livin' in this house. I mean, it was Harper's house, and that might bother you."

"Don't say another word," Stan said. "This isn't Harper's house anymore, it's yours. It has all the marks of you about it. We'll be married soon and I look forward to the life we're going to have together. This is just a house—a place where our hearts will find completeness."

"That's sweet, darlin'," Fanny said.

They sat silently for a few minutes and, then Stan sat up, took her hand and said, "Fanny, I want to make you my partner at the gallery and art center."

Fanny showed surprise as she responded. "Don't go makin' big decisions like that too fast, honey."

"It's not too fast—unless us gettin' married so soon is too fast. I want us to share everything together. You have skills and wisdom about running the gallery that I've seen over these weeks. You have a natural sense of how to do things. I want to have my attorney draw up partnership papers and for us to be legally, formally partnered in the Grayson/Plume Gallery. We can even change the name—"

Fanny interrupted. "No, that name has been visible in this town for nearly 30 years and it needs to stay just as it is. But I will accept the partnership, and I want you and me to have equal shares in the money and investments Harper left me—and on the deed to this house, too."

They spent hours discussing the details about the new life they were forging together, and then at nearly midnight, Stan went home. They had no idea what the future held, but they knew that whatever it was, they would share it together.

16

━━◆━━

Family Bonding

No sooner had Kate Sheppard announced the *Joyful Morning* concert to the congregation, than Sarah Jones began heating up the Dinkel Island grapevine about it. She laid it on thick about the lead female singer, Gracie Love, being the daughter-in-law of local artist, Stan Grayson.

"Can you believe it?"—she said when she called one of her Baptist friends—"we have a famous singer related to one of our own members, and nobody knew anything about it."

"Who says this singer is famous?"—her friend asked—"I never heard of her. What did you say her name is?"

"Gracie Love," Sarah said, impatiently.

"Strange name, if you ask me."

"Well, you know how it is with professional singers", Sarah said. "They always change their names to somethin' else for publicity. I don't know what her name really is, but her last name has to be Grayson!"

"Not necessarily, some of these young-uns keep their maiden name even after they get married."

"Well, anyway, she's married to Stan Grayson's son, Marty."

"And you say Stan didn't know his son was married to this gospel singer? There's gotta be somethin' wrong in that family, if you ask me. And tell me this—why are they comin' here just for a love offering? Those big outfits don't do things like that."

Exasperated with her friend's resistant attitude, Sarah finally found a way to end the call. Before she called anyone else she decided she'd better check some things out for herself. Her friend really had raised some good questions. Sarah called Margie at the church office since she figured they'd have the whole scoop there.

"I don't know any more than you heard on Sunday," Margie said. "I don't think Kate knows anything more either, but I know there aren't any secrets here. The singer's actual name is Mary Grace Love Grayson, and 'Gracie Love' is her professional name as a singer. She's married to Stan Grayson's son, Marty, and they live in Sarasota, Florida."

Although she was still curious about the details, Sarah decided she didn't have to know all the answers in order to stir up some excitement about the concert. She succeeded in doing just that! The conversation around the lunch counter at the drug store for the next couple of days was nothing but excitement and speculation centered on Gracie Love and the concert. It even spilled over into the conversation among the Old Geezers on Thursday morning.

"What's all this I hear about some big-time gospel singer coming to your church, Bob?" Doc Patcher asked when the Old Geezers gathered for coffee and conversation. "I don't know much about those kinds of groups, but the women folks sure are talking about this one. What's the big deal?"

Bob Drew explained what was going on, all of which the men had already heard from their wives. "Cheryl says Sarah Jones has stirred up questions about why Stan Grayson didn't know his son was married to this singer."

"That doesn't seem strange to me," Darrell said. "Sometimes kids break away from their family and it can be years before their parents know much about what they're doing."

"Cheryl and I were in the ceremony at the Wedding Pier when Stan and Lillie got married", Bob said, "and I remember Stan was disappointed that Marty refused to attend. I think it all goes back to Stan's divorce which happened before he ever moved to Dinkel Island."

"So what does Stan say about his son now?" Jimmy asked.

Doc answered, "I talked to him yesterday at the gas station. He's excited! You're right on, Darrell—Stan and Marty have had a reconciliation—but that's only half of his excitement—he told me he and Fanny Grant are getting married in a few weeks."

"Oh, yeah," Jimmy said, "my wife mentioned that, too. They've both been widowed for a while, so that's a good thing."

Darrell scoffed, "That Fanny Grant is something else, I'll tell you. She started out as a housekeeper for old Jauswell, and then inherited his house and money when he died—I always wondered about that!" Everybody nodded, and Doc raised his eyebrows.

"Then she married that guy from Richmond," Darrell went on, "and he died a couple of years later. Now she's latching onto another one! Her life sounds just like a soap opera to me."

They all laughed, then Bob said, "Seriously, guys, I've known Fanny a long time, too, and—."

"You've known everybody a long time," Doc said.

"Guess I have," Bob said. "Anyway, Fanny's a genuine person—nothing fake or put-on about her. She is who she is, and now she's about to be Mrs. Stan Grayson. I hope it's a good marriage for both of them. They both deserve it."

The conversation went on a bit longer, and then the group broke up and everybody went off to work. They hadn't talked much about Gracie Love, but they did agree that it was great for Dinkel Island to have a well-known personality connected to the town.

꩜

Stan and Fanny felt an irresistible pull to be together from the moment he proposed and she accepted. They both reveled in the excitement of a new chapter opening in their lives, and he began moving some of his things into her house, a little at a time. He slept at the condo, but that was about it. Early each morning he would go to Fanny's for breakfast after which they would both go to the gallery where he began showing her the ins and outs of his business.

They became concerned that as Molly saw Fanny stepping into the business she might feel pushed aside—and possibly quit. One day Fanny got Stan's attention when she said, "Honey, do you mind if I tell you somethin' I see goin' on here?"

"Of course not," Stan said. "What are you talking about?"

"Well," she paused, then went on, "you seem to be carryin' too much personal responsibility for day-to-day things both here in the gallery and at the art center. It looks to me like each one of these things is a big enough job for one person—and you're tryin' to do it all. I have an idea—."

Stan broke in, "I know what you're saying, honey. I just don't know what to do about it. I mean, when it was Lillie and me together, the art center was kind of her thing, and the gallery mine, but when she died I had to take on both things. Believe me, I know what you mean."

"Okay," Fanny said, I have a suggestion, but I don't want to be managin' stuff, you know, like takin' away somethin' that's impor-tant to you."

"Sweetheart, when I asked you share as my partner in this business, I wanted you to offer ideas and suggestions. So what do you think needs to be changed?"

Fanny took Stan's hand as she spoke. "I think you need to take charge of one thing, and let Molly take charge of the other. She's very talented and devoted to the gallery. I think you should turn that over to her, give her a raise and a new title, and you and me can spend our time doing somethin' more with the art center."

Stan stepped back, feeling a sudden release of tension he hadn't really admitted was there, and put his hand to his forehead. "You know," he said, "you're right! I never saw that! We've been worried about Molly feeling pushed aside, when she really needs to be drawn in more. Wow! Why didn't I see that?"

"You didn't see it because you was too close to it."

"Yeah, I guess you're right. So what you're suggesting is that we turn the daily operation of the gallery over to Molly, and we sort of supervise while concentrating our attention on the art center." Stan hesitated. "The only problem I have is with the extra cost of paying Molly more. She'd have to be full time and we'd need to increase her salary—plus benefits—frankly, I don't have the cash."

"How'd you get started with this gallery to begin with?" Fanny said.

"Well, Lillie had some money from selling her apart—." Stan stopped in mid-sentence as a light went on in the back of his head. "You're not saying you want to put money into this?"

"In so many words, yes!" Fanny replied.

"Well, you're already doing so much, putting your house and holdings in my name as well as yours. I just think it's asking too much …." Stan stopped in mid-sentence again as he saw an amused expression grow on Fanny's face. "What?…"

"Don't you see," Fanny said, almost laughing now. "It's not my money to loan you, it's ours together now, and believe me, we can afford to put some capital into these two businesses—and they really are 'two' different things."

They talked that out at length and then mapped out the details about how daily operations would be handled, with the result that Stan made a discovery.

"You know, now that I look at this, I've been frustrated at not having enough studio time. This way I could actually get back to painting more."

"Yeah"—Fanny replied—"and usin' your creativity feeds your soul. You'll feel more content and complete. And us gettin' married feeds both our souls, too, so you'll be the most complete person in town!"

They laughed about that, and the next day when Molly came in to work, Stan and Fanny invited her to sit down with them, have a cup of coffee and listen to some ideas they had. Stan began the conversation.

"Molly, you know Fanny and I are making a partnership out of the gallery and art center as we get married, and we want to ask your help with something."

Molly looked puzzled. She had seemed ill-at-ease when they all sat down together. "What kind of help?" she asked.

"You know, I couldn't have kept all of this going after Lillie died if it hadn't been for you. You know all the ins and outs of running the gallery, how to handle both artists and customers, and you generally keep things together. I know you have only wanted to work part-time, but we would like to ask you to take on a full-time position as the Grayson/Plume Gallery Manager. We'd like to offer you a higher salary and full benefits, as well."

Molly was obviously taken aback by the offer. "I—I don't know what to say," she said, fumbling for her words. "I guess I thought when you came into the business, Fanny, that y'all probably wouldn't need me anymore. Now you offer me this! Wow! I feel speechless."

Stan put his hand on Molly's wrist. "You don't have to answer us today, Molly. I know it's a big change for you, and we hope you'll see it as an opportunity."

Fanny added, "I knew you felt unsure about where you would stand with me around, and I hope you can see now that we both think a lot of you and and want you to keep workin' with us."

Molly seemed relieved, but still somehow troubled. "I guess I need to think this over," she said. "No, that's not it exactly—I'll be honest with you—something is changing in my life and I don't know if this is the right time to do something like this. I would love to do it, I really would, but I need to talk to someone first."

Stan and Fanny glanced at each other, knowing intuitively what she was saying. They turned to Molly and Fanny said, "Tell me if I'm out of place—but I think I know what you're talkin' about, and it's okay. Take your time and talk it over with Ed. We've both seen the two of you gettin' closer to each other. We know what a big change it is because we're goin' through it ourselves."

Molly seemed relieved. "Thanks"—she said—"you know exactly what I'm talking about."

Stan added, "Molly, if you and Ed want to work together at the gallery, we can also work that out, don't you think, Fanny?"

"Sure!"

"I've known Ed a long time," Stan said, "and I know how hard it has been for him to feel connected to a daily purpose since he retired. You two talk it over and just let us know."

The next day Molly came in and excitedly told Fanny about Ed's reaction. "At first he looked at me and said, 'Good old Stan— he's always been a good friend, ready to do anything for me, but he doesn't need to offer me a job.' So we sat down and had a long talk and I explained all that you and Stan had gone over with me, and Ed and I together decided this is a wonderful opportunity, and we'd like to do it."

～～

Stan wasn't in the room when Molly told Fanny that she would accept the job, because he was in the office talking with Marty on the phone. Marty was giving Stan directions to where the concert would be in Richmond on the twenty-fifth, and discussing how they might arrange to share some time together before or after the program.

"You know, that's only a few days before your concert here at Dinkel Island," Stan said. "As anxious as I am to see you and meet Gracie, I really wonder if, instead of us coming to Richmond, why don't you and Gracie stay here in town those days between concerts and we can have a much better time visiting each other. What do you think?"

Overhearing the last part of the conversation Fanny said, "Is that Marty? Here, let me talk to him a minute."

Stan handed her the phone. "Hi Marty, this is Fanny, and I just overheard your dad's end of the conversation when I came into the room. I want you two to come and stay at my house as soon as you get finished in Richmond and stay right on through the concert here. I've got plenty of room and I ain't takin' 'no' for an answer."

Stan chuckled, and imagined the response on the other end.

"Okay, then," Fanny said after a brief conversation, "it's settled! I'll be lookin' for you on Monday—in fact, I'll have lunch ready for you. I'm handin' the phone back to your dad and he can tell you how to get to my house."

Stan took the phone and finished the conversation, then hung up, got up from the desk and walked around to Fanny. "You're somethin' else, honey," he said, hugging her, and then they kissed, and she said, "So are you!"

༄

Gracie marveled at Fanny's house as she and Marty pulled into the driveway. "Wow!" she said. "I can see why Fanny said she has plenty of room. This place is like a mansion."

"A true sample of Victorian architecture," Marty said, admiringly.

They had no sooner turned off the engine than Fanny rushed out to greet them. "I'm so glad you two agreed to come stay with me," she said. "Gracie and Marty—what a pleasure to meet y'all and welcome you to Dinkel Island."

"Thanks for the invitation," Marty said. "We were just admiring your home as we drove in. It's magnificent."

"Oh, thanks—seems like I've lived here all my life. Since it got to be mine I've tried to freshen it up a little bit."

They went inside and Gracie said, "You've done a super job! It feels warm and bright in here, yet there's a kind of timelessness to it, like you've made the house reflect the flavors of different times."

"There's a small bathroom right down that hall," Fanny said, motioning toward it. "Y'all go freshen up. Lunch is ready so we'll go into the dining room and we can get to know each other while we eat."

Lunch included the best crab cake sandwiches Gracie could remember eating. They had a lively time of conversation and the after they ate Fanny showed them the rest of the house. "There are two guest rooms," she said, "so y'all choose the one you want, and you can move your things in when you're ready."

Gracie felt overwhelmed and grateful for Fanny's hospitality. "Won't this make extra work for you?" she asked.

"Oh, don't worry about that—I have a housekeeper and a gardener, and a lawn service that keeps up with the grass and such, so two more people won't cause any problem," Fanny said. Then she added, "I do cook my own meals, however, and it's no problem addin' more water to the soup, as the sayin' goes. Besides, we have some great restaurants here and I want us to use 'em while you're here."

"If lunch is any sample, you're a great cook, Fanny," Gracie said.

"Well I probably love cookin' as much as Stan loves paintin', and you love singin'."

∾⌒∾

That evening they went to the Yacht & Supper Club. As they ate, Stan said to Gracie, "You two make a beautiful couple. Now, catch me up on things. How did you happen to get saddled up with this guy?"

"Well, that's a long story," Gracie said, "but I'll shorten it up. He was a good tipper at the restaurant where I worked and I decided to snag him before he got out the door. I don't think he knows what hit him yet."

They all laughed, then Marty said, "Maybe that story needs a little embellishment."

"Okay," Gracie said. "I guess you knew Marty was singing with a gospel quartet called the *Son Shiners.*"

"Not really," Stan said. "I knew he was doing pretty well with that advertising firm and singing in his church choir." He looked at Marty. "When did you get into a quartet?"

"They were clients and one day they invited me to sit in on a working session with them—to get the feel of the atmosphere that surrounded their singing. As we got to talking I mentioned that I attended a Wesleyan Brethren church where I sang in the choir. Long story short, they asked me to sing a practice number with them and they were impressed enough that they asked me to join the group as a back-up singer."

"Wow, that must have been a thrill," Fanny said.

"You know it," Marty replied. "They were all part-time guys who just travelled around to churches in Florida for occasional appearances. I sing baritone, and when the baritone in the group was transferred by his company to another state, the guys asked me to step in as a regular. I had established enough contacts through the ad agency that I was able to quit working there and went out on my own, which I've done ever since."

Stan raised his eyebrows and said, "This is the first I've heard of you being on your own—I sure wish we had kept in touch more."

Marty glanced at Gracie, then looked his dad in the eye and said, "That's really my fault. I had some really deep anger when you and Mom divorced, and it literally took me years to get rid of that. Then, as my anger disappeared, I didn't know how to make things right with you."

"Son," Stan said, reaching over and putting his hand on Marty's shoulder, "you didn't need to be afraid of me—but I know I didn't give you any clues about that."

The atmosphere became emotionally tense for a few minutes as Stan and Marty talked about their estrangement. "I just felt guilty, I guess, and wasn't sure what to do about it," Marty said. He reached over and put his arm around Gracie and they exchanged smiles. "Then Gracie came into my life," he went on. "She helped me get past some of those feelings, but I didn't go the next step—confiding in you. After so many years I didn't know how to approach you."

"I certainly understand that," Stan said.

Gracie said, "Back to how we met. I was a waitress in Orlando and I served the table where these gospel singers were eating supper late one evening. They were cheerful, pleasant guys, and when I came around with their check, they talked with me a few minutes and found out I sang in a church choir."

"Yeah," Marty said, "that was when we were redesigning ourselves from an all-male quartet into a more diverse group and we were looking for female singers. She talked a little about her faith and we liked her personality, so we asked her to audition with us. Once we convinced her we were serious, she did it. We were so impressed with Gracie's voice that we offered her a job singing with us. We couldn't pay a lot, so she moved to Sarasota and worked in a restaurant there while we built up the new *Joyful Morning* group and began to market ourselves."

"In the middle of all that," Gracie added, "this guy here and I sort of fell in love. We felt God had drawn us together, and last May we got married. Now here we are at Dinkel Island, picking up some broken pieces from the past. A month ago I never would have expected this. Who knows what's next!"

17

Grief and Grace

*B*etween Fanny's cooking and the fare at local restaurants, Marty and Gracie were royally fed and entertained during the evenings of their week in Dinkel Island. Having rehearsed for the concert each day, the group took Friday off, which gave Marty and Gracie a chance to tour the gallery and art center with Stan and Fanny.

"We invite outstanding artists to come in and lead workshops several times a year," Stan explained as he showed them around. "We advertise those in Potomac City, Richmond, and other towns in the Northern Neck and beyond. In fact, we're in the middle of a two-day class on watercolor technique right now."

Fanny excused herself saying that she had to greet a touring group of senior citizens from Potomac City. "I won't be too long," she said as she went into the other building.

Molly Pringle was working the sales counter in the gallery and Ed Heygood was filing some papers in the office. While Stan was showing Marty and Gracie a painting he was doing in his studio, Ed went into the gallery, and then came back to Stan.

"Molly has a sale to a customer who wants to know what else is available from a particular artist," Ed said. "Where can I find the inventory sheets?"

Stan excused himself and went into the office with Ed, saying, "I like to keep things like that in the safe where they're not readily visible. Here," he said while unlocking the safe. Ed took the papers back into the gallery, and Stan realized he hadn't yet given Molly the combination for the safe. *I should probably leave this unlocked so Molly can put her receipts in here* he thought and went back into the studio.

When Fanny came back they all decided to go freshen up before meeting at the Seafood Pavilion for supper. Stan said, "I'll catch up with you over there—I really need to work on this painting a little longer."

A half-hour later Molly closed up, tallied the days transactions, and went over it with Stan as Ed went up to his apartment to get ready for supper.

"It sounds like you had a great day," Stan said. "I'll be glad to put that in the safe for you when I leave—just drop it on the desk."

Stan wanted to finish using some paint he had mixed and soon got wrapped up in his work, unaware of the time. Suddenly Ed came down the stairs.

"What, you still here?" Ed exclaimed when he found Stan still in the studio.

"Oh, gosh, I forgot the time," Stan said. "I'll clean these brushes and I've got to get home and change. Tell everybody I'm on the way."

Ed left and Stan cleaned his brushes, clicked off the office light, pulled the door shut, rushed out and locked the back door on his way home to change. He was only a few minutes late getting to supper and everyone gave him a hard time about being the absent-minded artist. Then they settled down to a delicious meal, and soon it was time to leave for the church.

When they reached the church they found the community center room was filled, with people standing along the walls. Others were making themselves as comfortable as they could outside hoping to hear from there. The concert lasted over an hour, and nobody even thought about the time. It was one of the biggest events ever at Dinkel Island.

After initially introducing themselves and singing several numbers, the quartet stepped back while Marty and Gracie sang "Love Lifted Me." Then Gracie sang "How Great Thou Art," and "Jesus Hold My Hand." Next the group members disbursed to the sidelines while Gracie gave her testimony.

"My name is Mary Grace Love Grayson," she said with warmth, waving toward Marty and adding, "Marty's my husband. We're newlyweds—."

She was interrupted by a huge round of applause. "Thanks," she said. "We were married in May, and so far the honeymoon isn't over!" Again she was interrupted by applause.

When the room quieted Gracie went on, "I'm here because God literally gave me a brand new life through Christ. Some of you may understand what I'm about to say, and some may not—I grew up not knowing anything about God except a profane expression."

As she spoke, Gracie looked around the sanctuary and saw a few heads nodding. She went on, "I heard the name 'Jesus Christ' used as a curse word, but had no idea he was real and wanted to be my savior. Christmas was a time for decorations, partying and getting stuff, but that was it. I knew *Jingle Bells*, but had never heard *Joy to the World.*"

Again she paused as these words brought total silence and rapt attention within the audience. "Not only that, I was abused—in every way you can imagine—by my father and people who surrounded him."

There was a stirring among the people and some expressions of empathic concern. She continued: "At 16 I was taken out of school and put to work in my family's business. Then one night about the time I was 18 I ran away, and never turned back. I was caught in a storm right out here in the Chesapeake Bay and nearly drowned when my boat went down, but I made it to shore." Again she noticed rapt attention.

"When I got to shore, I needed rest, but I was wary of people who might see me or approach me, and I found a place to hide for a day while I got myself together. I had an overwhelming sense that God had saved me, was with me, and would lead me. It was strange, because I had no church experience to fall back on. I just knew God was with me."

Again Gracie paused while people were responsive, some applauding, others responded verbally. "I hitch hiked south," she said, " and one day I was dropped off in a small North Carolina town where I met a couple who had more sensitivity and compassion than I could have ever imagined."

Unlike her usual talks, Gracie suddenly broke down emotionally, excused herself a moment, then spoke again. "I—I'm sorry—being at Dinkel Island has brought back some memories that are painful. I'll give those to the Lord—so forgive me—okay," she said, and smiled with a radiance that said God was working in her spirit even as she spoke.

"The couple I met were missionaries from Virginia who were traveling back to a very unique senior citizen center they ran in South Carolina. To make a long story short, I was trying to go to Florida because I'd heard it was warm and I didn't think I had any relatives there. Uncle Bert and Aunt Millie—that's who they became to me—persuaded me to stay in their home with them, and hired me to work on their staff.

They saw that I got my GED certificate, and later even a couple of years of college. But most of all they gave me a Savior, Jesus Christ, who already knew me and loved me and had just been waiting for me to love him back so he could open up my life for me. That happened through music, and by the grace of God, I began to sing in churches and wherever else I could."

Gracie felt the love and support flowing to her from the audience. "Uncle Bert and Aunt Millie not only gave me hope and helped me find myself," she said, "but they helped me deal with my painful past by trying to find my family. We learned that my dad had died and mama and the other kids had gone on somewhere else. So I wasn't able to tell them about my Lord, or forgive them to their faces."

The congregation responded with empathic murmurs. "Finally, I legally changed my name. I asked God for a name and he gave me three words: *Mary*, for Mary Magdalene who was Jesus' close companion and was totally changed by him; *Grace*, for the grace of God that saved me through Christ; and *Love*, for the fruit of God's Spirit that I want my life to express and give to others. So my name is my testimony—*Mary Grace Love*—and now God has added the name *Grayson* through my marriage to Marty, whom I met when I was a waitress in Florida."

As Gracie spoke, Marty walked over to her, put his arm around her and when she finished she looked at him and they embraced. The people in the audience stood and applauded, then without accompaniment Marty and Gracie sang together the Bill Gaither song, "He Touched Me." They motioned for people to sing with them, and the words were flashed on the overhead screen. The room was filled with praise. They finished singing again the refrain, "He touched me, O he touched me, and O the joy that floods my soul! Something happened, and now I know, he touched me and made me whole."

When they had finished, Marty sat back down and Gracie went on. "I know some of you here may be as lost or broken or desperate as I once was. You might be carrying burdens you think can only be eased by money, or power, or connections with different people. You might have grief so deep that it robs your body of sleep and your soul of peace. You might feel lost in a dark dungeon of pain and fear that there is no way out."

Emotions were strong and visible in the room. Gracie concluded, "Wherever you are in your life, just take heart and hope from one small Bible verse, Psalm 30:5 'Weeping may linger for the night, but joy comes with the morning.' That's where we get the name of our group, *Joyful Morning*. We want to invite you into that joyful morning God has in his heart for you. I'm going to sing a little, and we'll all sing another number or two, and then we'll close with an invitation for you to come and talk and pray with us before you leave tonight. God has some miracles to work at Dinkel Island, and some of them might happen in *your* heart and soul."

The accompanist moved over to the piano and Gracie said, "Now I'm going to sing my favorite hymn, ' Amazing grace, how sweet the sound that saved a wretch like me,'" and I want you to sing with me. The words will be up on the screen. Let's sing praise to God!"

Gracie sang the first stanza, then the rest of the group joined her and they began singing the rest of the hymn, motioning for all to join in. The sound of praise was electrifying. People were standing and swaying as they sang, and when they finished *Amazing Grace*, they sat down and Gracie sang three more songs.

The quartet came back and led everyone in singing a familiar hymn that was often used in revival meetings over the years, "Just as I am, without one plea, but that thy blood was shed for me...." A radiance seemed to fill the room as they all sang. Finally Mark, who acted as lead spokesman for the group, invited Kate Sheppard to step up and lead them all in an invitational prayer.

"I don't know when I've felt so much warmth and love in a room in my life," Kate said. Turning to the group she said, "Thanks, all of you, for coming to share your talent and your faith. Gracie, thanks for your story. I'd love to talk with you more about that sometime if you're willing." Gracie nodded that she was, then Kate prayed, and offered a benediction along with an appeal for people to come and kneel in prayer and stay as long as they needed. She indicated she and Herb Melloman would be there to talk to anyone who wished and Mark added that the same was true for each member of the *Joyful Morning* group.

People did come forward, and it was some time before the evening was over, equipment packed up, chairs put away, and the lights turned out. Everyone went home with a deep sense of peace and hope.

Ben Wartman had kept a low profile at Dinkel Island, carefully obeying the traffic rules, avoiding drinking too much, and keeping his reddish hair dyed black. In public places he talked little and listened a lot. So when he heard that a major southern gospel group was coming to one of the churches in town on the last Friday in September, he took notice—not because of a personal interest in such things. He had no faith at all, didn't believe in God, and thought churches just ripped off peoples' money and stirred them up over things.

What captured his attention was the enthusiastic and widespread interest the event stirred among people everywhere he went. There were posters on power poles, and in store windows, and the *Island Sentinel* carried articles and pictures. It seemed like everybody in town was going to be there. To Ben that meant a new opportunity to get that mystery money he was sure was stashed away somewhere in the art center.

On the day of the concert he switched work shifts with one of the other maintenance guys at Wal-mart and did some reconnaissance. Parking in the lot at the Grande Hotel, which was also the parking lot for a nine-hole golf course that surrounded it, he pretended to make some cell phone calls from the cab of his truck. His real task was watching the activities at the Community Art Center across the street.

When two vans from a senior citizen facility in Potomac City pulled into the parking lot, he had an idea. The people from the vans began to assemble into a group and it occurred to Ben that he might try to join in with them so he could get inside the building. He jumped out of his truck, walked quickly over to the parking lot and tucked himself in at the back of the group as they were ushered inside the building, trying to look like one of the volunteer staff.

He found himself in a large multi-purpose room with art on the walls, tables and chairs both set up and stored along the walls. A woman who looked to be in her sixties entered from a side door, walked over to the group and introduced herself as Fanny. She then talked briefly about the different programs that were offered, and asked for questions. She motioned toward a hallway that she said led to a number of resident artist's studios and invited the group to visit among them later.

In a corner of the room a woman who had been leading an art class told her group to take a break, and a couple of dozen artists got up from tables where they had been working and began to stretch, talk and go toward the restrooms. No one seemed to pay much attention to the senior citizens, and when Fanny finished answering questions she invited the group to follow her through the door from which she had entered the room. Ben again tacked himself onto the fringe of the group.

Ben could see now that there were two buildings that were part of the same business. He now found himself inside the Grayson/Plume Gallery where paintings were hung on partitioned walls, and exhibits were placed around the room with pottery, sculpture, jewelry, and other fine art and craft items displayed. In the back was a counter where a woman was processing the sale of a small painting. He picked up a folder describing the work of a potter and pretended to read it as he observed his surroundings.

His attention was drawn to a closed door on the back wall to the right of the sales counter, which suddenly opened and a man that Ben judged to also be in his sixties, came out and went to the counter. He wondered if that was this "Stan" guy Lucy Mac was chasing. The man and the sales person talked a moment, then he went back through the door, emerging a few minutes later with some papers that he handed to the customer.

Ben noticed a computerized cash register and credit card terminal, and he looked around for evidence of a security system, but saw no cameras or motion detectors. When the sale was completed the two people behind the counter looked through some papers and talked a moment, then the man went back through the door and closed it.

The senior citizens with whom he had entered were scattered around, and some were taking small purchases to the sales counter, so Ben decided it was time for him to exit. He folded the papers he was holding, put them in a pocket, walked around a bit more looking at things, and then left the building. Once outside he walked back across the street to his truck and drove to the small trailer he had rented back a dirt road in a wooded area off of Tranquility Bay, near the campground.

The rest of the afternoon Ben spent drawing a rough map of the two buildings he had been in, and memorizing where things were. He wasn't sure where he would look for the money. Remembering the door behind the counter in the gallery he guessed that it led to an office—and maybe even a rear entrance from the alley. He laid back on the bed, closed his eyes, and tried to envision the building's features. Deciding it was best to go in from the alley, he relaxed and took a short nap. When he awoke, he fixed himself a couple of hot dogs, drank a beer, and decided it was time to go.

Ben stuffed an old pair of work gloves into the pockets of a dark hoodie he intended to wear, and looked for his flashlight, which he couldn't find. The sky was overcast, but darkness had not fallen completely, so he decided he could probably get along without the flashlight. He drove back to the gallery, found a parking spot not too far away, and then got out of his truck and joined in with people who were walking from their cars toward the church for the concert

It was a cool September evening and his hoodie felt good. He checked the pockets to be sure the gloves were still there. As he walked up Bank Street toward Dinkel Avenue he came to a gravel alley that went in behind the gallery and art center. He stopped, knelt down and began retying his shoe laces, considering his next move, while people walked on by.

When the people hurrying toward the church had moved past him, Ben slipped up the alley, walking quietly. The overcast sky and deepening darkness began to envelope the alley with its board fencing, shadowy trees and building walls, in a thickening haze. Ben was almost up to the building he thought was the gallery, when he heard a sudden sound like someone moving fast on the gravel behind him.

Ben dropped down and ducked behind a trash dumpster, then watched as the same man he had seen working in the gallery earlier sprinted right past him, went to a door with a small sign that identified it as the gallery building, unlocked it, and went inside, turning on a dim light and then Ben saw a light come on upstairs. He felt an adrenalin rush as he pulled on the work gloves, stepped out from his hiding place and ran across the parking lot to the door, and tried the handle.

The door was unlocked so Ben pushed it open, stepped inside, then shut it and took in his surroundings. There was a short hallway that led to a door he thought might enter the gallery itself, plus a door on the left he thought might be an office. Opposite that door was the stairway where he heard a door shut and footsteps begin to descend. Spying a stack of cardboard boxes to his left, he quickly hid behind them just before the footsteps produced the man he had seen enter the building, who seemed intent on leaving quickly and did not even glance around the room. As he went out the door he turned off the light, closed and locked the door, and disappeared.

Ben was alone in the building and he hadn't even had to break in! He waited a few minutes until he decided the coast was clear and then began to explore his surroundings more carefully. It was very dark, so he pulled out a book of matches and lit one, hoping to see a flashlight lying about, but there was none. Ben made his way forward to the office door and tried the door knob. It was locked.

He turned back to the area into which he had entered, lit another match, and saw that it was a large room used for storage as well as an art studio and workshop. There were easels, canvases, paintings in storage slots, stacks of paper, brushes, jars and tubes of paint, and tools of various types. He didn't see a flashlight, but did find a hammer and screw driver which he then used, without benefit of light, to force open the office door, splintering some of the frame.

He had guessed right, it was an office. Stepping inside he was tempted to hit the light switch, but noticed a small window behind a desk and wasn't sure if the light would show through the draperies. He lit another match and then saw a flashlight on a shelf which he used to search the room. He saw a small safe on top of a two-drawer file cabinet beside the desk and wondered how he could open it, or if it was too heavy to carry out with him. He went around to the safe and pulled on the door. It opened easily. "Ha!" he muttered to himself. "Anybody dumb enough to leave a safe unlocked deserves to be robbed."

The safe quickly proved to be a disappointment. There was nothing in it but a bunch of documents that he didn't take time to read because he was sure he wouldn't understand them if he tried. Ben shuffled through papers piled up on the desk and discovered a small manila envelope with some folding money and coins inside. This was nowhere near the $5000 he was looking for. Angrily he grabbed he money, stuffed it in his pocket, and then with a sweep of his arm across the desk sent everything there careening around the room.

Pulling the door closed behind him as he left the office, Ben decided to go into the gallery and look behind the sales counter. That also proved fruitless. The cash drawer was open and obviously empty, and rifling through the cabinets under the counter produced no money. Again a sweep of his arm sent everything on the counter flying off into the room. He turned abruptly and went back out through the door and stormed up the stairs, thinking there must be another office up there.

As with the safe, the door at the top of the stairs was unlocked. He opened it slowly and then realized he was in some kind of an apartment. "Aha!"—he said aloud—"this is where that money will be." He moved through the apartment, rifling through closets and furniture drawers, but found nothing. It was getting late and he became more irritated. He knocked over a couple of lamps and a wooden chair, and threw a heavy bookend into a mirror in his rage, leaving shattered glass all over the floor.

Ben thundered down the stairs, and then out the back door which locked when he pulled it shut. He still had the flashlight in his hand, so he threw it off across the parking lot where it made a loud noise hitting the side of the trash dumpster. Ben ripped off his gloves and stuffed them into his hoodie pockets, and then ran back up the alley. He was enraged that every time he tried to get that mystery money he was somehow done in by things he couldn't control.

As Ben got into his truck and drove back to his trailer his anger began to subside. He was disappointed that he had not found the money he was after, but he did have something for his efforts and he would count it when he got home.

"One more time," he said aloud to himself. "I'll try one more time to get that money and then I never want to see this stupid town again."

18

A Shocking Discovery

After the concert Ed and Molly sat in the living room at her house drinking coffee and basking in the afterglow of a very moving and inspiring evening.

"I was really impressed with the quality and range of Gracie Love's voice," Ed said. "She almost rivals Barbara Streisand."

Molly laughed, "Well, I hadn't made that connection—but she is exceptional. What impressed me more than her voice was her testimony. Can you imagine someone with that much against her becoming who she is today?"

"Actually, I can," Ed said, leaning back and stroking his memory. During my years in ministry I came across that kind of deep spiritual shift a couple of times—the first time, in fact, happened right here at Dinkel Island."

Molly perked up, "Really! That's fascinating. Tell me about it."

Ed had never forgotten the trauma when CJ Crumbold, who was now a well-known pastor, had been a young man with criminal intent who had masqueraded as Harper Jauswell's nephew in an effort to steal his money.

"It was a long time ago, so I don't recall all the details, but it was a very complicated situation," Ed said. "Essentially, a young man came to Dinkel Island claiming to be Harper Jauswell's nephew—Harper, as you probably know, was a powerful and often negative man, and Fanny was his housekeeper. The young man was so persuasive that Fanny fell in love with him, but Harper had a heart attack and a spiritual experience in the hospital that changed his character—he became a man of strong, genuine faith for several years after that. Anyway, the plot got exposed and Harper not only forgave the young man, but was instrumental in leading him to the Christian faith. In fact, CJ Crumbold became a pastor who specializes in prison ministry. That was a dramatic change."

Listening intently Molly sat back, exhaled and said, "Wow, that must have been something to go through. I've never been around anything like that—that is until I heard Gracie talk tonight. It is amazing what God can do, isn't it?"

"It is, indeed," Ed said. He thought a moment, and then went on, "I wonder, really, how different something like that is from what you and I—and Stan and Fanny—have been going through in overcoming the negative power of grief?"

"Hmmm," Molly said. "Grief does come in all kinds of flavors, doesn't it? It gets into the middle of things and causes you to hold yourself back." She looked at Ed with an expression of affection and added, "I sure was holding myself back—until I met you." She saw understanding and warmth in his expression.

Suddenly Molly became animated, jumped up, pulled on Ed's hand and said, "Come on, let's go into the kitchen and have an ice cream sundae—while I tell you just how much you mean to me."

Ed was surprised by her suddenness. "Okay"—he said—"on one condition, that you return the favor and let me tell you how much you mean to me, also."

"You got it," she said and they started toward the kitchen, stopped, embraced each other and kissed with a passion neither had known in a long time. After eating sundaes and sharing their feelings, it was hard to disengage from the power of the evening. Finally at midnight, Ed said, "I need to get some rest. I'll see you first thing in the morning and in the meantime—"he paused, drew her to himself, kissed her, and continued—"in the meantime, I love you, Molly Pringle. Good night."

As Ed unlocked the back door of the gallery he felt a strangeness that sent a shiver down his back. He closed the door, feeling very alone, wishing he and Molly could have stayed together longer. Then he realized the strange feeling hitting him was somehow different—foreboding—*but why?* He started up the stairs to his apartment, then stopped short. *What...?* he thought. He turned and looked at the office door and saw shattered pieces of door frame on the floor. He was immediately on heightened alert.

He was shocked to discover the disarray in the office when he pushed the door open and turned on the light. Papers were scattered around the room and the safe next to the desk was open. "We've been robbed!" he exclaimed, and immediately called 911.

Within minutes a squad car pulled up behind the gallery, and Chief Draper pulled up in front. The two officers made a surveillance of the building, then went inside where they talked with Ed and began to check out the interior.

Ed described how he had come in and discovered the shattered door and then the ransacked office with the open safe. Chief Draper asked him what was missing.

"I don't know," Ed said. "I live upstairs and I've been helping out in the office a little lately, but I've never had anything to do with the safe."

Chief Draper called Stan, who had already gone to bed, and he soon arrived. "What's going on?" he asked Ed as he came into the building. Ed filled him in on the details and then showed him the damage there in the gallery. Stan was in shock.

"Can you believe this?" he said. "First that explosion back during the art show, and now this. In thirty years of running this gallery I've only had one other incident, and that was when some guy skidded his car into the front window during an ice storm."

Stan shook his head and Ed put a hand on his shoulder. "I don't know what to think, either," he said.

Just then Chief Draper called down from the apartment. "You guys better come up here," he said. "This place is a wreck."

In a state of shock and disbelief Ed and Stan went through the apartment, seeing the broken glass, overturned furniture and ransacked closets and drawers. "What the heck is this about?" Ed said. "What was the guy looking for? None of this makes any sense."

Chief Draper called in some extra help and they began to go over things, looking for fingerprints or any other evidence they could find.

"Do either of you use book matches?" he said.

"No."

"Well here's a match book cover we found on the floor in your studio, Stan." The chief held it up revealing an advertisement for *Harry's Hash House* in Potomac City. "I've found several stubs from matches that probably came out of this book. What's really puzzling is that we don't see evidence of forced entry to the building itself—only the office door. Who can you think of that might have a key to the building, but not the office?"

"Uh—nobody," Stan said. "Fanny and Molly have keys, but we were all at the concert together tonight. As far as I know none of us has lost our key." Stan looked at Ed, "Was the door locked when you came home?"

"Yeah," Ed said. "You know, I had an eerie feeling when I came in the door, though, and I've never had that before."

"That's just your subconscious telling you something's wrong," Chief Draper said. "That's not uncommon."

They talked more about who might have a grudge or what of value might have drawn someone to break into the gallery.

"What's missing from the safe?" the chief asked.

Stan had looked over everything in the office. "The only thing is the petty cash envelope."

"How much money was in it?" the chief asked. "And what about your sales receipts for today?"

"Molly showed me the sheet," Stan said, and he sifted through some of the papers that had been on the desk. "Here it is—mostly credit card or debit card sales. It looks like she took in about $50 in small cash sales. That would be included in the total in the cash envelope—here it is: $329.87."

"And that's it?" Chief Draper asked, puzzled. "You know, this just doesn't make sense. I can see somebody breaking in to steal a few dollars, but why all this trashing of the place? And how did he get into the safe in the first place?"

Suddenly Stan's face flushed. "Oh, no! That's my fault. I told Molly to put the money and receipts on my desk and I'd put it in the safe before I left. Then I got busy painting in here, and forgot that I had left the safe open. I just switched off the light and pulled the door shut when I left. I never put it in the safe—in fact, I left the safe unlocked. Stupid!" Stan said, slapping his palm against his forehead. "I've never done anything like that before."

They talked this over and then the deputy came in with a work glove he had found on the gravel in the parking lot, near the door to the gallery. He was holding it on the end of a stick. "Found this outside. Might belong to the robber. Maybe we should check it out."

They took that and the match book cover with them, and said they would be back in the morning.

"I really don't think anything else will happen tonight," the chief said. "Are you okay here by yourself, Ed?"

"Hey, come on to the condo for the rest of the night," Stan said. "We can clean all this up tomorrow."

Ed agreed and they left. It had been a night with the wildest range of emotions Ed could remember, from the elation and joy of the concert, to this craziness of a break-in. After a good night's rest they could tackle the situation with freshness in the morning.

∿

After the concert everybody was tired, and Marty and Gracie went to bed almost as soon as they came into Fanny's house. "It's been a wonderful night," Gracie said, "but we're both exhausted. I think we'll just go on to bed, if that's okay with y'all." She looked at Marty who nodded and yawned.

"You've earned a good night's rest," Stan said.

"I'll say," Fanny said. "That's the best concert I've ever been to—and that testimony of yours was fantastic. We'll talk some more in the mornin'. G'night, y'all."

"Good night," Gracie said as she and Marty went upstairs. They fell asleep quickly.

As Gracie slept her mind began to tap into images she had long ago pushed away—images related to Dinkel Island and her experiences there 22 years earlier. A voice began to echo in her mind. "It's just the wind and some trees fallin' in the storm."

Gracie's body stiffened, and she made a muffled sound, turned over, and then she heard frightening sounds—pounding—an axe against wood. She felt panic as she smelled the musty dirt under a building where she was crawling on her belly, pushing a backpack in front of her. She stopped, dug out something—a vinyl bag—pushed it into the backpack—kept crawling.

"Keep moving," the husky voice behind her urged. "When you get out from under the building stay low and run down through the woods to the boat. Run! Don't look back. I'm right behind you." Rain was falling hard and the wind whistled in the trees. What was that? A crashing sound. Thunder? She looked back. Tom was on the ground, crying at her to run fast. A man's figure, his face magnified with an expression of evil contempt, snarled like a rabid dog behind Tom. "Crash!" That sound again—he had just fired a shotgun—at her! The pellets whizzed overhead, tearing into the trees just above her. "NO! NO! NO!" she screamed.

"Gracie! Honey—what's wrong?" It was Marty, pulling her to himself, an expression of deep concern on his face. "You were screaming, honey. What's wrong?"

Opening her eyes, Gracie saw that she was in bed with Marty, who was now holding her close to him, rocking her. The warmth of the room in Fanny's house seemed to enfold her with a sense of safety. She sobbed, then looked into Marty's face. Her lips trembled as they kissed.

"I had a terrible dream," Gracie said. "It's one I used to have a lot a long time ago, but then over the years it went away."

"What kind of dream? What was it about? You seem so frightened."

"It was here!" Gracie exclaimed. "It happened right here, right outside Dinkel Island."

"What happened, honey? You're not making sense."

Gracie trembled. "Pray with me," she said. They prayed together and she began to relax and grow calm.

"I realized it while I was giving my testimony tonight," she said. "You don't know what I'm talking about. Turn on the light and I'll explain."

Marty turned on the light. They sat up in the bed and pulled the covers closely around themselves and she said, "I've never told you much about the details from my childhood and my escape from home."

"You said your real name was Cybil Froster, and your daddy was an oysterman in Maryland. I never felt it was necessary to ask more than you wanted to tell me."

"That's right—that was my birth name. Do you remember, I said I ran away from home one night and never went back?"

"Yes—you mentioned it in your testimony, too."

"That's right. That's when it hit me about Dinkel Island." Gracie then told Marty the whole story of how Tom Brewster had taken her to the cabin at Lighthouse Point, and about their love there, and the raid when someone shot Tom, and she escaped, which led to her boat wreck in the storm. She told him about the fire she saw where the cabin was located after she got the boat away from the creek. She cried from the pain of remembering all the trauma. Marty comforted and consoled her.

"I'm glad you told me. I'm so sorry you had to go through something like that. It has to be a deep scar in your spirit, but we've given that to God now and maybe it has served a purpose. I love you dearly, Gracie, and nothing that can happen, or ever has happened, can change that."

Marty held her tightly and they turned out the light.

19

Memories and Evidence

"Are you okay?" Fanny asked Gracie when she and Marty came downstairs for breakfast Saturday morning. "I thought I heard a noise during the night, but I figured if you needed somethin' y'all'd let me know."

"I'm okay," Gracie said. "I had a strange dream that woke me up, that's all."

Fanny hugged her. "Sometimes I think we tuck stuff away in the back of our minds and then one day it pops up—like in a dream."

"I'm glad Marty was there," Gracie said as she squeezed his hand. "His love and God's grace got me through the rest of the night."

"Well, I hate to bring up more trouble," Fanny said, "but Stan ain't here this mornin' because there was what you might call a nightmare over at the art gallery last night—probably happened during the concert." She told them about the robbery.

Gracie shivered as Fanny spoke.

"What's wrong, honey?" Fanny said.

Catching her breath Gracie said, "I just had a strange feeling when you mentioned the robbery. It's like it connects with my dream—but that seems far-fetched."

"Really! That must have been quite a dream you had!"

"Tell me about the robbery"—Gracie said—"what was stolen?"

"I don't really know yet," Fanny said. "I'm goin' over there as soon as we finish breakfast. Why don't y'all come along?"

"Yes!" Gracie said. "Yes, I want to do that. It doesn't make sense, but I feel some kind of connection with whatever is happening."

They arrived at the gallery at the same time as Molly. Stan and Ed had begun cleaning up the damage and it didn't look as bad as it had earlier. Ed told Molly about the strange feeling he had when he entered the building.

"I didn't think about it last night," he said, "but do you remember when we got to the church I reached in my pocket and my cell phone was missing?"

"Yeah," Molly said, "and you ran back to the apartment to see if you had left it there—which you had!"

"Right."

"So what does that have to do with anything?" Stan said.

"Well, just this," Ed said. "I unlocked the back door and ran up to the apartment. "I wasn't in the building more than a couple of minutes." Ed paused, then went on, "you know, the back door doesn't automatically lock once you open it from outside, and I'll bet I didn't lock it when I came in."

Fanny said, "If you were only there a couple of minutes, that doesn't seem long enough for somebody to get inside before you came back out—unless, of course, they were already there watchin' the entrance."

"But I would have seen or heard something—still, it could have happened that way. Maybe I should call Chief Draper and tell him about it." Ed called on his cell phone and left a message for the chief.

"So what's the bottom line?" Marty asked Stan. "What was stolen?"

"About $300, that's all. No art works were taken, but the place really was trashed. They didn't take anything that had sensitive information, like credit card receipts. It was really weird."

Molly repeated the amount. "You know," she said to Stan, "I started to put the money and paperwork in the safe instead of on your desk when I left yesterday. Sure wish I'd done that now!"

"Well, it's not your fault. You just did what I told you to do. It's my fault"—Stan said—"if it's anybody's. I know better than to do things that way. All the more reason to get the whole gallery operation turned over to you as quickly as we can, Molly."

Fanny stepped into the conversation. "It don't matter who done what. A mistake was made, and it's not a big one. Sure, there's some cleaning up to do, but $300 is not a big deal."

"Actually," Ed said, "the missing money seems out of sync with the other damage done in the building. I'm not sure what this was all about. I think the money just happened to be there so the thief took it. Do you remember when we talked about motives after the explosion and fire? I think these two things might be related and I'm wondering what's behind all of it?"

Gracie and Marty looked surprised and Marty said, "Explosion? When was this?"

Stan explained about the excitement that had occurred during an apparent break-in effort while the Art Extravaganza was going on.

Ed said, "One of the motives we discussed then was that money Stan and I found in the backpack in Tranquility Bay last July. You remember…"

"Oh, yeah," Stan said. "Maybe this is the same person, and maybe that's what he or she is looking for."

"Money in a backpack?" Gracie asked. "What kind of a backpack?"

Stan answered, "Oh, just some grungy thing Ed caught that we thought was a skate until we got it to the boat. It had been in the water a long time and there was some money inside of it. We turned it over to Chief Draper and he never has been able to find out how it got there."

"It got to be quite a hot topic on the community grapevine," Ed said. "Even the guys in the drug store Old Geezer group got into speculating about it. It *was* a lot of money—nearly $5000 as near as we could tell—all in small bills."

Gracie looked shocked.

Ed went on, "We figured it might have drifted into Tranquility Bay from somewhere else. The money was in a sealed plastic container, something like you would use to store things in a refrigerator, and that was inside a vinyl bag."

Gracie looked nervous. Marty said, "What's wrong, honey?"

"I'm remembering something I haven't thought about in a long, long time," she replied.

They all looked at her and at each other.

"I'm sorry," she said. "Please excuse me a minute." She went back toward the bathroom.

"What's going on with Gracie?" Molly asked. "She seems upset."

Marty excused himself, and went after her. Everybody was confused. They bantered around a little small talk for a few minutes, and then Gracie and Marty returned. She seemed to have collected herself, but Marty seemed concerned about her.

"This is quite a shock for me," Gracie said, "and what I'm going to tell you is something I literally haven't remembered until now." She paused, took a deep breath and continued. "Do you remember when I gave my testimony about being in a boat wreck when I ran away from home?"

They all nodded, and gave her their full attention.

"Well," Gracie said, "I wonder if the money you found, Ed, might be from that boat." Her remark hit everyone like a shock, and she could feel their curiosity escalating.

"Wait a minute," Ed said. "That had to be years ago."

"It was 1989—which was what—twenty-two years ago?"

Stan and the others looked at each other, and then asked her what she was remembering from that experience.

Gracie said, "I ran away with a young man who worked for my daddy. He brought me to a little cabin up in some creek near here—I can still see that place in my mind. He didn't abuse me or attack me or anything, and we fell in love—or what we thought was love, at least. We spent a couple of months living there and we used to come to Dinkel Island for supplies. It was the first time in my life that I felt free and loved, and I wanted it to go on forever."

"What an awful thing to go through," Molly said.

"Actually, that was the good part. 'Awful' was what life was like at home before I left—and 'awful' was what happened next."

"Can I get you something, honey?" Fanny said, "How about some water?"

"This is hard to talk about," Gracie said. "Yes, water would be good." Fanny got the water and after drinking some of it, Gracie went on with her story.

"It seems to me it was November—near Thanksgiving—and a huge storm blew in from the sea with high winds, rain, thunder and lightning. We were in the cabin and I remember how loud the noise sounded outside. Then I heard a different kind of noise, but Tom said he couldn't hear it. He had a habit I didn't like—he would steal money—and put it along with a lot of what he earned into a plastic box in a vinyl bag like you described. I don't know how much it was, but he was saving to get a new boat and make a better life for both of us."

Gracie paused. She had everyone's rapt attention. "The noise sounded like somebody trying to break in. Tom had a trap door and we slipped away under the house and out through the woods. I threw some clothes into an old backpack, and on the way out under the house I grabbed the money bag and put it in there, too."

She looked around, keeping eye contact with everyone. "I don't know why, but Tom stood up instead of going down through the woods the way we had agreed, and a wild looking man shot him and then they came after me. I managed to get to Tom's boat and tossed the backpack on the deck as I started the motor. I got the boat out of the creek, but the storm was the worst I'd ever seen and something under the water struck the boat and it broke apart. I managed to swim to shore, but the backpack disappeared with the boat."

"What an awful thing to go through," Molly said. "And that man shooting your friend—did you ever find Tom again?"

"No," Gracie said. "Actually, I didn't even try. I knew he was probably dead and I was afraid to go back there. I saw flames and smoke where the cabin was, so I'm sure they burned it down. All I wanted to do was get away from that—and everything else in my past."

"I can imagine," Ed said.

"Just surviving the boat wreck was a miracle," Stan said.

"Yes, it was," Gracie said. "But the bigger miracle was that somehow, for some reason, when I got to shore I had this strong feeling that God had saved me. I didn't know God—didn't know anything about him—but I felt that way."

"Wow!" Molly said. "We were just talking about the miracle of being where you are now, singing and sharing your faith, after what you had told us about your background. You overcame even more than we could imagine. What a blessing!"

Gracie said, "There's an old saying I hear in church a lot, and it's true: *God is good, all the time.*" God's goodness is the only hope we have, but it's all we need. I do feel blessed." She turned to Marty and they embraced, and as she looked deeply into his eyes she said, "Part of the blessing is that he sent you to be in my life. I'm so thankful. When I was living in that cabin, I thought that was bliss—completeness, joy and fulfillment. But it wasn't! I know that because what you and I have—our life and ministry together—this is bliss. This is God's blessing."

~⁓

No sooner had Gracie finished her story than Stan's cell phone rang. Grayson/Plume Gallery," he said, "Stan speaking."

It was Chief Archie Draper returning Ed's earlier call. "So y'all think you know how the thief got into the gallery last night," he said. "Tell me more about that."

"Actually, we've got a lot more than that to talk about, Chief," Stan replied. "Can you drop by here?"

"Okay—what's going on?"

"It's a little complicated, but we're putting some pieces together and I think you'll want to get in on this."

Chief Draper arrived a few minutes later. He recognized Gracie from the concert and introduced himself. "Ms Love—oops! I guess its Mrs. Grayson, isn't it?"

Gracie smiled and shook his hand, then gestured toward Marty. "This is my husband.

"It's a pleasure to meet you, ma'am—both you and your husband. The concert last night was wonderful. I enjoyed your singing, and I was intrigued by your testimony."

"Thank you," Gracie replied. "I guess my testimony has some deeper roots than I remembered up until now." She gestured at the mess in the gallery. "I don't know anything about all of this, but I might be able to help you solve the mystery of some money my father-in-law and Ed found out in the bay last summer."

Chief Draper looked surprised. "Oh? What connection do you have with that?"

Gracie told him the whole story and the chief grew pensive. "You say all of this happened back in 1989—and you and this boy you say was killed lived in a cabin near a lighthouse?"

"Yes, sir. It wasn't a working lighthouse, just the ruins of one. The cabin was near there, but kinda hidden in some thick woods."

"That would be Lighthouse Point," the chief said. He took out his smart phone and called his deputy. "Can you do a quick check back in the files from 1989? I'm looking for a storm, a fire on Lighthouse Point, and a boat wreck. Also, do we have anything on a Tom Brewster back at that same time? E-mail me what you find. I'm over at the Grayson/Plume Gallery and it looks like there might be some deeper background to this robbery and some other things that have been goin' on."

Chief Draper stood up and paced around a moment. "Now, Gracie, tell me more about this money that Ed and Stan found last summer."

She told him about Tom's box of money, the backpack, and the escape in the boat.

"And you threw the backpack into the transom of the boat when you escaped?"

"Yes. All I could think about was getting away from there. It never occurred to me that the boat might wreck and I would lose it. When all of that happened I was too busy getting away from the boat and swimming toward the shore to even think about the money."

"Is there anything else you can remember that might help us get to the bottom of all this?"

"No," Gracie said. "But if I think of something I'll let you know."

"You say you saw the person who shot Tom. Could you describe him?"

"I can still see that horrible face with the evil look in his eyes, a wild expression on his face, and that awful reddish hair that stuck out around his hat."

The chief looked up suddenly. "Reddish hair?" he said.

"Yes," Gracie answered.

Chief Draper looked at Stan. "That rings a bell—do you remember the kid that saw the person running away after the explosion at the art center—didn't he say the guy had wild, reddish hair?"

"You know, he did," Ed said.

Turning back to Gracie the chief said, "I know it's been a long time, but can you describe him?"

Gracie thought about it. "He had on a kind of yellow slicker, like watermen wear, and boots, I think—and a grungy looking dark baseball cap."

"Was he white, African American, Hispanic? Could you see the color of his eyes?"

"It was raining hard and I was scared to death, but I believe he was white. All I remember about his eyes was that they were dark and evil."

"Stan, could you stand up a minute," the chief said, as he got up and went over to Stan. "Do you think he was as tall as Stan here?"

"Probably," Gracie said. "As you say, it was a long time ago, but that would be my impression looking back. I guess you could say average height and build."

"How old do you think he was?"

"I would guess in his late twenties or early thirties."

"Thanks," the chief said. "Y'all have been helpful." He called the station again. "I want you to contact the sheriff and ask him to put out a description of a man we'll call a person of interest. He's Caucasian, dark reddish hair, probably not well trimmed, dark eyes, medium height and build, probably around fifty years old. Might be a waterman."

"Okay, folks. With all the suspicious activities goin' on around here lately I think that same guy might still be around. The chief turned to Gracie. "Would you be willing to go up to Lighthouse Point with me and see if we can find where that cabin was?"

Gracie looked at Marty, who said, "Are you up to all this, honey?"

"Sure," Gracie said. "It will be hard, but I think it will help me to break the power of memories that have been surfacing." She turned to the chief and asked, "When do you want to go?"

"How about right after lunch today, say 1:30?"

Stan looked at Fanny, who read his mind and nodded as he said to the chief, "Why don't we all go—Marty, Gracie, Fanny and me?"

"That's fine," the chief said. "I'll come by here and y'all can follow me up there."

❧

After lunch they all headed out to Lighthouse Point. When they came to the gate the chief found the lock had been broken. He went back to the others and said, "Somebody's been in here ahead of us—the lock's been busted. Could have happened some time ago, but it could also be something recent. Let's keep an eye out for recent tire tracks or foot prints when we get up to the lighthouse."

The chief opened the gate, got back in his car, and they continued on. They did find tire tread marks and shoe imprints. The chief called the sheriff and asked him to send out someone from forensics, explaining what they were doing. Dinkel Island and the county shared jurisdiction for the property along Lighthouse Point Road since it was so closely related to the town and isolated from the rest of the county area.

The chief's phone rang. "Chief Draper."

It was his deputy at the station who said, "I went back into some old records and found a report about a fire up at the lighthouse during a nor'easter back in 1989." He paused a minute while he leafed through some papers. "Here it is—they found a guy with red hair and a pickup truck who said he was scrounging in the area for old tools and stuff. Said he was a part-time waterman, but was vague about any other employment. Do you want more?"

"Sure, what else do you have?"

"Well, he said he came out of an old shed up there and saw a fire and thought lightning had struck something, so he ran up to check it out. When the fire department arrived he came back to the shed."

"I doubt if the guy still lives there, but what was his address—and what name did he give."

"Name was Ben Wartman," he said, and gave him the address.

"Thanks—put that report on my desk—I'll be back in soon."

The chief closed his phone and said, "Seems there was some guy up here when a fire occurred during a storm about the time you're describing, Gracie. What's interesting is he had red hair! Ever hear of the name Ben Wartman?"

The name didn't ring a bell for anyone. "Okay, let's walk on up there," the chief said, pointing up the hill from the lighthouse. "Gracie, can you remember how you got to the cabin?"

"Probably not," Gracie said. "Everything looks so much different—so overgrown."

The chief got a chain saw out of his trunk. "Just in case we have to cut our way through thick brush." At the edge of the woods he turned to the women and said, "Y'all don't need to go in there if you don't want to. It looks pretty rough."

They had all worn jeans and boots and said they had come this far, they wanted to finish the trip. They all began making their way through the dense brush.

"See those broken branches up ahead?" the chief said after they had gone a ways. "I think somebody else has been in here, and not long ago."

They found shoe prints that looked like what they had seen down by the lighthouse. Stan asked, "Do you think this is the same guy? That was all so long ago."

"Could be a vagrant," the chief said. "Don't know why anybody'd want go to this much trouble getting through the woods, though, unless they had some reason to be here."

They came to an area that showed the blackened rubble in the remains of what had obviously been a small building that had been destroyed by fire. Everything was overgrown with weeds. After poking around they found some identifiable items, including some badly rusted coils that had once been a bedspring.

"Oh," Gracie exclaimed as they pulled some debris away from one end of the area, "that's a cinder block like Tom stuffed the money bag under. I think we crawled out right about here."

"I don't see any reason to see any more," the chief said. "We have the site, and I'll look through the reports from the fire when I get back to the office. If we need to explore any more I'll send in a crew with some equipment. The property owner lives in Richmond and was very cooperative when I talked with them about needing to search the area."

With that they made their way back down to Lighthouse Point Road where they disbursed. "We've got something to go on now, so I'll let you know what develops. Oh, Ed and Stan—you guys can come by and pick up that so-called "mystery money" now. I'll be glad to get rid of it. We have pictures of it and plenty of supportive evidence building up."

Stan and Ed looked at each other. "You pulled it up, Ed—why don't you go on by the station and pick it up on the way back. See y'all at the gallery."

20

Dead End

It was Friday night after the concert when Joe Truvine heard the report on his police scanner about a robbery at the Grayson/Plume Gallery. He arrived on the scene just as Chief Draper and his deputy were doing their surveillance around the building.

"What's up, Chief?" Joe asked.

"Good heavens, Joe—don't you ever sleep? You must wear ear buds from that scanner even when you're in bed."

"You know how it is—early bird gets the worm. So I'm here looking for a scoop. Anything you can tell me?"

"I'd tell you to go on home and check with us in the morning, but you wouldn't do it. Actually, we just got here and don't know any more than you do."

"Just from lookin' around, I don't see any signs of forced entry," Joe said. Maybe it's another thing like that explosion last summer."

"Could be," the chief said. "We're goin' in to talk with Ed Heygood and we'll let you know what's goin' on in the mornin'. You might as well go get some sleep. All we have now is a reported break-in—nothing else."

"Oh, so it wasn't the gallery, but Heygood's apartment that was robbed?"

"I didn't say that," the chief replied. "What I said was that I don't know the details. Hey, Joe," chief Draper said slapping him on the back good-naturedly, "it's not like you had a daily paper here. Before you go to press we'll have plenty for you."

Joe didn't like being put off, but reporters often had to sneak around in the background to get to the heart of a story, and he knew Chief Draper could be as hard to get through as a stone wall. "Okay," Joe said. "Guess you're right."

After the chief went into the gallery Joe decided to wait around outside in his car and see who else showed up. It wasn't long before Stan Grayson arrived and lights came on throughout the gallery and the adjacent art center—and that was it. After a time the lights went out and the police, Stan and Ed all left at the same time. Joe decided there was nothing to be gained by waiting around, so he went home.

The next morning before he went to the *Island Sentinel* office, Joe drove back by the gallery and saw the "closed" sign in the front window. He could make out Stan and Ed inside, apparently cleaning up something, so he got out of his car and went to the door. By the time he got there and knocked, they had gone back into the building and didn't respond. Joe decided to park over at the hotel and see what else transpired.

He watched as Fanny, Marty, Gracie and Molly all arrived, and then a little later saw the chief return and stay for a while. A bulletin came over his scanner describing a person of interest that the Nor'easter County Sheriff and the Dinkel Island Police were looking for related to a robbery. Joe noted the details about the man they were seeking, and cursed himself for not having persisted when no one answered the door at the gallery. He got out of his car and walked over, arriving just as Stan and the others were coming out."

"Hey, Stan," Joe called out as he approached them. "Looks like some excitement around here—what's goin' on?"

Stan and Ed told the others to go on while they talked to Joe in front of the building. "We had a little incident last night—nothing serious. A minor theft, and some vandalism."

"So what was stolen?"

"Actually, not much—a little cash, but that was it."

"You mean nobody was tryin' to rip off those great art treasures you guys have in there?"

Stan laughed. "Always the joker, eh? No—no art was stolen—or even damaged. We don't know what they were looking for."

"They?" Joe asked. "There was more than one?"

"Don't know"—Ed said—"it doesn't look like it."

They talked a few moments, and then Stan and Ed met up with the others and they went to lunch while Joe went back to the *Sentinel* office.

❧

Kate Sheppard seldom went to the church office on Saturday morning, but this particular weekend she still had some work to finish. She had always found the sanctuary to be a special "prayer closet" when no one was in the building, and she headed there first, sitting down in a chair about halfway back where she had a view of the "Return of the Prodigal" stained glass window. As usual, the image captivated her attention. A sense of healing symbolized by the father's embrace of his penitent son seemed to vibrate within her spirit.

Kate closed her eyes, raised her hands, palms open, and prayed aloud, "O Father, I feel something in my spirit today. There is pain, yet also healing and hope. I feel that something unknown, that has lurked in the shadows, is spilling into the open. Lord, if there is a need where I might serve, please show me the path to take, and grant your healing grace through Christ." She went on with her prayer, not sure where it was all coming from, but certain that God was present and opening some kind of door for her. She prayed for all the needs she knew among her flock, and as she left the sanctuary she felt buoyant and energized.

In her office Kate pulled out her notes for the next day's sermon. The theme was from the story in Mark 8:22-24 where a blind man begged for Jesus to touch him. When Jesus rubbed saliva on his eyes and touched him, the man said he could see people, but they looked like trees walking around. When Jesus touched his eyes again, the text read, "he looked intently and his sight was restored, and he saw everything clearly."

Those words, "saw everything clearly," began to press themselves into Kate's mind. "Lord, what am I missing? What am I not seeing clearly? Touch the inner eyes of my spirit that I might see things clearly." She didn't really know what this prayer was about, but she felt it flowing from deep within herself. Suddenly her phone rang.

"Wesleyan Brethren Church," she said. "Kate Sheppard speaking."

"Kate, this is Sarah Jones. Have you heard about the robbery?"

"Uh—no. Who was robbed? When?"

"My son heard somethin' on that police scanner of his about the art gallery bein' broke into."

"You mean Stan Grayson's gallery?" Kate said in disbelief.

"Yep! From what he heard he figured they didn't get much, but trashed the place."

"Oh, no! I'll give Stan a call right away. Thanks for telling me, Sarah."

"That ain't all! Willy said they done put out a lookout fer some red-haired guy that they wanna question."

"Really! Well, I'm glad they're working on it. Maybe they'll find this person right away."

Kate and Sarah talked a little longer, and after she hung up Kate said a quick prayer for Stan, wondering if this had something to do with the feelings she had experienced in the sanctuary. She called Stan's cell phone.

"Hello, Stan," she said when he answered. "I hope I'm not catching you at a bad time."

"Oh, hi, Kate," Stan replied. "No, I'm kinda tied up with something right now—but we're just goin' to lunch, so I can talk a minute. What's up?"

Kate looked at the clock and realized it was almost noon. "I'm calling because Sarah Jones just called me and said your gallery had been robbed last night. Is that true?"

"Afraid it is," Stan replied. "Kinda put a sour note on the end of that fantastic concert at the church last night. We think this happened while the concert was going on."

"Oh, no! I'm so sorry."

"It kinda shook Ed up when he came in and found the mess," Stan said. "Whoever did this didn't get much money, but they sure tore the place up."

"Please let me know if there's anything we can do at the church. Do you need help getting things cleaned up?"

"Thanks, Kate, but what we need are prayers to find who did this and why. We've been talking with Chief Draper, and he and the sheriff are working on it. We'll get things cleaned up okay, it's not that bad of a mess. Just keep all of us in your prayers."

"You know I will," Kate assured him. "Is it okay if I ask Herb to put this on the prayer chain?"

"Sure. Pray that we find whoever did this and for God's grace to touch that person's life. Confidentially, there seems to be more involved than we can understand at the moment—and pray for Gracie and Marty. This was kind of a rough way for their visit with us to end."

Kate said she would honor his requests, and she prayed with him before hanging up. Gracie Love came into her mind. She had enjoyed the concert immensely, and had felt an unusually strong pull toward Gracie. She had been touched by Gracie's testimony. She felt something there—some kind of tie—and she wanted to talk with her. It suddenly dawned on her that *Joyful Morning* would be moving on to their next concert engagement in North Carolina. The only way she knew how to reach Gracie was through Fanny or Stan, and she'd just talked with Stan. Kate dialed Fanny's cell number.

"Hello," Fanny answered cheerfully, as always. "This is Fanny Grant."

Kate identified herself and asked if she knew how to reach Gracie.

"She's right here," Fanny said. "We're all just eatin' lunch together. You wanna talk with her?"

When Fanny handed Gracie the phone, she told her who was calling. Gracie said, "Oh, Pastor Sheppard, thanks for calling. I remember you said you wanted to talk to me after the concert last night. I'd be happy to do that, but we're a little tied up this afternoon."

Gracie told Fanny that they would be at Dinkel Island through Monday, and then the group was headed for their next concert. They decided to get together Monday morning. Kate hung up feeling that somehow in all of this Jesus was rubbing her eyes and she would come to see something clearly. She didn't know what it was, but she was excited about it.

Ben Wartman awoke on Saturday morning with a headache that made him sick. After the robbery, and fueled by the anger he had felt at still not finding the money from the backpack, he had stopped at a convenience store and bought enough beer to put him into a stupor.

Now he was a mess. His body felt grungy and his mouth tasted foul, and when he looked in the mirror he saw not only bloodshot eyes, but red roots starting to appear under his dyed hair. He cursed. What the heck did it matter, anyway. He'd been careful not to leave any evidence he could think of, but you never knew what some enterprising cop might find, so he decided he needed to pack up and leave town. By noon he had gotten everything together and was hungry. He fixed a makeshift lunch, drank another beer, and then laid down to rest and fell asleep.

When Ben awoke it was after three o'clock in the afternoon. He threw his belongings into the truck and headed out to Lighthouse Point Road. Suddenly he slammed on the brakes. He was still in a brushy area, not quite out to the road, when a police car and two other cars came from the direction of the lighthouse. He felt a cold sweat as he wondered if they'd found that the gate had been forced open. He had a sinking feeling that something was way out of control, and he'd better get out of town fast.

After the vehicles went around the curve up past the Yacht and Supper Club, Ben hit the gas and sprayed gravel as his truck bolted forward. He didn't even stop at the road. He did a hard right turn and peeled rubber as he accelerated. As far as he knew, the only way out was to go into Dinkel Island and then take a left and head out across Crabber's Creek on the main highway.

Ben Wartman, you idiot, he said to himself. *Slow down or you really will have trouble.* He caught the red light at the main road. Two sheriff's cars rolled through the intersection, headed out of town. *Slow down, dummy,* he told himself. *They ain't after you. They don't know who you are. Just take it easy.*

When the light changed, Ben turned left and crossed the drawbridge. He decided he'd better get some gas, so he pulled into a Shell station. While he was pumping gas one of the Dinkel Island police cars zoomed past, heading out the way the sheriff's cars had gone. *What's them boys doin' out here?* he thought to himself. He decided there must be an accident up ahead. *Just be cool,* he told himself.

A mile past the gas station Ben came upon a road block. Both town and county police were there, stopping traffic going in both directions, checking drivers licenses and registration cards. *So that's where those boys was goin'!* Ben got his documents ready and eased up to the first cop as traffic inched its way along.

"What's goin' on, officer?" Ben asked as he rolled down his window.

"Just a routine traffic check," the policeman replied. "Let me see your driver's license and registration, please."

Ben handed the documents to him, and after looking at them, and then at him, the officer walked around and looked the truck over.

"You got a lot of personal stuff in this truck, Mr. Wartman," he said. "Are you moving out of town?"

"Actually, just travelin' through. Stopped here Friday to hear that gospel choir that was singing. I'm headed up to Maryland where I got a job waitin'."

"Really! I wouldn't take you for a gospel music fan—but then you never know about folks, do you?"

"Guess not," Ben said, beginning to feel nervous.

"Mr. Wartman, did you know you have a broken tail light?"

"No, sir," Ben said.

"Please get out of the truck, sir," the officer continued. "Let me show you what I'm talking about."

Ben was really nervous now. He got out and the officer watched him as they walked to the back of the truck. To his surprise, Ben did indeed have a broken tail light. He pushed his hat back on his head, put his hand to his forehead, and said, "Well, I'll be darned. I never noticed that. I'll stop and get it fixed first place I can."

When he pushed his hat back, his red hair roots suddenly showed, and the officer saw it. He looked at his clipboard where he had notes on the person of interest they were seeking, and saw "wild, reddish hair" written there. The man in front of him seemed to fit the description, having probably dyed his hair black to change his appearance. He also noticed how nervous the man was becoming.

"Mr. Wartman, I'm going to have to ask you to pull your truck over to the side up there," the officer said, pointing to a space behind the Dinkel Island police cruiser. "We want to check the cars behind you, and I need to write you a citation for improper equipment."

Ben lost it. He bolted for the cab, jumped in and started the engine and hit the gas at the same time. As he dug his wheels into the pavement and aimed past the police car in front of him, he lost control and sideswiped it. This brought an immediate response from all the police who were present, and as he broke free and pushed for speed, all three police cars behind him took off in pursuit.

Having the advantage of surprise gave him a slight lead at the outset. Coming around a curve he saw a gravel road to the left and spun onto it. He gunned his truck up through the cover of some cedar trees. As he broke into the clear again, he saw some small frame homes, barns and outbuildings along the road. People near the road jumped back as he sped past.

Looking in his rear view mirror, he saw that the police had recovered from his evasive maneuver. They were in hot pursuit up the gravel road. Their lights flashed and sirens screamed. A sharp right curve lay ahead amidst thick cedars and brush. Ben's thoughts raced. *There's gotta be someplace to turn off. Maybe I can double back to the highway and lose them.* Too late he realized it was the end of the road. Dead ahead was a ditch, fence and a large barn with some cattle grazing off to the side.

Ben slammed on the brakes. At ninety miles per hour it did no good. He hit the short ditch with a jolt. His speed took him through the fence. Almost instantly he plowed into the side of the barn. He hadn't bothered with his seat belt when he jumped into the truck and took off. Ben felt his body being crushed as he hit the steering wheel and then went over it into the windshield with his right side and hip. The old Ford Ranger began to cave in and twist around as it hit the barn wall. It rolled and then ended upside down in a stack of hay bales.

Ben lost consciousness when he hit the windshield. He never knew it when he was transported to the hospital in Potomac City.

21

<hr/>

Missing Pieces

$\mathcal{T}$hursday's *Island Sentinel* carried a front page headline: "Robbery, Arson Suspect Captured," with a sub-headline: "Gospel Singer Tips Police." The article by Joe Truvine spelled out the rapid series of events that had led up to the identification, and capture of Ben Wartman.

> "Ben Wartman, an on-and-off waterman who had been living recently in a trailer on Lighthouse Point Road, has been identified by Dinkel Island Police as a suspect in the fire at the Community Art Center during the Art Extravaganza in August, and also in the robbery at the Grayson/Plume Gallery on Friday night.
>
> "Stopped during a routine traffic check on Saturday afternoon, Wartman reportedly fled the scene, sideswiping a Dinkel Island patrol car. Witnesses on Grimes Farm Lane reported Wartman speeding in an apparent effort to elude pursuing police. Unable to stop at the road's dead end, the suspect's car bounced over a ditch, went through

a fence and crashed into the side of Jeremy Grimes's dairy barn.

"The Dinkel Island Rescue Squad responded to the scene and called in a med-evac helicopter that transported the badly injured Wartman to Nor'easter General Hospital in Potomac City, where he is in intensive care and under guard.

"According to police records, Joyful Morning gospel singer Gracie Love provided evidence linking the so-called "mystery money" found in Tranquility Bay last July, to a boating accident she experienced during a storm twenty-two years ago, in 1989. A connection between that incident and the arrest of Ben Wartman appears to exist and a fresh investigation into the mystery money is underway.

"When approached by this reporter, Gracie Love declined comment. She and the Joyful Morning group were preparing to leave town, continuing their concert tour. Undoubtedly Gracie Love will return when Wartman is brought to trial."

∿

Joe Truvine's article rivaled Sarah Jones' phone calls in stirring up the town grapevine. Conversation was lively at the drug store lunch counter and over the telephones. With the mystery money now at the heart of the whole thing, speculation was rampant. People wanted to know who Ben Wartman was, and how a beautiful and talented woman of faith like Gracie Love could be involved. In the course of one week, from the Joyful Morning concert to the arrest of Ben Wartman, Dinkel Island had experienced a spectrum of excitement that ran from elation and praise, to violence and scorn.

Kate Sheppard found herself in the midst of it all in a very personal way. She had talked with Gracie Love after the worship service on Sunday morning. Sarah's grapevine had guaranteed that the congregation would be abuzz about the robbery and arrest. At that point, however, Gracie's role in identifying the money hadn't been revealed, so that never entered the conversation.

What had captured Kate's attention during the concert was when Gracie had talked about the missionary couple who had enabled her to find a fresh, new life through her faith and music.

"I find it so fascinating," Kate said, "that you had absolutely no faith background, yet you felt drawn toward God when you went through a boat wreck and could have been killed. What do you think made you turn to God?"

Gracie had pondered that a moment, then said, "I think I knew there was a God, but I had no personal experience of worship or faith. Somehow, from somewhere in the depths of my spirit, when I realized I had nearly been killed a couple of times that night, some sense of a greater power than I knew anything about emerged inside of me—and the only word I had for all of that was 'God.' I knew God had saved me. From that moment on I wanted to know more about God, and that opened me up to a whole new world."

"You said you were nearly killed a couple of times. What else happened besides the boat capsizing?"

"That's another whole story that I didn't really talk about in my testimony," Gracie said. "It's no secret—but it was a very painful part of my life and I guess God enabled me to park it somewhere in the back of my mind."

"Oh, I didn't mean to pry," Kate said. "You don't have to go into that if you don't want to."

"Really, I don't mind," Gracie said. "Maybe I should start by telling you about the way I grew up. My daddy was a Maryland waterman. He and mama ran an oyster packing house, and he had a buy boat. He hired some guys to work with him and they went out and bought oysters from tonguers, then mama and us girls culled and packed them for restaurants. It was a rough life, and I never was happy with it."

"I think you said you were abused when you gave your testimony."

"Yes, I was," Gracie replied. "The worst part was that my daddy didn't stop other watermen or friends of his from playing around with us girls. He thought it was great sport. They all did a lot of drinking, and sometimes had some wild parties. My sisters and I learned to go along with it, but I would never let them go but so far and then I'd fight back. They thought it was funny."

"You mean the men made fun of you."

"Yes, they did. That's why I noticed one guy who was older than me but who seemed to treat me with respect, and when he offered me a boat ride, I gladly accepted. I hadn't meant to run away from home, but Tom—that was his name—Tom brought me over near here to a little cabin."

Gracie went on to tell Kate about the brief time she had lived with Tom and the attack on the cabin that led her to try to get away in Tom's boat during the storm.

"I really see the hand of the Lord in your life, Gracie. Time and again God was there. Maybe you just knew that in your heart."

"That's true," Gracie responded.

"I was also fascinated when you talked about your name during your testimony. What was your actual name—if you don't mind telling me?"

"No, not at all. It was Froster. Cybil Froster."

Kate started as she heard those words. She tried to speak but the words caught in her throat. She coughed. Finally she said, "Cybil Froster—and who were your mama and daddy?"

"Daddy's name was Ernest—but he went by 'Tumble.' Momma's name was 'Mo,' which was short for 'Morene,' I think. She came from someplace in Virginia."

Kate Sheppard's face turned white. She was stunned. Tapes from old conversations ran rapidly through her mind. *I'm sitting here talking to my long lost cousin!* Tears welled in her eyes. She reached out and embraced Gracie so suddenly that Gracie was thrown off balance.

"What—what—" Gracie stammered."

Kate backed off. "I'm sorry—I didn't mean to frighten you. Gracie, you and I are cousins! We're related!"

"Cousins!" Gracie exclaimed in disbelief. "Who are you in relation to my family?"

"My mother's sister ran off with a waterman from Maryland that nobody in the family wanted her to go with," Kate explained. "Morene was always very independent and defiant. She and a man named Ernest Froster ran off and nobody ever heard from her again. I never heard him called 'Tumble,' but I believe that was your daddy. Your description of his behavior certainly fits what I remember hearing in the family."

Kate and Gracie embraced and shared tears and joy as they sat together throughout the afternoon, talking about their families and putting missing pieces together. When Gracie went back to Fanny's, she felt a warm sense of having found her home at Dinkel Island.

~∾~

Monday was Marty and Gracie's last day before moving on with the tour. They spent it seeing the town and the area with new eyes. Stan took them out on his boat and showed them the area from the perspective of the water. They even found the creek that Cybil and Tom had used to get to the cabin.

On Tuesday morning after Fanny served breakfast for the whole *Joyful Morning* crew, the two RVs left town for North Carolina. Stan and Fanny set the date for their wedding to mid'December. They wanted both Marty and Gracie to be involved, even though it would be a small ceremony. When the group pulled away from the church it was with joyful anticipation of a speedy return. Fanny looked at Stan.

"Well, that's it!" Fanny said. "The wedding's set and we've got a lot to do."

Stan nodded agreement and then they walked back to the gallery in a refreshing sense of bliss.

Ben Wartman was in a coma throughout the weekend. His right shoulder and forearm were broken and he had a lacerated left thigh as well as a concussion. On Monday he began to regain consciousness and take in his surroundings. Opening his eyes and looking around was frightening. He had never been in a hospital Intensive Care room, and the maze of digital gadgets and screens unnerved him.

"Well, Mr. Wartman, I see you decided to wake up," said a smiling woman in hospital garb who was studying the screen of a computer plugged into a console on the wall opposite his bed.

Ben's right shoulder and arm were in a cast that immobilized that side of his body. His leg was bandaged and he felt pain throughout his body. His thoughts became fuzzy and he started to speak, but withdrew his words before they left his mouth. Dimly he had a sensation of being hurtled through the windshield of his truck and then feeling crushed by pieces of its twisting body. He closed his eyes and felt the pain of his ordeal as he relived the crash.

"Oww!" Ben muttered.

The nurse came over and moistened his lips with a sponge, and then asked if he wanted an increase in pain medication, reminding him at the same time how to squeeze a button that would provide relief. Ben felt the relief he needed was something deeper than the pain of his broken body—he needed relief from his life suddenly being turned upside down. He tried to remember how it had happened, but his mind clouded up and he drifted back to sleep.

On Tuesday he was disconnected from some of the tubes and wires radiating from his body to various pieces of digital equipment. After lunch the doctor came in and introduced himself. "You've had a rough time of it," he said. "You are making progress and later this afternoon we will move you to another floor for progressive care. You'll be hurting for a while, Mr. Wartman, but you'll recover from all your injuries."

The doctor asked him if he had any questions, but Ben felt something like panic inside his mind, and he shut himself down without responding. Just before 3:00 p.m. he was moved to a private room that looked out on the colorful fall scenery of Potomac City. He noticed that they kept the door to his room closed and that there was a uniformed policeman guarding the entrance. Ben's heart sank and deep depression set in as he realized he was actually a prisoner.

His thoughts went back to the traffic stop and the broken tail light. *If I just hadn't been so stupid,* he said to himself. *Running like that was dumb! Dumb!* He hit his left fist hard against the bedside tray and sent the water jug and a cup flying. The sound produced an instant opening of the door, and a nurse came in.

"What happened?" she said. "Are you all right?"

"Just knocked that water jug off the table," Ben muttered.

The nurse picked it up, brought in a fresh one and cautioned him about moving so aggressively. She needn't have bothered— the pain his actions caused in his body told him not to do that again. Ben felt despair. *What do they know about me? Who's payin' for this hospital? How am I gonna get out of this?*

He continued to stew over things in his mind. *You idiot! You had it made. All you had to do was take the ticket and tear it up when you got outa town. You wasn't comin' back anyway. Now look what you've done—now they'll probably figure out it was you that robbed that art gallery.*

Feeling depressed, Ben shut down his mind and fell asleep. He was awakened some time later by the doctor and two uniformed police officers, one from Dinkel Island and one from the county Sheriff's office. The doctor said, "These two gentlemen are here to speak to you. I've told them that you have progressed sufficiently to be able to talk." His manner was crisp as he stepped back and the two officers stepped forward introducing themselves.

"Mr. Wartman," the sheriff said, "you are in this hospital to recover from injuries suffered at the time of your apprehension. You are being held on charges of hit and run, flight to avoid arrest, reckless driving, speeding, and trespassing on private property."

Ben, seething inside, said nothing.

Chief Draper spoke next. "From Dinkel Island you are also being charged with arson, robbery and destruction of property."

After reading him his rights, the sheriff said, "A grand jury has been convened to determine whether or not there is probable cause to indict you on these charges. When you are released from jail you will appear for arraignment."

Ben's heart sank. Then the real blow came when they told him an investigation was underway to determine if he would also face charges for crimes committed twenty-two years earlier that also involved trespassing, arson, and murder. Ben's heart raced and he wanted to run, but his injuries held him in place. As if on cue the doctor came back into the room and said the policemen would have to leave. Ben felt sick at his stomach as he closed his eyes and listened when the door closed. He was furious. He felt trapped.

How'd they find out about that stuff at Lighthouse Point? That was so long ago. Ben muttered to himself—then a thought struck him. *"It was Lucy Mac—it had to be!"* he said aloud. It was his worst nightmare. Lucy Mac said she'd turn him in someday, and now she'd done it.

Wait a minute, he thought. *She wasn't there for any of it. She didn't see nothin'.* Ben had seen enough crime shows on TV to know that would just be her word against his. If that's all they had he figured he could beat the rap on that old stuff. *What evidence could they have after so long? If they really got somethin' on me then why'd it take 'em so long to find me?* Ben felt a touch of relief.

22

Spiritual Warfare

CJ Crumbold's interest was piqued by an article in the Potomac City paper about Ben Wartman's crime spree in Dinkel Island. Here was a confused and blundering man who was in a lot of trouble and needed his help. He called Rev. Kate Sheppard in Dinkel Island and asked if she or any pastor there was ministering to Ben.

"Not to my knowledge," Kate said. "You would probably have the blessings of most folks here if you wanted to approach him. I'm sure you wouldn't be stepping on any toes."

The next morning Ben was surprised when a man in a sport coat, with a van dyke beard and wavy graying hair, came into his room. "Mr. Wartman," he said, stretching out his hand with a gesture of openness, "my name is CJ Crumbold. I'm pastor of the Wesleyan Brethren Church here in Potomac City."

O no, Ben thought. *Some durn preacher! What's he want?* Ben grunted and turned his face away. "You're in the wrong place, man. I got no use for religious goody-goodies. I got enough trouble without somebody trying to make me feel guilty."

223

"I'm not here to make you feel guilty," CJ said. "When I read about you in the newspaper, I remembered myself about thirty years ago. So I thought I'd offer to be a friend in your time of trial."

Ben turned toward him and said with a snarl, "Yeah, sure, you was arrested for some crime, right? You expect me to believe that crock?"

"You don't have to believe it," CJ said, smiling and raising his outstretched hands in a gesture of amiable surrender. "I undertstand." Ben turned his face away again and said nothing. CJ waited patiently and then said, "Well, it looks like you're not up to talking. Sorry to have bothered you."

As he turned and started toward the door he heard a sound behind him and then Ben's voice. "Wait—sometimes I'm a little hot-headed, which helped get me in this whole mess to begin with."

CJ turned and saw evidence of deep spiritual pain in Ben's face.

"What kind of a crime did you commit?" Ben asked.

"Oh, just a little identity theft, and a scheme to steal a rich man's money. I also did time when I got mixed up with the wrong crowd when I was young."

This doesn't add up, Ben thought. "So how'd you get to be a preacher?"

"The guy I was tryin' to rip off forgave me and withdrew all the charges against me. The scheme had failed, so he wasn't out anything, and he taught me to know the God who had forgiven him, and in whose name he forgave me."

"Forgave you? So you walked free?"

"Well, more or less. There are always consequences to the things we do, but the love of God is greater than those things."

CJ waited silently while Ben turned away and became withdrawn. After a few moments Ben saw him still sitting there and said, "So what are you waitin' for?"

"Oh, I just thought maybe we had a little more to say to each other."

"Not likely. I'm glad you had such a great way out of your trouble—I don't have anything like that."

"Let me ask you a question," CJ said. "Who's your lawyer?"

"Ain't got one—guess I gotta git one though. Them cops will be back to ask me a bunch o' questions."

"Well, I know a good one who defends criminals all the time. He was my lawyer when I was in jail. I could ask if he'd be willing to at least talk to you, and he might offer his services."

Ben choked out a half-laugh. "Sure! I ain't got no money to pay nobody for nothin'."

"Who mentioned money?" CJ said. "That's a small problem from what I hear about the charges you're facing. There's always a way to handle that."

Ben softened a little. "I wouldn't kick him out if he came to talk," he said. "I really don't have much choice, do I?"

"You don't have to accept this man, so you do have a choice. But it's the choices you made along the way that are limiting your choices now, it seems to me."

Preacher talk! Here comes the sermon. "My choices are my own business."

"They sure are. Well, you think this one over. I'll check back with you tomorrow and you can tell me if you want help getting a lawyer. In fact, here's my cell phone number," CJ said as he pulled a business card from his pocket. "If you decide you want help before tomorrow, you just give me a call. CJ wrote a name on one of his business cards and gave it to Ben. "Or you could give him a call yourself—here's his number."

Ben put the card on the bedside table and said, "I'll think about it."

"May I offer a prayer for you?"

"Wastin' your breath," Ben said.

"Well, that's my choice." He spoke a brief prayer seeking God's healing power in all aspects of Ben's life, and then turned and walked out the door.

Ben grunted and covered his face. Tears seeped from his eyes.

∽

"Good mornin' sweetheart," Fanny said as Stan came into the house for breakfast. "You look like you had a rough night."

"Does it show?" Stan said. "I kept waking up thinking about that Wartman guy. It was like he would pop up in the middle of whatever I was doing and I couldn't get rid of him."

Fanny drew him into a deep kiss, and then they walked into the kitchen. When Stan sat down at the table she said, "That man's like a demon. That's somethin' you gotta get rid of. Have you prayed about it?"

"Only all the time. The answer I hear is 'wait.' That's one of the hardest answers to get from God."

Fanny already had breakfast on the table so they sat down, bowed their heads and she prayed. "Thank you for another day, and for fresh hope. Please calm the inner turmoil Stan is feelin' and strengthen him. Help us to see past problems to solutions, and past pain to healin'. We put this day and all its pieces in your hands, Lord. Amen."

They discussed the recent events while they ate. Fanny said, "When was the last time you felt God told you to wait when you wanted some problem solved?"

"There have been numerous times—let me think, the last one—oh, I guess that was when I was feeling so overwhelmed about the Art Extravaganza that I was ready to throw in the towel. The problems just kept increasing. Nothing seemed to make any difference until you came along."

"Exactly!" Fanny said. "You've said before that God told you to wait when you wanted instant solutions to those problems. And then he told me the same thing when I felt so alone in this house. We know how God finally answered those prayers—."

"Yeah—we found each other. He put us together. I kept trying to get over the grief of losing Lillie and finally God just opened a door and poof! You showed up and that problem dissolved. But how is that happening in this situation?"

"Too early to tell, I expect," Fanny said. "I believe God will take care of Mr. Wartman just fine, so you and me gotta take care of us and forget about him. We gotta pray for him, but after that it's in God's hands. I guess that's how to get rid of the demon—just let go. Stop givin' him so much power over you."

"I guess you're right," Stan said. "I never thought of it that way." They finished breakfast, cleaned up the kitchen and went to the gallery. Molly and Ed were already there when they arrived.

"You just had a phone call from Kate Sheppard," Molly said. "She wants you to call her back."

Stan went right into his office and dialed her number. When Kate answered she said, "Wow, that was quick. I wanted to let you know that CJ Crumbold called me about Ben Wartman. He's going to visit him. I know that man created a lot of stress for you and I just wanted to offer you my prayers and support."

"Wartman again!" Stan said. "I was up half the night with nightmares about that guy."

"I can imagine. You must be struggling with conflicting emotions. I want you to know I'm praying for you and I'm available if you need to talk."

"Thanks," Stan said. "I probably do need to sit down and get this off my chest. I hate to dump it on you."

"You're not dumping on me. I'm offering to walk through it with you. Do you mind if I come over and talk with you sometime today?"

"Sure, come anytime."

"How about a half-hour from now?"

"Okay. I'll look for you."

∼⌣∽

Stan hung up and walked back into the gallery. Fanny had gone next door and Ed had stepped out. Stan and Molly were going over some of her plans for the gallery when the door chimes tingled. They looked up to see Lucy Mac walking in looking angry. She strode forcefully into the shop.

"Well, I'm surprised to see you again," Stan said. "I thought you had left town."

"Don't fall all over yourself greeting me, Stan," she said sarcastically. "Don't worry I didn't come back to see you. I heard about that scoundrel Ben Wartman gettin' arrested and I came for some revenge."

"Well we don't have him here," Stan said, uncertain why Lucy Mac had come to the gallery. "I'd suggest you go up to Potomac City and check at the hospital or the jail."

"He musta really banged himself up if he's in the hospital. I came here because I wanted to know what they got on 'im before I go and tip the scales."

"Tip the scales?" Stan said. Molly, looking on with interest, stifled a snicker.'

Lucy Mac turned on her. "What's your problem?"

Stan knew Molly was equal to most challenges, but wanted to keep her out of this one. "She doesn't have anything to do with this. I don't know if Wartman's been charged with anything. I know he is a suspect in several things that have occurred here at Dinkel Island."

"Well I can testify about some stuff he did a few years ago," Lucy Mac said.

Molly and Stan looked at each other. "You need to talk to Chief Draper about that," Stan said.

"Oh, I will, believe me. I'd like to see that worm brought down to where he belongs." Lucy Mac looked around a few moments, then said, "Ain't changed your mind about puttin' some of my stuff in here, have ya? Dress the place up a little, ya know,"

"The answer's still the same, Lucy Mac. I don't think your work fits here."

"Don't know how you stay in business with such a limited view, Stan. Well, I'm off to the prosecutor's. Caio." With that she walked out.

"I wonder what kind of testimony she has against Wartman?" Molly said. "Was she around here back in the eighties?"

"Sounds like she must have been," Stan said.

The door jingled again and Lucy Mac was back. "Oh, I meant to tell ya," she shouted. "Ben Wartman set off that explosion during the art show to create a diversion so he could come and harrass me at my tent. Just thought ya outa know that." Lucy Mac turned abruptly, slammed the door and disappeared.

Stan and Molly looked at each other, then laughed. "Sounds like she's an explosion all by herself," Molly said.

Stan and Molly had hardly gotten back into their discussion when the door chimes jingled again. This time it was Kate Sheppard.

"Oh, Kate," Stan said. "I almost forgot you were coming by."

"Are you busy? Do you want me to come back later?"

"No, that's fine," Stan said.

They went back to his office and Kate said, "How are you doing with all of this, Stan?"

"I'm okay, I guess. Struggling with some anger. The stuff this guy did is maddening. Out of the blue he blows up my storage shed and starts a fire, and then comes back later and breaks into my place and trashes it. It would be impossible to not feel angry after all of that."

"Of course. Things like this just set up a spiritual battleground."

"That's a good phrase for it," Stan said. "It sets up a conflict. I hear Jesus say we should love our enemies and pray for those who persecute us. I've done that in some other situations, but this one is too fresh, I guess. 'Love your enemy' bumps right into the freshness of my pain."

"That's spiritual warfare," Kate said. "The key is to keep struggling with it until you can let go of the anger. I will be praying for you to get through the struggle."

"Thanks," Stan said. "You know, I'm glad you talked with CJ. What do you know about him?"

"Not much, but I know he came into the ministry from some kind of criminal background. That's why I encouraged him to talk to Wartman."

"You're right about that. Lillie and I were there when CJ went through that whole thing, and we saw how God changed his heart and his life. If anybody can make a difference for Wartman, it will be CJ."

Kate seemed thoughtful for a moment and then said, "Maybe fixing your prayer focus on Wartman will help you let go of your own pain."

Stan turned that over and then said, "A man I once learned to respect a great deal said the answer to most things was to let go of ourselves so God could get hold of us and our problems. I guess it's time for me to get that process going."

"I'll pray for you," Kate said.

"Thanks. And I will pray for CJ and for Wartman. Who knows what God will do with this crazy situation?"

23

God's Fingerprint

*S*aturday morning dawned with a bright October sun that soon warmed the breeze that whispered among the fallen leaves in the yard. Stepping from his car, Stan breathed in deeply and walked up to Fanny's back door. "Hi, honey," he said as he entered the house.

Fanny appeared from the kitchen just as he closed the door. "Hi, darlin'. You look fresh today!"

"I feel fresh. I got a good night's sleep. I think I'm getting past all that stuff about Ben Wartman. In fact, I feel so good that I came up with a fresh idea I'd like to share with you during breakfast."

Fanny served the waffles, fried apples and bacon she had prepared, and then sat down. "So what's your idea?"

"It's about our wedding. I've been wondering why we're waiting until nearly Christmas to get married. We've just been talking about a ceremony at the altar instead of a big event. How would you feel about moving it up as soon as possible?"

Fanny smiled. "Funny you should say that. I've been havin' those same feelin's. In fact, I was gonna say somethin' the other day and then we got sidetracked."

"No kidding! Wow! What would you say to two weeks from today?"

Fanny got out a calendar and checked the date—October 22. "Since we're trying to keep this small there shouldn't be a lot to do to get ready. Of course, we have to see if Marty and Gracie can come back then, and we need to see if Kate can do it that day—and Ed and Molly are going to stand with us, so we need to check with them. What time should we set it?"

Hmmm, Stan thought, w*e did ask Gracie if she could sing at the wedding.* "Let's talk about time in a minute. Right now I'm wondering how important it is to have Gracie sing? I mean, I love her singing but this is such a small wedding that I wonder if it would be too much?"

"Let's ask Gracie about it," Fanny said.

Stan got out his cell phone and called Gracie. When she answered he told her what they were thinking about. "Is that a date when you could be there?"

"Actually, October 22 won't work for us. Being on tour does have its drawbacks."

Stan told Fanny what she had said. "Here's an idea," he said, "if December is still okay for them maybe they could come stay with us for a couple of weeks right at Christmas? We could really have a family get-together—maybe start a new tradition. How do you feel about that?"

"I love it!" Fanny said. "See what Gracie says."

"Oh, that's such a good idea," Gracie said when Stan relayed the message. "Let us know the time of the wedding and we'll pray for you then. Mid-December is the beginning of our winter break, so I'm sure that part will work out."

Having that settled, Fanny called Kate Sheppard who said she was free on the twenty-second. They set the time for two-o'clock in the afternoon. The next step was to get Molly and Ed on board, which they did when they got to work at the gallery.

"Fantastic!" Molly said. When Ed came in, he agreed, so it was set—or so they thought. The next day after church Ed and Molly went to the Seafood Pavilion for lunch with Stan and Fanny. "Got a question for y'all," Molly said. "Since we're going to be there for your wedding anyway, Ed and I were wondering—"

Fanny interrupted. "Do you two want to get married at the same time?"

"Yes!" Molly said. "That's what I was about to ask. Would we be stepping on your toes?"

Fanny looked at Stan and he smiled, took Molly's hand and said, "That's such a great idea! I didn't know y'all were that close to tying the knot."

"Neither did we until we talked about things last night. Y'all mean so much to us that it just seems natural to do it this way. Glad you agree."

◦⌇◦

Ben Wartman was released from the hospital the next week and placed in the Potomac City jail awaiting a preliminary hearing. He had taken CJ's advice and retained Percy Monichase as his lawyer. He wasn't sure how to pay for all of this, but CJ assured him there would be a way. The next day he met with Percy to prepare for the hearing. Ben was scared and asked, "What's gonna happen to me?"

"You're in deep trouble, Mr. Wartman. The grand jury has indicted you on some serious charges. At the hearing the prosecutor will present his evidence on those charges, and we will present evidence why the court should not find probable cause. I'm going to need for you to be totally honest with me—answer my questions, and don't hold anything back. If you hold back you will tie my hands." He went on to explain how the hearing would work and what Ben could expect.

"Okay," Ben said, hesitantly. "I'll tell you whatever you wanna know."

"To begin with, why don't you tell me in your own words what happened the day of the explosion at the Art Extravaganza?"

Ben told him about trying to get into the gallery where he thought he could find the money that had been found in the bay. He admitted trying to blow a hole in the wall and running away when he realized it was going to get out of hand. Ben went on to tell about casing the gallery and figuring out where the office was, and then about going in and trashing the place in anger when he couldn't find the money. "My mama always told me I was a hot-head and it was gonna git me in trouble some day. I never listened but she was right. Everythin' I done was dumb—jest plain dumb."

Percy let that ride as he turned to the charges about events in 1989. "What's that all about? Did you do those things? Why?"

"Well, it all started with this guy I knew in Maryland who called me about some girl that he said had been abducted by a guy that was livin' in Virginia. He wanted me to see if they was in Dinkel Island. I figgered out who they was and thought if I could catch that girl they'd give me a reward, and maybe I'd git me some respect. I hired me a couple drifters to help out and then things went wrong and we ended up burnin' down the old house."

"Did you kill the man who lived there?"

"Last time I seen him he was alive. I shot at 'im, all right, but he weren't dead."

"So what happened after you shot him?"

"I sent Bubba—one o' them drifters—after the girl cause she done run away."

"And the man you shot—Tom Brewster I believe—what happened next with him?"

"Me and Roland carried him down into the woods and shoved him under a big ol' root ball. Figgered that'd give us time to git away before he come to and started lookin' fer us."

"So he was alive the last time you saw him."

"Yessir, so far's I can remember."

"Did you intend to kill him?"

"Not when I shot at 'im. Jest meant to scare 'im."

"And when you and, who was it—" he looked at his notes "—Roland. When you and Roland put him under that root ball, did you intend to kill him then? I have to know the truth about this because the prosecutor will try to prove your intent was murder."

"Puttin' him there was Roland's idea. He didn't wanna kill nobody and said that way the guy would have a chance." They talked some more about the storm and the fire at the cabin and about the fact that Ben thought Tom was a thief and had some stolen money at the cabin.

"I remembered that girl had a backpack and I figgered she took the money with 'er, so when them guys found money in a backpack in the water last July I figured it was from when that girl wrecked her boat."

Percy shook his head and sat with a blank stare for a while, which made Ben uncomfortable. Finally the lawyer said, "Mr. Wartman, this is the most bizarre story I've ever heard. I hate to ask this, but are you sure you've told me everything?"

Ben felt scared again. "I think so, yessir."

"Okay, here's what I would suggest. You need to plead guilty to the explosion and fire that resulted and the attempted robbery at the art gallery."

Ben was shocked. "Guilty! I thought you was s'posed to git me off, not git me hung."

Percy calmed him down and explained. "A relatively small amount of damage was done by the explosion and fire, and you stole a small amount of money from the gallery, even though you lost your temper and made a mess of the place. I think the issues from farther back are going to be much harder to clear up, especially since I understand you are being charged with murdering Tom Brewster. It's going to be hard to prove that you did, but harder to prove that you didn't. We need to concentrate our attention there."

"So what happens if I plead guilty? They jest gonna throw me in jail, right?"

"Not necessarily. You're already in jail. I tried to get you out on bail but you're considered a flight risk. What I will do is to plea bargain on those charges."

"What's that mean?"

"I'll try to get you a reduced sentence on a lesser charge. Can't do much about the arson charge, but maybe we can get the robbery charge reduced to petty larceny, and work out some arrangement for you to pay back the costs you created."

After more discussion Ben agreed to the guilty plea. Then Percy brought up the charges from side-swiping the police cruiser at the checkpoint and his flight and the pursuit that followed. "I doubt that we can plea bargain about those things. Now, on to the serious charges from back in the eighties. I'll have to see what kind of evidence is presented and we'll have to build whatever case we can."

Ben returned to his cell and spent a very restless, depressed night feeling like a wild animal that had been caged.

❧

CJ Crumbold went to visit Ben the next day. He found him depressed and lethargic—almost unresponsive at first. They were in a visitation room and Ben sat with his head slumped forward, staring at the floor. CJ tried to start a conversation several times with no response. He made one last effort to connect.

"Ben, I understand your preliminary hearing is tomorrow and I had hoped we might talk about that, but I see you're not interested."

Ben looked up, blinked and said, "Talkin' don't do no good."

"Oh?" CJ said. "Why do you say that?"

"I done talked with that Percy guy and he's got me pleadin' guilty. So what good is he? I thought you said he helped you get outa your trouble. He ain't helpin' me."

"I'm not a lawyer, Ben, but I think I understand about pleading guilty. He knows you don't have a strong defense for your actions so he'll try to get you a reduced sentence. You really are in a lot of trouble here and there aren't any easy solutions. A plea bargain is what he did for me and it helped, but your issues are different, more complicated than my case was. You have to level with him and trust him. He will work for your best interests."

Ben seemed agitated. Suddenly he jumped up, pushing over his chair in the process, and began to pace and flail his arms around. "My best interests! What does that mean?" Ben's eyes flashed as he paused and then said, "Ain't neither one o' y'all got anything to lose in this."

"Well, bravo!" CJ said. "At last a little feeling here! Go ahead, Ben, get that stuff off your chest."

Somehow that seemed to dampen Ben's outburst. He set the chair upright and sat back down. "I don't figure you at all. What do you get outa this?"

"What I get is a chance to help somebody sort out their stuff and maybe find their soul—you, Ben—your soul."

"What concern is my soul to you? Maybe I ain't even got one."

"Everybody has a soul. That's the inner core of who you are. It's what makes you unique. And it's also what connects you with God."

"God!" Ben spat. "God ain't got no use for me—if there is a god. Where is he?"

CJ leaned across the table and looked Ben square in the eyes. "He's right here in this room, Ben. He's in your cell. He's everywhere. He'll be in that courtroom with you tomorrow. And do you know what—he was there at the art center when you broke into the office, and he was there when you ran from the police—he's always present."

"So why didn't he do something to stop all that stuff? I thought God had so much power. Looks to me like he's a wimp."

"That's because you're trying to take his place, Ben. I used to be just like you, that's how I know. You can't really find God's power until you stop getting in his way."

"I ain't tryin' to be God."

"That's just another way of saying you're putting yourself first, and when you do that you can't really make good choices, or understand or even love other people. Your world gets twisted up and you do things you regret later. God doesn't want it to be like that for you."

"So you say. I ain't good enough for God to care about me. Never have been."

"That's where you're wrong. God has been loving you and wanting the best for you ever since you were born. But God doesn't force you to do things his way. He loves you enough to let you make your own choices. And that means he lets you suffer the consequences. But God is always there with you no matter what you're going through."

Ben seemed confused. "I ain't never heard nothin' like that. How do I know that's true?"

CJ picked up a Bible he carried with him. "Because it isn't just what I say, Ben. It's here in this Bible. Everything we're talking about is in here. Have you ever read anything on the Bible?"

"Shoot! That's just a book. I ain't got time for no books."

"Let's say it's God's book."

"So, did he write it? No! People wrote it. It's just a bunch o' words."

"Ben, God inspired the people who wrote it. He gave them the wisdom to write it. They wrote it out of their own experiences with God. It's God's signature on the world he created."

All of this seemed to be too much for Ben to take in, but he did soften a little. "You got another one o' them Bibles handy? Maybe I oughta look at it."

"Here, take this one. I have others." CJ handed the Bible to Ben. "You know, we were talking about your soul. Do you know what a fingerprint is?"

"Sure. Everybody's got fingerprints and they're all different. The cops use fingerprints to find people."

"Okay," CJ said. "Now, I need to leave but before I do I want to give you something to think about. Your soul is God's fingerprint in your life. You didn't know it, but you've been trying to cover up that fingerprint. Now it's time to uncover your soul and let God's fingerprint mark your life from this time forward. When you're in that hearing tomorrow, listen to what your lawyer and the prosecutor and the judge have to say, and however it comes out, ask God to help you find his fingerprint of love."

"Ask God! How'm I s'posed to do that? God ain't gonna listen to me."

"Ben, God's already listening to you. He's been listening to you all your life, but you didn't know that because you haven't been talking to God. Talk to him now. Then listen for his voice. I'll be back after the hearing and we'll talk about that some more. Okay?"

CJ saw that Ben seemed freer than when their conversation had begun.

"Okay," Ben said and CJ sensed a slight opening in his soul.

24

Off Dead Center

$\mathcal{T}$he preliminary hearing was held the next day. The Commonwealth's Attorney tackled the lesser charges of arson and robbery first. Chief Draper testified about evidence he had found which pointed to Ben Wartman as the suspect in both crimes. He mentioned the matches and match book cover they had found at both scenes, and the work gloves they had found outside the back door of the gallery. A neighbor had found a flashlight by the trash container in the alley that Stan identified as from his office. The chief said no fingerprints had been found on any of the items.

Stan was called as a witness and gave his account of both incidents. Next the prosecutor tackled the events at the road block, all of which was corroborated by police records. Finally he took on the events from twenty-two years earlier.

"There was a nor'easter blowing on the day in question, which we have verified from old weather records," he said. "During that storm it is alleged that Mr. Wartman and two other men broke into a cabin in a thickly wooded area of Lighthouse Point, startling the people who were inside so that they ran from the cabin. Mr. Wartman then shot one of the occupants while the other ran through the woods and escaped in a boat. Following that Mr. Wartman and his cohorts set fire to the cabin, burning it to the ground."

As this was presented Ben Wartman became despondent. He had a vacant expression on his face. Percy knew the power of body language in a courtroom and nudged him. "Ben, you need to sit up and look alert. You're not helping yourself by slouching in your chair."

"Sorry," Ben said, straightening up a bit. "I jest can't stand hearin' all o' this stuff. How they gonna prove any of it? That all happened so long ago and they weren't nobody there to see it."

"You just sit tight and don't panic. Remember, you have to trust me in this and you have to be strong. They will introduce evidence soon, you can be sure."

Almost as if choreographed with Percy's comments, the prosecutor called to the witness stand Lucille McCall, also known as Lucy Mac. Being a preliminary hearing it was permissible to use witnesses who might offer second-hand information if it seemed to connect with the issues at hand. Lucy Mac had gone to the Commonwealth's Attorney and told her story about Ben talking in his sleep. Percy was quick to point out that this was hearsay evidence, and the judge reminded him that it was acceptable. Ben Wartman shook his head and seemed to sink deeper in his chair.

"Ben Wartman was screamin' in his sleep about some guy he shot, and some fire, and then two guys he threatened to shoot. I remember him yellin' 'jump or I'll shoot ya.' When I asked him about it later he said it was somethin' that happened when he lived at Dinkel Island, and he saw those two men floatin' away in the stormy water after they jumped off the cliff."

"What makes you believe these things Wartman said in his sleep were real, instead of just part of a bad nighmare?"

"Because he was spaced out. We used to drink and party a lot and then he started usin' some drugs, and he got nasty and went out of his head. I wouldn't have no part of that. He never had no other nightmares while I was with him. The drugs brought this out of him."

"So you believed him because of the drugs. You must have been afraid for your own safety. Why didn't you report this at the time?" the prosecutor said.

"You just said it—I was scared. I seen the look in his eyes, and I'd seen him get in rages before, so I kicked him out and said I would turn him in if he ever bothered me again."

"I see, and did he bother you again?"

"Yes, during the art festival this year. I'm an artist and had my tent set up at the end of the show area because I registered late. When that explosion happened and everybody ran up toward the Grande Hotel to see what that was about, Ben Wartman showed up at my tent. He led me to believe that he had set off the explosion as a diversion so he could harass me."

Percy cross-examined Lucy Mac. "How many years ago did this confession of Ben's happen? Can you remember what year it was?"

"Well, sure. It was ten years ago."

"Now these crimes allegedly happened twenty-two years ago, so you're saying the guilt or whatever it was in Ben's mind was still strong enough to come out in a nightmare?"

"Yes! He was like a crazy man. I was afraid of him after that dream. I will never forget that."

Percy did not pursue any further questions, and Lucy Mac was dismissed. Next the prosecutor brought evidence provided in an affidavit by Gracie Love Grayson who was unable to attend the hearing because of her concert schedule. The prosecutor read the sworn testimony Gracie had prepared before returning to Florida.

"Mrs. Grayson was a teenager at that time," the prosecutor said. "Her birth name was Cybil Froster and she was living in the cabin with Tom Brewster with whom she had run away from an abusive home situation in Maryland."

The prosecutor thumbed through some notes on a clipboard. "When Mrs. Grayson came to us with this information," he said, "we showed her a number of anonymous photographs of men which included Ben Wartman. She identified him as the person who shot Tom Brewster and also fired a shotgun at her.'

"Did Mrs. Grayson actually see that Tom Brewster was dead after he was shot?"

"As you heard in her testimony, he was on the ground in pain and yelled at her to run, which she did. No, we do not have a body, but the state believes by trial time we will be able to prove beyond a reasonable doubt that Tom Brewster was killed by Ben Wartman. We believe there is probable cause to try him for murder."

"Is that everything you have to present?" the judge asked.

"It is, your honor."

Turning to Percy he said, "Is there anything else you wish to say?"

"Yes, your honor. I would like a brief recess to confer with my client."

"I have many more cases on my agenda today, so I will give you fifteen minutes after which I will expect both of you to be prepared to make a plea so we can dispose of this."

Percy said to Ben, "Well, you've heard what the prosecutor has to offer. It does not prove anything, and this hearing was not meant to do that. It does indicate that these crimes occurred, that there is evidence linking them to you, which means there is probable cause that you are guilty of the charge."

"Is that all you're gonna do?" Ben said. "You ain't argued much for my side."

"That was not the purpose of this hearing. When the case goes to trial then we will have formed a defense and I will speak for you. What I want you to do now is to plead guilty, as we discussed earlier, so I can plea bargain for you." They discussed this more and Ben reluctantly agreed. When the judge called them back into session Ben made his plea.

"Your honor, the defense would like to enter a plea bargain on the felony charge of robbery and request a reduction to a misdemeanor charge of petty larceny. Mr. Wartman has also expressed a willingness to make financial restitution for the damages caused to the property in question. He pleads not guilty on all other counts."

The judge weighed the request, and the prosecution offered no objection, so the plea bargain was accepted with a one-year jail sentence. Trial was set for January. Ben returned to jail with mixed feelings about his welfare, but not as scared as he had felt before the hearing.

That evening Stan, Fanny, Ed and Molly went out to supper at the Seafood Pavilion and discussed the hearing. "You know," Stan said, "I feel like I'm getting off dead center now that things are coming together and the trial date has been set. Justice will be done."

"Off dead center," Ed repeated. "In other words, unstuck! Good for you. Does that mean you can see Ben Wartman now with some sensitivity to him as a person—and not just from the perspective of a victim?"

"Yeah, you could put it that way. Sure," Stan said with a spark of insight.

"What a question!" Molly said, looking at Ed.

Picking up the implication that Ed was being hard on him, Stan said, "No, I'm glad Ed put it that way. He and I have talked about my spiritual struggle. I've also been talking to Kate Sheppard about it. It just became clear to me—I've been thinking like a victim rather than like a disciple of Jesus Christ. What I saw in the hearing today was a man who is deeply troubled, maybe not too intelligent, or who at least has never developed his thinking skills. He wouldn't know a boundary if it hit him in the face—and several of them have! I feel compassion for him, now, not anger. All of that just sort of came together today."

"Bravo!" Ed said. "I knew that's where you would come out, Stan. I've known you long enough to know it can sometimes take a while for you to get through the personal impact of things before you see the large issues."

"God has a way of not lettin' us stay stuck," Fanny said. "We just gotta give him some room to move around inside our brains and hearts, and then he shows us the way."

"Well spoken," Stan said, giving Fanny a hug. "It took me forever to get over feeling victimized when Lillie died, but then when I finally let go, I found you right there on my doorstep—or should I say I found myself on your doorstep!"

They all laughed. "I had that same problem in my own way," Ed said. "I came back to Dinkel Island feeling totally lost and looking for something to help me get beyond my loneliness. I put on a good front, but retirement on top of losing Sally really made me depressed."

Ed looked at Molly. "Then I got involved around the gallery a little bit, and got to know you," he said. Next he looked at Fanny and said, "I watched you and Stan discover your love for each other." He looked back at Molly and took her hand. "Somewhere in all of that I stopped thinking about my losses and found a new blessing by falling in love with you, honey." He pulled her close and their eyes met, moistened with tears of joy.

"Fanny and I could both say the same things from our side," Molly said. "I just thank God for opening new doors for all of us so that we all got off dead center."

They finished their meal, and as they left the restaurant Stan said, "You know, I hope this trial, in spite of how hard it's going to be for him, will get Ben Wartman unstuck from a very sad and destructive life. I'm going to pray for CJ as he works with Ben over the coming months. I believe God can turn that guy around. Maybe this trial will be the thing that gets him off dead center so that it can happen."

≈

The next day Gracie called Stan. "Marty and I prayed for y'all yesterday when the hearing was going on. How did things turn out?"

"It was an interesting outcome," Stan said. "He pled guilty to the arson and robbery charges, and he got a one-year sentence for that. He'll go to trial in January on everything else."

Gracie was silent. "You still there?" Stan said.

"Sorry, I was just feeling something in my spirit when you said that. I just have a feeling that man has no real understanding of himself—or even of his own soul. He seems like someone totally lost." Gracie paused again. "There are so many people like him stumbling around, running into brick walls of all sorts, never knowing what's happening in any deeper way. I know this trial and whatever follows will be hard for Ben Wartman, but I wonder if there's a soul window that might get opened for him in the process?"

Stan couldn't believe how closely he and Gracie were thinking. *Must be your spirit working in us, Lord.* "Those are my thoughts, too," he said.

"Maybe they're God-thoughts," Gracie said.

"I think so. You know, as I heard your testimony where you talked about seeing the evil in Ben's eyes when he had shot Tom and turned and fired at you, it occurred to me that God has been doing a lot of healing already. You shared facts, but not anger or vengeance—of course, it was a long time ago, but some people would hold onto something like that for a long time. Listening to everything that was said I feel like Ben has been holding onto the guilt from that day for all these years."

"It only takes a moment for me to realize what God has brought out of that day in my life," Gracie said. "I was young, foolish, desperate and lost. I thought I'd found perfect bliss with Tom, but if we'd gone on like we were it would have been disastrous. The events that day sent me into a boat wreck that opened my own spirit to hear God's voice. Now I just pray that Ben Wartman can hear God's voice as he puts all of that stuff behind."

"Something to pray for!" Stan said. They talked on a few more minutes before hanging up. Stan sat for a while and pondered everything that was going on. *"Thank you Lord,"* he said softly. *"Thank you for loving us even before we know you're there."* Fanny had gone on to the gallery to work. She had sensed the movement in his spirit and quietly gone on so he could continue his spiritual quest. He looked outside and saw how brilliantly the sun was shining. *Think I'll walk to work today,* he thought.

Once outside he was glad he'd made that choice. He could hear God's voice of hope in the sounds of the birds, and see God's radiance in the colorful leaves. It was one of those warm fall days when you feel a slight crispness in the air and the very pores of your skin become sensitized to the wonder of a changing season. Stan walked briskly. Since he had been coming to Fanny's every morning for breakfast he had gotten away from his ritual of a morning jog. The exercise was invigorating.

How could anybody stay stuck on dead center on a day like this? Thank you, Lord, for stirring me up in mind, body and spirit. Thanks for your healing grace. I pray that you will touch Ben Wartman just as you have touched me. As he finished his prayer thoughts, Stan whispered, "Amen." *So be it.*

25

—◆—

Fresh Air

As usual at Dinkel Island, word spread quickly about Ben Wartman's arrest. The newspapers carried the story about his guilty plea and jail sentence. They also raised speculation about other crimes he had allegedly committed back in 1989. Over at the drugstore, Bob Drew joined with the Old Geezers as they poured coffee, selected sweet rolls, and began talking about the latest news.

"Looks like we've had us a little crime spree here in Dinkel Island," Jimmy Charles said. "Can you imagine something like that going on right here in our peaceful little town?"

"Don't know why our town should be different from anyplace else," Darrell Tellerson said. "You read about stuff like this happening all the time."

"Yeah, but not here," Jimmy said. "This is supposed to be a safe place to live where everybody knows everybody, and people can trust each other."

Doc Patcher had a twinkle in his eye as he said to Jimmy, "How many watermen do you know?"

"What's that got to do with anything?" Jimmy said. "I know a couple of guys who work the bay."

Darrell said, "Do they own their own boats?"

"Sure."

"I'll bet you don't know the guys who hire out to work on those boats," Doc said. "You see, I run into these guys when they get sick or injured, and I find that many of them drift around from place to place. They don't have roots anywhere. There's no way for anybody to really know who they are outside of their own little group. Trouble sometimes follows in the wake of people who live like that."

"Good thought," Bob said. "What surprised me in the news reports was the stuff that happened back in 1989. Cheryl and I had been living here about five years then. I remember that storm—one of the biggest we've had. But I don't remember anything about a fire at Lighthouse Point."

"We get nor'easters here every year and they're always rough storms," Doc said. "I was here in eighty-nine, too, but a storm doesn't stand out in my memory."

Jimmy shifted the focus. "Forget about storms. One thing is sure—now we know where that mystery money last summer came from. Wartman must be a little on the dense side if he thought Stan Grayson would have had it. Everybody knew Archie Draper had it and was trying to find out where it came from."

"It's not so much that he's 'dense,'" Doc started to say.

Jimmy interrupted. "No—more like stupid!"

"Okay, guys, get real," Doc said with irritation. "What I'm saying is, maybe nobody ever taught this guy how to think things through. Or maybe there's something else going on. People who work with addicts talk about something called 'stinkin' thinkin,' which is a twisted way of thinking where they put themselves or something that 'feels good' at the center of everything. They get so they can't think straight and that leads them to do things they wouldn't otherwise do. This just might be what's going on with Ben Wartman."

Darrell said, "Well—I guess that's something to think about, Doc."

"Yeah," Bob said, "and here's another thing to think about. I'll bet this guy doesn't have any kind of spiritual life."

"Oh, now you're gonna get religious on us," Jimmy said.

"Maybe I am," Bob said. "If you have a personal sense of connection with God, it changes the way you see yourself and everything that goes on around you. That sense of God is kind of like a GPS, it shows you how to get through life without getting side tracked or lost—or if you do get lost, it helps you change your course. I'll bet Ben Wartman's spiritual GPS isn't turned on."

They all laughed at the reference to a GPS, but agreed Bob was probably right. "So what hope is there for a guy like that, anyway?" Darrell said. "I mean, he's in so much trouble now that the only road open to him goes straight to hell."

After sharing a few thoughts about that, Bob said, "I've got to get to work, guys, but I'll leave you with one more thought." He paused a moment, and then went on. "Even on the road to hell, God can step in and change your direction. Just sayin'—"

Kate had been keeping in touch with Gracie since their discovery that they were related. Once the word was out about Ben's hearing and the date for the trial, Kate called Gracie.

"How's the tour going?" she said. "We miss you around here."

"You know, I'm amazed how much I miss y'all—and Dinkel Island. I once thought that was someplace I'd never want to go back to. Now all of that has changed."

"We've got our share of trials and blessings," Kate said. "Speaking of trials, they set Ben Wartman's trial for January seventeenth."

"Yes, I know—Stan told me about that. I'm glad they got him before he harmed anyone else."

"Actually, I don't think he's a danger to anyone now, but he sure doesn't seem to have any boundaries, either. It's sort of like he's possessed by evil that distorts his thinking."

"I'll say!"

"Stan heard that Wartman said he had a right to that money they found in the bay, because it was in the backpack from the cabin he raided back in eighty-nine. That's pretty distorted thinking."

"It sure is! Didn't you say a pastor up in Potomac City is working with him?"

"Yes—CJ Crumbold, who was a criminal himself when he was called to the ministry. CJ spent years doing prison ministry, so I imagine he can get through to Ben if anyone can. I think we should pray for both him and Wartman."

"I agree," Gracie said. "Everybody has a potential for redemption by God's grace, and I have been praying that he will find his."

"I'm going to ask some of our prayer warriors at church to take on this concern," Kate said."

"Now," Gracie said, "have you got a few more minutes to talk? I'd like to tap into our newly discovered kinship by sharing something special with you."

"Sure," Kate said, and with that the doors of familial bonding began to open fresh vistas of relationship for both of them.

Ben Wartman was escorted from his cell to the visitation room to meet with CJ Crumbold. It was a week after his hearing and CJ had met with him once since then. Ben wasn't thrilled about the visit because he wasn't used to thinking about things on a deep level. At the same time, his only other visitor was his lawyer, so he tolerated CJ.

He wasn't sure how his tolerance was going to hold up, however, when CJ asked him an uncomfortable question. "Ben, what were you thinking when you decided to raid Tom and Cybil's cabin?"

"I don't know—It just seemed like the thing to do at the time."

"Really! Didn't you think about the consequences? Didn't you think about what would happen next?"

"I didn't think it was gonna be any big deal." Ben said. "I jest wanted to scare that guy away and git the girl for the reward. I needed money and that looked like an easy way to git some."

"But there wasn't any reward. That was just something you made up in your head, wasn't it?"

"There shoulda been a reward!" Ben said, with anger. *Everybody seems to be on that girl's side,* he thought. *She and that guy was up there hidin' money he stole. I was jest doin' somethin' to help out. Ain't my fault things got outa hand.*

CJ didn't respond, and Ben felt awkward with the silence. He calmed down.

"Somehow them two sneaked outa that cabin and when I saw 'em I got scared they'd git away and I had to stop 'em. It all jest happened. I didn't nean to hurt nobody."

"Now wait a minute—you fired a gun at those people, but you didn't think it would hurt them? That doesn't make sense! What were you *feeling*?"

"What do you mean, 'feeling'?" Ben said.

"What did it feel like inside you when you faced Tom and pulled the trigger?"

"It was like—I can't explain it. It was like a thrill, like ridin' on a roller-coaster. It felt good. I was in charge of somethin'. I had the power, man."

"Power!" CJ repeated. "I'll bet most of the time you don't feel like you have much power, do you?"

"Sometimes." Ben was getting agitated. *I oughta tell the guard to take me back to my cell.* He stood up and said, "Look, I don't wanna talk about this stuff, okay? If that's all you're gonna do, then I'm outa here. I don't understand you, man. What's it matter to you what I think or feel."

"What are you afraid of?" CJ asked.

"I ain't 'fraid of nothin'!" Ben said as he glared at CJ, who had remained seated.

"I'll tell you why I'm asking you these things. Fear is one of the most normal feelings people have. Everybody's afraid sometimes."

"Are you afraid of me?" Ben said.

"No, Ben, I'm not afraid of you. If I were, I wouldn't be in here talking with you. I'm here because I believe there's a positive part of you deep down inside that you've never let have any power in your life."

Ben rolled his eyes. *Here comes the sermon!* He looked away from CJ.

"That spark of goodness inside each one of us is our soul. It's a little piece of God himself that he has given us. I care about you because I'd love to see how much better your life would be if you'd get in touch with that spark. I've been where you are now, and I know what a difference God made in my life." CJ smiled. "I'd just like for you to find that same thing. God won't take away the consequences of what you did, but he just might help you not do anything like that again. Wouldn't that be great?"

Ben didn't answer. He walked over and asked the guard to take him back to his cell. CJ's words stayed with him, however, churning around in his mind. *Nobody ever talked to me about anything like that. I wonder if there is somethin' to this God stuff.*

❧

Over the next few days Ben wrestled with feelings he had never let surface before. He dug around in his stuff and pulled out the bible CJ had given him. It was a New Testament and Psalms. CJ had explained that the Psalms were about peoples' struggles with God in their own souls, and that they went back to ancient times. He had told Ben to just thumb through and see if he could connect with any of the feelings expressed there.

When Ben opened the Bible his eyes fell on Psalm 51. Scanning through the words, verse 10 seemed to jump off the page. "Create in me a clean heart, O God, and put a new and right spirit within me." Ben pondered the words. *A clean heart? I wonder what that means.* He began to thumb back through the pages and soon came to one where the corner was turned down. Highlighted toward the bottom of the page were the words, "For his anger is but for a moment; his favor is for a lifetime. Weeping may linger for the night, but joy comes with the morning." He turned back another page and words from Psalm 27 were highlighted: "The Lord is my light and my salvation, whom shall I fear?"

Ben wasn't sure why, but he couldn't get some of the words out of his mind. *A clean heart—joy—light—salvation. What's this all about?* Ben wanted to push it all aside as Bible mumbo-jumbo, but the words haunted his mind. To make it worse, CJ didn't return for over a week. Then one day a guard told him the preacher was in the visitation room to see him, if he wanted to go. Ben went.

"Where you been?" he asked CJ when they sat down. "I thought you gave up on me and wasn't comin' back."

"Ben, I'll never give up on you. I wanted you to have some time to think about our last conversation."

"Well, I done thought about it. I been readin' some of that Bible you give me. I don't want to go soft, but sometimes I wonder if there is somethin' to this God stuff." He didn't like to deal with his feelings, but here they were spilling out of him. He didn't know how to put them into words. Somehow the words from the Psalms seemed to be doing the job for him. He decided to talk about that.

"There's some words in that Bible that I can't figure out," Ben said.

"What words?"

"Weeping, for one. That ain't a word I ever heard much."

"It's just another word for 'crying," CJ said. "A lot of people don't like to admit that they cry. They think it makes them sound weak."

Ben understood. "That's the way I feel," he said.

"Actually, crying is like opening a window in a stuffy room to let in some fresh air," CJ said. "Crying can be good for you. It can open your soul to let God's spirit come in. It can make you feel fresh on the inside. That's the joy that comes in the morning. It's like fresh air, only its spiritual."

In spite of himself, Ben was fascinated. "I never heard nothin' like that from no preacher before," he said. "All I ever heard was how bad I am, and how God don't like sinners, and punishes people like me by sendin' 'em to hell when they die. What you're sayin' don't sound like that."

"What you've heard starts at the wrong place. It gets you stuck on the idea of how bad you are and then threatens you with punishment. We can talk about heaven and hell sometime, but first you have to start at the right place."

"What's the right place?"

"The right place is with the love God has for you. God created you for a good purpose, but he doesn't force himself on you. Because he loves you, he gives you the freedom to make choices in your life. Sometimes they're bad choices, and sometimes good choices. One of the good choices is to get to know God in your own heart and mind, so you can find his guidance and blessings. Everybody sins. Our sins might be different, but they're always against God. He gives us the freedom to do that. He also gives us the freedom to ask his forgiveness. He wants to make us whole in spite of our sins that cause brokenness."

This was a lot for Ben to grasp. "Wait a minute," he said. "You're tellin' me that God's gonna forgive my sins, but he ain't gonna take away my jail sentence, or whatever else happens—and I'm still s'posed to think he's bein' good to me?"

"That's right. His goodness is in his love for you. You chose to do some things that were crimes, and there are consequences from that—but God's love goes way past those things. Ben, God has loved you since the moment you were born. He's been sending you signals so you would love him and find the blessings he wants to give you. But you have to listen to the signals and ask for his help. If you do, you don't ever again have to be where you are today. If you want, I can help you find that path of God's blessings. That's the joy God has waiting for you, if you give him a chance in your thinking and your feelings."

It was a lot to think about. CJ didn't seem to offer any more than he thought Ben could handle at any time, but in the visitation room that day a door was opened into Ben's soul. From that moment on Ben had a chance to become a new person in Christ. His weeping soul had a chance to find the joyful bliss of God's gracious love that had been reaching out to him all along. It would be up to him to open the door for God's forgiving love to enter his life, but at least now he knew the door was there. He knew CJ had been where he was now. With his help a very small light became visible way down through the dark tunnel of Ben's life, and he knew he had a chance to turn some corners.

26

Return of Bliss

On Thursday morning before their Saturday wedding, Kate Sheppard met with Stan, Fanny, Ed and Molly in her office to go over the ceremony. Kate had met with each couple separately, and since it was a double wedding she needed this time to coordinate details. Both couples were off from work at the gallery for the next ten days. Cheryl Drew was filling in there, and the resident artists were handling the art center. Everything would be closed for the weekend.

"I really appreciate Cheryl taking care of things at the gallery," Stan said, "but I wonder why I didn't think of inviting her and Bob to stand with us during the wedding? I've been close to them since they came to Dinkel Island—and so have you," he said, turning to Ed, who nodded agreement.

"Why don't we do it?" Fanny said. She looked at Molly, "What do you think?"

"That's fine with me. I don't know Bob that well, but Cheryl helps out at the gallery so often that I feel she's part of it."

Kate reminded them, "I think you were concerned that if you started inviting people you'd end up having to bring in the whole community, and you just wanted to keep this simple."

"Yeah," Fanny said. "That's why the Women's Association is doing that reception the next Sunday after we all get back from honeymoonin', instead of after the weddin'. I'm okay with havin' Cheryl and Bob stand with us, though. They are almost like family."

"I'd be glad to extend the invitation if y'all agree," Ed said.

They agreed and Ed called Cheryl, who said it was an honor to be asked and she'd check with Bob. A few moments later she called back and it was all arranged. Kate took both couples into the sanctuary where they walked through the ceremony. Each couple would take their vows separately while standing together as a foursome. Kate decided the arrangement had a good feel to it. After a prayer, everyone left the church.

～♪

On Friday evening each couple found a special way to spend their time together. Stan and Fanny spent a peaceful interlude on her porch swing. The mid-October weather, which had been warm that afternoon, became cool after the sun went down. Stan pulled Fanny closer to him when he felt her shiver. "Do you want to go inside? It is kind of chilly out here," he said.

"In a minute," Fanny said. "I love the feelin' of freshness in the evenin' air, especially now when we're about to start our life together. I feel so good. I don't know how to describe it—sort of complete, I guess. I just want to enjoy this a few minutes."

"I feel the same way," Stan said. "You know, there's a word for this feeling—it's called *bliss*."

"Bliss," Fanny said. "I think that fits what I'm feelin.' Life seems so good right now. It feels like everything is in its place and at its best."

"You know, I never thought I'd feel this way again," Stan said. They sat a few more minutes, swaying back and forth as the swing's anchor chains squeaked. A nearly full moon cast shadows in the yard and a few stars twinkled overhead. "I thank God for opening this new season of life for both of us."

Fanny leaned back, closed her eyes and then said, "Just like you, only a short time ago I thought I would be alone forever. Thanks for lovin' me." She shivered again. "Let's go inside," she whispered. They went in and lit a fire in the fireplace and continued to bask in the bliss they had found together until it was time to separate for their last night apart.

〜

Ed and Molly decided to spend the eve of their wedding with an elegant dinner at the Yacht and Supper Club. They took the long way around to Lighthouse Point Road, passing the entrance to the Dinkel Estate, Pappy's Place and the condos where Stan had been living.

"This was a unique place to live as a young pastor," Ed said, reminiscing. "So much has changed here over the years, yet it still feels like a small, private community away from the big-city hustle."

"I had a hard time getting used to that when I first moved here," Molly said. "Now I love it."

Ed thought for a moment. "When I moved back to Dinkel Island after so many years away, I felt like I was on a boat adrift in the water. I felt an incompleteness that was overwhelming. Falling in love again was the farthest thing from my mind. Then I met you."

Molly squeezed his hand. Ed pulled into a parking space, turned off the engine and reached toward her. Looking deeply into her blue eyes he said, "You are a gift from God, sweetheart. You make my life feel rich in ways I never imagined before." He kissed her. "Thanks!"

Molly melted into his embrace and said, "You have all the right words, because you've just described how I feel tonight. When Carl died I said I would never fall in love with anyone else." Her eyes glowed as she went on, "I guess we have to feel that way at first, in order to put the past away with love and respect, and wake up to a fresh tomorrow. I love you so much."

"You sound poetic," Ed said admiringly. "Have you ever tried to write out your feelings?"

"As a matter of fact, I have. I just haven't had anybody to share them with, so now maybe I'll hook you for that!" They laughed as they walked into the restaurant. They were seated where they could watch the lights from Dinkel Island dance across the surface of Tranquility Bay. "This view paints a mural of peace and tranquility in my spirit," Molly said.

"There you go being poetic again."

They laughed and settled down to their dinner. Molly's warm smile ignited an aura of well-being between them. She said, "What a difference this time in life makes. When I was young, my hopes and dreams were mostly about me—about being successful, having the things I wanted, making a good impression. Now those things don't matter—they're just decorations. What matters is who we are and how we enrich others, and are enriched by them. What matters is being healthy in every dimension. I think that's what God is giving us in our marriage."

Saturday morning a light frost glistening on the grass and shrubs disappeared quickly under a warm sun in a cloudless sky. The temperature climbed into the sixties by afternoon. Everyone arrived at the church with time to spare, so they stood inside the entrance talking while they waited for Kate.

"Maybe this is none of my business," Cheryl said, "but I'm a romantic. Where are you guys going for your honeymoons?"

Molly spoke first. "I'm glad you asked. Ed and I have decided to do a little family bonding. We're going to his children's homes to introduce me to them, and them to their new step-mom and step-grandma."

"Yeah," Ed added, "but we're not staying with them. We're staying in hotels and acting like newlyweds should."

They all laughed. "I guess we're more traditional," Fanny said. "We've both always wanted to go to Hawaii, so we decided this would be a great time to do it. We're flying out from Dulles Airport tomorrow."

Kate entered the sanctuary and called everyone to the chancel. As they exchanged a few words of small talk, Ed reached into his pocket and produced the paperwork she would need to fill in and return to the court after the ceremony. "I used to sweat what I'd do if couples forgot their paperwork," he said.

"I had that happen once," Kate said. "We just delayed everything while the groom went back home to get it. It was a big wedding, too, so that was *fun*." Stan and Fanny handed their papers to her as well, and Kate asked them to take their places.

The women had decided to wear casual jacket dresses since it was a small private wedding. Fanny's dress was magenta with a white floral pattern, while Molly's an amethyst jacket with a floral print dress. Stan and Ed wore khaki pants and navy blazers. Each bride carried a small bouquet of peach and pink roses. Kate admired them as they stood before her, knowing what their unions meant in the wake of grief that all of them had experienced in recent years.

Kate began the ceremony. "We are gathered together in the sight of God to witness and bless the joining together of Stan and Fanny, and of Ed and Molly, in Christian marriage." She spoke of marriage as a covenant established by God as a part of his creation design, and of Jesus's sacrificial love as an example of the love shared between a husband and wife.

As an aside, Kate said, "We used to have another question we would ask at this point—'if anyone knows any reason why these couples should not be joined in holy matrimony, let him speak now or forever hold his peace.' Of course," she added, "we don't really use that question today."

At that moment the sanctuary door suddenly burst open and a couple stepped inside. Everyone gasped at the unexpected intrusion and turned to look toward the door. The brightness of light behind the couple prevented them from seeing who it was. Then the door behind them closed—it was Marty and Gracie Love Grayson.

"What?" Fanny said.

"Marty?" Stan said.

Ed looked puzzled. "What's going on?" He looked at Kate who broke out laughing. Then Marty and Gracie charged down the aisle shouting, "Surprise!"

As the two couples, Marty, and Gracie all embraced they began to both laugh and cry. Bob and Cheryl appeared to be totally confused. Finally Kate spoke up. "It was their idea. Gracie talked me into this on the phone. I hope you don't mind."

"Mind?" Fanny said. "It's wonderful. But how did you two get here. What happened to your concert this weekend?"

"It was cancelled," Gracie said. "We just hopped the first plane we could get and then rented a car from D.C. to here. We're so glad we could make it."

"And right on cue," Kate said.

Ed laughed. "I wondered why you threw in that old line about anybody who objects speaking up. That hasn't been in our ritual for decades."

"That was my idea," Kate said. "It just seemed to make such a great entry cue. I hope you didn't take offense."

"No, no—now that we're over the shock of it, I'd say it was a good piece of staging." Ed said. "Do you write stage plays in your spare time?"

Kate laughed. "No, ministry is about all I can handle."

Everyone recovered from the exciting interlude and Kate resumed the wedding vows. She had each bride and groom make their declaration of intention to their partner, then she shared some thoughts from scripture and offered a prayer. Marty and Gracie stood beside Stan and Fanny, and Bob and Cheryl stood next to Ed and Molly as each of them spoke their vows to their partner.

Stan took Fanny's hands in his and said, "I take you to be my wife, to have and to hold, from this day forward, for better, for worse, for richer, for poorer, in sickness and in health, to love and to cherish, until we are parted by death." Next Fanny spoke her vows to Stan, and then Ed and Molly followed the same procedure.

As she led the couples in assuming these vows, Kate always felt sensitive to their potential impact. *Better, richer, health,* she thought. *That's the easy part. That's what everybody looks for when they take this step. Worse, poorer, sickness—that's the hard part. I wonder how these couples will fare with the hard part?* In the recesses of her mind paraded the images of the couples she'd seen fall apart under the weight of 'the worst.' *By your grace, Lord, bless them with wisdom and strength when the hard times come, and joyful bliss beneath all else.*

After they had spoken their vows, joined hands and exchanged rings, Kate pronounced each couple man and wife, offered a prayer and pronounced the benediction. Everyone lingered briefly after the ceremony.

Gracie said, "I want y'all to know just how much each of you, and all the people we've met at Dinkel Island, have meant to me. I had a very dark and frightening experience here when I was young. Then a crime happened while we did the concert in September. Those are not the things that resonate with me now. I know God is with us through all of our experiences, both good and bad. His Spirit has been especially strong for both Marty and me since our concert. Hard times and suffering do happen, but those things pass and the joy of God's victorious love shines with the morning. We wanted to be here today because we know this wedding is one of those joyful morning times."

Marty put his arm around his dad's shoulder and said, "Gracie speaks for both of us. It is so wonderful to have had my relationship with you restored. No matter what is past, God's love is solid and we rejoice with you and Fanny for all that is to come."

The two newlywed couples said their 'goodbyes,' and charged out the door toward their cars. Suddenly Gracie and Marty pulled out small bags of rice and tossed it at them. "We just couldn't resist," Gracie said. Everyone called out with joy.

Their cars were already packed, so each couple drove off for their honeymoon destination. Crossing Crabber's Creek bridge, Stan had a glow in his eyes as he looked at Fanny and said, "You know, honey, I truly believe God's blessing of bliss has returned! Hallelujah!"